MW00875463

A CIP catalogue record for this title is available from the British Library.
Edited by Cas Peace
Cover model: Ray Holmes, photo copyright Morag Holmes.
Cover by @CoverGirl

Please note: The thoughts and opinions expressed in this fiction novel are not the author's own.

A MATTER OF TIME:

The Dying of the Light

JUDITH ARNOPP

For Richard,
my noble warrior

<u>Late summer 1539 - Greenwich</u>

Time has stopped. I do not know how long I've been standing here, staring into the cooling darkness of her eyes. They are slightly slanted, her fine brows are arched, and the nose is well-proportioned, in a kindly, heart-shaped face.

She is perfect.

Her lips are pink, plump and kissable, her mouth curved upwards as if amused by the fools around her.

How foolish, she seems to say. *I've no idea what all the fuss is about.* It is as if she casts ridicule on those who compose sonnets in praise of her beauty. I have written them myself; my own lines penned in the lonely depths of night when sleep was elusive, and I was ... filled with longing.

Ah, the discomfiture of love. I've been in love with one woman or another since before I reached manhood. I first met Caterina when I was a boy of ten, and when I tired of her, Anne was waiting who, in turn, was usurped in my heart by Jane.

I had not yet wearied of Jane when she was taken from me after giving me my heart's desire – my son. I was not ready to lose her, and there was no woman waiting to take her place as my queen. Now, there is just a void where she once was and, according to my Council, it is a queen I need.

I have my son, my heir, but one boy is never enough, not for any king and especially not for me. They tell me a political match will not only secure the realm against the threat posed by the Holy Roman Emperor, but will also provide a brother for Prince Edward; a young Duke of York who will stand at his sibling's side in times of crisis – a younger stalwart brother such as I never had.

Although I did well enough.

A door opens, the curtain drifts in the movement of air, but I do not take my eyes from hers. I will make this woman my queen; she will warm my bed, she will soothe my aching need and she will further strengthen the Tudor line. She will bear my children. If anyone can give me strong sons, it is she.

A footstep, a light touch upon my arm.

I turn, still dazed by the painted vision of Christina.

"Anne," I say, my voice husky from prolonged silence. "Is it that time already?"

I look about the chamber and realise it is no longer day; the sun is sinking, and night shadows are creeping across the floor. She smiles, pert and dark. Tantalising.

"The chamber is so dimly lit, I thought at first there was nobody here and you were still with the Council."

"No." I stretch my back, yawn and reach for my stick, turning at last from the portrait that has enthralled me for more than an hour.

Anne Basset looks reproachfully toward the painting.

"Is this the woman you will choose?"

Her face is clouded, and I realise with a degree of satisfaction that she is jealous.

"Possibly. She is very handsome."

"And very young too."

"At sixteen, she is old enough."

I do not miss the hint of resentment in her tone and reach out for her. At twenty years old, it isn't as if Anne herself is yet in her dotage.

"I am expected to wed a foreign princess, Anne, or you know I'd take you to wife. I'd rather have you than anyone else."

"So you say."

She pouts prettily, looks up through her lashes, prompting me to hook a finger beneath her chin and raise her face to mine.

I kiss the end of her nose.

"Don't spoil the evening with dissention, my dear. Supper will be here anon, and I want to play you a tune I've been working on."

Her arms slide about my waist, or as far as they can reach, and she presses against me.

"Is it about me?"

I look down at her head, which reaches no higher than my chest.

"Of course it is, if your skin is softer than a new dawn, and your laughter merrier than a lark."

"It must be about me then."

She spins away and comes to a stop beside the painting.

"Very well, but can we draw the curtain over the portrait, so I don't have to put up with the Duchess glaring at me all through the meal."

"She doesn't glare. She is soft, winsome…"

She shrugs her shoulders and moves toward the supper table.

"It seems so to me. Perhaps it is because I dislike her. I daresay she will dislike me too."

I gasp, throw up my hands.

"She will soon be your queen."

Anne turns and smiles, tantalising dimples appearing on her cheeks.

"And when she is my queen, I will love her devotedly. I assume you will ensure I am given a good position in her household."

"Of course. I wouldn't want you too far away."

She sits down without waiting for my permission and plucks a handful of grapes from the bowl, popping one into her mouth.

"I hadn't planned on becoming a king's mistress, Henry. I had hopes of a husband, a fine country estate and children ... plenty of sons."

She looks at me slyly as I take my seat at table, but I know her well enough by now to realise she is teasing. Even so, she is entering dangerous territory.

"And you have someone in mind? Tell me, who is this fine rich gentleman?"

She cracks a nut, picks the kernel from the shattered shell.

"I've nobody in mind at all. I only have eyes for you, Your Majesty."

The saucy minx doesn't even try to disguise her sarcasm.

I open my mouth, about to parry with a sharp quip, but I am forestalled when the door opens and the servants file in with our supper.

The spaniels, who have been sleeping at the hearth, pull themselves up and come to sit at my feet in the hope of scraps. I sit back and wait in anticipation while the dishes are uncovered, my mouth filling with saliva as the chamber fills with the aroma of roasted duck and capon. I help myself to one of each and Anne chooses a bird and begins to tear off strips of meat and place them on her tongue. She chews slowly, her eyes on mine.

"I do worry," she says, her eyes sliding away, "that the new queen will not show me favour once she learns of my ... role here at court."

Anne has no official position as royal mistress. She is just a girl who has been good enough to offer her king comfort. I have no intention of drawing attention to that fact by endowing her with the office. I drop a stripped capon bone onto my plate and rinse my fingers, dab my lips.

"Nothing has been decided yet. I may choose not to marry Christina of Milan at all. I might decide to remain a bachelor, or I may marry a wench from the royal kitchen. Whatever I decide will not be influenced in any way by you."

She drops her knife, a devastated expression flooding her face, then, as her countenance thaws, she picks up a cloth, wipes her hands, straightens her back and clasps her fingers in her lap. Her pent-up words may not be spoken but I hear them just the same.

Damn, I had not wanted a fight. Not with her, not tonight. I reach across the table.

"Anne, come, come. I don't want to argue. Look at this lovely spread. Can we not just enjoy the evening? It is not often we have the chance to be completely alone."

Her eyes are awash with unshed tears. I sometimes forget how young she is, how unschooled in matters of the heart. She is not yet old enough to have become jaded with love. After blinking the moisture away, she lifts her chin and smiles blithely through her unhappiness.

That's my girl.

She retrieves her knife, and we begin to eat again, the silence broken only by the sound of Cut and Ball slobbering at a bone beneath the table. The chamber has every appearance of tranquillity, but the evening is spoiled. Anne will try not to sulk, she will oblige me with every appearance of joy, but I know inwardly she will resent it.

I decide to approach the matter again.

"You must try to understand. It is the council, not I, who is keen for this marriage, and nothing is decided yet. There are other candidates and much negotiation to be dealt with before a decision can be made. Even then, it will be months before the new queen arrives. It would be silly of us to worry about it now. We should enjoy ourselves while we can. Make the most of things…"

I lean forward, willing her compliance, and she nods, but unenthusiastically. I can feel my temper growing short. I toss down my napkin.

"Speak then, speak freely. I will not mind what you say. Out with it!"

She puts down her knife, picks up her wine cup and rinses her mouth, licks her lips.

"Very well."

She looks at me directly, unflinchingly. "I understand that you are to remarry, I understand the reasons why it can't be me, but it will be hard for me to relinquish you. Oh, I know you say you want me close by and you will continue to visit me when you can but…"

Her gaze falls to her lap, and I notice her chin wobbling. She is trying very hard not to cry. I reach out and place my hand on top of hers. She takes a deep breath and finishes her sentence all in a rush.

"How will I bear it, Henry, thinking of you lying with her where I have lain, knowing the jokes you will share, the things you will do with her, the fancy little love tokens you will bestow upon her. The pretty poems you will write for her … How can I know all that and still be civil? How can I tolerate her being hailed by all and sundry as your queen when it could be..."

She leaps up, tears the curtain aside. "Look at her, Henry, she is beautiful. I can never compare! I would not be human if I were not jealous."

She stops suddenly, lowers her head, realising how far she has overstepped the margins.

"Anne."

She looks up and we stare at one another, unblinking. I move toward her, take her hand.

"As I said, I may not marry her at all. There is another, preferred by Cromwell for her Protestant background, her political connections. Her brother, the new Duke William, is part of the Schmalkalden League and an alliance with him will bolster our defence against Europe. You see, my personal preferences are not considered; it is all about politics, my dear."

She frowns into a wine cup and waves a hand toward the portrait of Christina.

"But all that has nothing to do with this one. She is related to the King of Spain, why are you even considering her?"

Anne is very well informed. I wonder who has been enlightening her. She is right, of course; Christina is not the best political choice. Besides that, she has refused me and aligned herself with … but I am not going to admit to that. It is simply that I can't seem to stop looking at her image; no matter how hard I try to push her from my mind, I cannot help imagining her in my bed. She would be so perfect, and she may yet be persuaded.

My mind slips away, re-examining the soft hue of her painted cheek, the moist promise of her lips … until Anne clears her throat, and brings me back to the present. I smile, take her hand again and lead her back to the table where our food is growing cold.

"I am not considering her. Cromwell has made it clear where my duties lie, and envoys have already been sent to Düsseldorf to sound out the idea of an alliance between me and the Duke of Cleves' sister."

She frowns.

"And her name is?"

I roll my eyes, shake my head, making a joke of it.

"Anne. Her name is Anne. I am plagued by Annes."

It has been a trying year. Not just for England but for Europe too, the treaties and alliances that have been in place for decades are broken. Change is in the air, innovation taking precedence over convention. I am not certain it is a good thing. There is security in tradition, and I find myself inclined to baulk at certain adjustments that have recently been made to the way in which we worship. I question whether God would approve.

When Bishop Gardiner returned after three years working as our ambassador to France, he complained of many changes in England.

Not all of them were to his favour.

Saddened by the death of my brother's widow, the Dowager Princess, Catherine, he shook his head over the tardiness of Mary's acknowledgement of the royal supremacy, but he brightened somewhat at the death of Anne – my late, enchanting, faithless queen.

I saw all this in his demeanour when he gave me condolence on the loss of Jane, quickly followed by his joy at the birth of our prince, Edward, who thrives even now in the royal nursery.

But no comment at all was made on the plight of the monasteries; there was no need for him to speak of it, his conservative religious leanings are no secret. He knew better than to voice his abhorrence of the new learning.

We have an English Bible now, with my image on the frontispiece. I am pictured seated just below God, whose face, of course, disappears beyond the top of the page. No man has ever looked on God, and his image will forever be a mystery.

It is I, King Henry VIII, who is centrepiece, enthroned in glory, handing out the word of God to the populace. Cromwell and Cranmer also grace the page but in a far less prominent position than I. Which is as it should be.

A copy of the Bible is to be placed in each parish church to enable every man to read God's word, or, in most cases, have it read to him, without the intercession of a priest. Gardiner does not remark on this, or on the steady dismantling of the abbeys, or the destruction of the icons. He knows it is wiser to keep his own counsel. I would never admit it but even I am saddened by the dismantling of some tombs.

It seems only yesterday since I stood in reverence before Becket's tomb. It has gone now, the saintly bones scattered, the costly shrine demolished. Sometimes, I fear these men of the new faith will tear apart the very bones of England. My Catholic heart is full of fear but, if we are to be free of Rome, there is little I can do to stop them.

I've always found it necessary to keep an eye on Gardiner. Distrust for the wily bishop runs deep, but it cuts even deeper when he doesn't even voice an opinion on the subject of Reginald Pole's treason, or the fact that his family are now marked traitors. He must be plotting something. I resolve to keep a keener eye upon him.

Pole, exiled for his continuing offences against me, recently defected to Rome and now works in unison with the Pope against me. They call me a heretic, and they believe that since I am excommunicated, my position as king should also be forfeit. They imagined, quite wrongly, that my cousin, Henry Courtenay, could be placed upon my throne but, by God, I wasn't having that! I swore to see them all in hell first.

In December, we took Courtenay's head, and in January Henry Pole was executed for his part in the Exeter Conspiracy. In March, Nicholas Carew followed them to the scaffold. And there will be others. As long as

Reginald Pole remains at large … other traitors will be taken. All who conspire against us, or shelter our enemies, will be hunted down.

With popish Europe ranged against us, we are now vulnerable to attack on several fronts. Spain, France, Scotland and the Low Countries pose an immense threat, so I lose no time in raising new coastal defences, and troops are mustered across the country. I am unaccustomed to vulnerability and it tortures me; the idea of invasion keeps me awake at night and I take all precaution against it.

I have been forced to make decisions that prick my conscience, and I am consumed with dread about the road ahead. I do not *need* Rome or the Pope, but I need God on my side. I have no wish to offend the Heavenly Father and pray the ten articles I recently signed do not bend our nation's faith too far.

Cromwell is ailing, I suspect he seeks to avoid the issue so, with some relief, I seek out the advice of Norfolk, who is traditional in all manner of things. A great debate commences: matters of faith, matters of conscience are bounced like tennis balls about the Privy Council chamber.

After lengthy discussion and much disagreement, we refine the ten articles of faith down to six; the guidelines now reaffirming matters of transubstantiation, the reasonableness of withholding the cup during communion. The permission for private masses and the importance of confession also come under review, as do the rules on clerical celibacy and the observance of vows of chastity. Before the matter is passed into law, Archbishop Cranmer hastily and reluctantly scurries back to Kent to pack off his wife and children on an extended journey overseas.

And now, cut off from Rome, with the world I once knew in chaos around me, I await the arrival of a new wife, a new queen for England, and a new mother for Edward and his sisters.

29th December 1539

While my dresser laces my left sleeve, I extend my other arm and squint at the letter in my hand.

"The lady has arrived on our shores, safe and sound," I announce. "They report that she is tired after a perilous voyage but was very merry at supper. Ha! She sounds like a woman after my own heart for as you know, I too am always merry at supper."

Lowering the letter, I imagine her at table. If she is even one tenth as fair as her portrait promises, she will be far fairer than my three former wives. I crumple the letter, crushing it to my heart.

"I cannot wait to meet her."

It has been an unsatisfactory Christmas season. The players were lacklustre, the musicians mediocre and the half-hearted celebrations have left me jaded and impatient for life to begin again in full measure.

"Why should you wait, Sire?" Anthony Browne asks as I hold out my other arm for the attention of the dresser. "We are all bored and there is nothing like a good canter across country to stir the blood. Your Majesty could surprise your bride, as you used to in your…"

He was going to say 'in my youth' but remembered in time that I am still in my prime. I pretend I haven't noticed his near slip while I consider the idea. I picture myself striding into the chamber and Anne, my mysterious lady, throwing up her hands in delight, recognising me at once and our hearts instantly entwining.

My excitement roused, I lower my arm and turn away from the gentleman who is holding out my coat in readiness.

"We should go in disguise. I could enter her presence dressed as ... as a humble squire, perhaps. Think of the great joke it will be when she discovers my deceit. She will fall instantly in love with me and fear herself to be enamoured of a lowly servant, until the moment I reveal myself as her future husband."

The gentlemen laugh and nod, all agreeing that it would be a lark if I were to ride out and meet the new queen in this unconventional manner.

"Pick out some plain clothes for me to wear and we will do it. You shall all come with me, dressed similarly. It will be a welcome change and cheer us all in this dreary season. I have a few tasks to finish but we can be ready within the hour. Give the order to make ready the horses."

It has been so long since I acted spontaneously that I can scarce remember the last time, but my heart is light as I allow them to help me into my coat. Denny passes me my stick and I limp from the room, a servant at my heels. In the passageway, I encounter Cromwell's man, Rich. He sweeps off his hat and bends his lithe body almost in half. I envy his youthful energy, his strong limbs, his scanty beard, the years that stretch unblemished before him.

"Ah, Rich," I say, "How is your master this morning? Any better? We have missed his counsel."

"He is up and about now, Your Majesty, but not well enough to present himself to you."

"No, no. Tell him not to rush back. We don't want to risk contagion."

He follows me, slowing his pace to match mine while he reads from a list of instruction from Cromwell.

Even in sickness, Cromwell is never lax in his duty to the crown. After working so hard to bring the Cleves match to fruition, he will be sore at missing the opportunity to greet the new queen. The boy continues to speak, but I lose concentration and his voice floats in the periphery of my mind, like a bee in a window.

It will be a relief to have a woman in my bed again. I have forgotten all about Christina of Milan now, from the looks of Anne's portrait, she will be a far better vessel for the son of a Tudor; and since she bears the same name as my mistress, I need have no worries about injuring either of their sensibilities if I confuse their names.

I halt when we reach the hall, and Rich continues a few paces without me before he notices my absence. He stops talking, turns enquiringly toward me with one finger still poised above the paper he carries. When it becomes apparent I had stopped listening some time ago, he lowers the paper.

"Is everything well, Your Majesty?"

"Yes, yes. I just have other matters on my mind. It is a momentous day for us, for England. I am preparing to ride out and greet my bride. Inform Cromwell that I will be leaving within the hour, would you?"

He bows again and backs away, skipping and hopping to avoid the barking spaniels who, having just noticed my arrival, come running to greet me. For a while I am engulfed in hair and tongues and wagging tails, the odd tooth snagging unintentionally at my clothes.

I ruffle their coats and slap their haunches.

"I am off to greet your new mistress," I tell them, and they bark delightedly at the news. I stand up, the dogs bouncing around me. I hope Anne likes dogs as much as I do. Anne … the other *faithless* Anne, had loved them but Kate had preferred her monkey and Jane was not enamoured of animals at all, although she tolerated them for my sake. Perhaps this Anne would like a spaniel of her own, or maybe two. We must look about for a likely litter.

I stride toward the open doors, the dogs skittering along behind. With the wind cold in my ears, and my eyes streaming, I hasten the hounds around the gardens, holding imaginary conversations with my new bride. She is witty, of course, and funny and careless of muddying her skirts on the mired paths; she tucks a ghostly hand beneath my elbow and relates the wonders of her brother's court which, of course, is nowhere near as glorious as mine.

With a small company I ride across winter-locked countryside where great oaks stretch skeletal branches across angry pewter skies. The world smells of decay: dank leaves, lank wet undergrowth, tangled dead briars, and ... mud. At this time of year there is not yet a sign of spring, and no hint of the glory of summer that must surely follow. The ditches that flank the roadside run deep with water; the speed of its journey as frantic as my own.

Steadily we canter on, my horse flicking clods of mud from his hooves, my cloak flapping behind me, my hat jammed hard upon my head to keep it in place. Soon, I tell myself, this journey will be over, and I will at last be united with my queen.

It is years since I have done this; too long since I concealed my regal status behind a common disguise. Kate and Anne loved such games. I never failed to surprise them. I recall how Kate used to laugh, fold herself into my embrace the moment she recognised me, and exclaim in wonder at my cunning.

Anne would pout and frown, claiming she knew who I was all along. She never did like being taken for a fool; never enjoyed a joke if it was against her. As for Jane ... I can't recall having ever played the courtly game with her.

In my early years as king, I was always playing Sir Loyal Heart and the whole court joined me in the game. Each gentleman would choose a lady, the more unattainable the better, and spend his every waking hour wooing her. He would write lovelorn poetry, strum plaintively at his lute in praise of her many virtues, with no real hope of reward. I remember Brereton, for a lark, choosing the Dowager of Norfolk as his lady and she, not in the least amused, cracked him over the head with her fan.

There was rarely any harm in it. Only occasionally did these platonic games stray into something more serious. In my case, there was Anne ... at first my pursuit of her was just a game like all the rest but ... her constant rebuffing, her refusal to play along taunted me into earnest courtship long before I realised I had actually been free to offer her marriage all along.

Had she yielded straight away, it is very likely I'd have forgotten her in a month and the whole fiasco of the years that followed would have been avoided. Had I known her for the harlot she was, I'd have chosen another to sport with. Her sister Mary never caused me so much trouble. But Anne is gone now and I will not let her spoil this happy moment. I am soon to meet another of that name, and I hope to God this one is worthy of my affection.

It is a cold day, and it is not long before I regret my hasty decision to ride so far. Somer, who pleaded to join us, is snivelling before we've travelled twenty leagues. If truth be told, most of us feel like joining him. When we spy the low thatch of a hostelry, I am glad to stop for a break. My gentlemen precede me through the door, and when I too duck beneath the lintel, the innkeeper, wide-eyed with surprise, falls over himself to serve us. Although we only plan a short stop, he piles the table high with bread, cheese and pastries. I pull up a chair and prepare to tuck in.

A boy barges in from the back room, his arms full of pots, and pulls up short, stumbling into a table, knocking a tray of cups clattering to the floor. He draws his forearm across his mouth.

"'Ere," he says, waving a rude finger in my direction. "Ain't that the king?"

As we titter at his incredulity, the innkeeper cuffs him round the head and sends him scurrying back to the kitchen. When the ale comes it is rich, cool and welcome after our ride. Somer, with his scarlet nose dripping, downs a jug of ale without coming up for air. He thumps his cup on the table and asks for more.

"Slow down," I say. "You'll be begging us to stop so you can piss before we've travelled half a league."

Somer pulls a face and drinks deeply again from the fresh cup the innkeeper places before him.

"Not long to go now, Sire." Culpepper comes to my side and offers me a tray of pastries. I take one and when I sink my teeth into it, warm honey runs down my chin. Taking a proffered stool I ease my leg onto it, stretch it out, hiding the griping pain that attends the movement.

"Darkness is not far away. It will be late when we arrive but I daresay I can wait until tomorrow to meet the lady."

I do not miss Denny's look of concern.

"Why not rest the night here, Sire?" He looks doubtfully about the dim interior. "Perhaps it is more accommodating upstairs…"

Slapping my knee, I stand up, put down my ale.

"I'm not in the least tired but if any of you are not man enough to complete the journey, feel free to catch up with us in the morning."

I look pointedly at Denny and his face reddens in embarrassment as he drains his cup and places it beside mine.

"I was only thinking of others. Young Culpepper over there looks very green about the gills."

Tom is in fact in fine fettle, bestowing unwanted attention on the innkeeper's daughter. Our laughter draws his notice and he lets go of the girl's hand and straightens up, his face a picture of innocence. With our mockery redirected toward Tom, Denny cheers up and helps me shrug into my cloak. He hands me my riding gloves, and I accept them with a wink.

We drag Culpepper from the girl and troop outside. The innkeeper follows us, a plump purse in his fist courtesy of Denny. He tugs his forelock.

"'Twas an honour, Sire. A great honour."

A lungful of good English air chases away the fug of the hostelry. I look at the sky. The daylight is already dwindling. As I clamber into the saddle, trying not to grimace as I ease my feet into the stirrups, my mind turns toward roaring fires, groaning tables, soft cushions. Despite the prospect of fleas and the discomfort of inferior beds, the idea of sleeping the night at the inn was tempting, but I'd never admit to it. I cannot appear weak so I spur my horse on, reminding myself that Sir Loyal Heart would never flinch from adventure in favour of a soft bed.

Give him his due, as we ride Culpepper does all he can to keep my spirits up. He cannot help but be aware of the pain I suffer in my legs since the accident. The intervening years have done little to ease it. Each day, it is his job to remove the bandages, and gently anoint the oozing wound before rebinding it. We have tried any number of ointments and salves, but none of them have much lasting effect. Tom is a good boy. Attentive without being fussy, good company but always subservient. He knows his place. He is discreet. He keeps my secrets. Of all my companions this night it is he who notices my fatigue but has the sense not to draw attention to it.

"I think my horse is going lame," he claims after an hour's ride. "Can we slow our pace for a while?" We rein in our mounts to a walk for the last few miles. I make a private note to reward him for his thoughtfulness – he deserves a small manor perhaps, or a fine new set of clothes. It won't be long before he is ready to marry. He is a handsome boy who clearly has an eye for the ladies.

By the time the lights of Rochester come into view I am aching in every bone, my frozen fingers are melded to the reins, and my arse is sore from the saddle. When we finally dismount in the castle yard, I am hard put to conceal my discomfort any longer.

"Well, I for one am in dire need of supper," I say, drawing off my gloves. I look about the hall, which is almost too warm after the bitter night outside, and my cheeks burn as I thaw, my fingers tingling.

But we are here and I am glad of it.

During the meal, my mind drifts away from the conversation, and the clatter of plates dwindles. I pay little heed to anything but my dinner, for I have earned it. As I work steadily through the courses, I run through the lines of a verse I have been composing for Anne, to mark our first meeting. The trouble is, every time I try to picture the face from Holbein's portrait, that I carry now in my pocket, there is another who supersedes it.

That other Anne.

Boleyn.

I force her image and the rhyming couplets away and concentrate determinedly on the moment.

Dabbing my lips with a napkin, I push my plate aside, lean back in my chair and rest my hands contentedly on my full belly.

"There is nothing like a day in the saddle to give a fellow an appetite," I say, and although I have not said anything particularly witty, the company break off their conversation to titter, and push their own plates away.

The next day I rise early, and everyone congregates in my chamber while I am dressed. By prior arrangement, we have all selected similar clothing so, apart from my height and noble bearing, there is nothing to distinguish me from my gentlemen.

I turn to the company.

"How do I look?"

I hold out my arms. The clothes are comfortable, lighter and far plainer than my usual garb.

"Like a humble messenger, Your Majesty. The lady will be amazed when she discovers the lowly servant to be none other than her future spouse."

Somer shuffles forward, similarly dressed, although we could not persuade him to part from his favourite green coat. His monkey leaps up and down on his shoulder as Will reaches out and tests the quality of my jerkin. He rubs it between finger and thumb and looks up at me, his brows quirked.

"Ha ha! Even our fool is fooled," I quip.

"Perhaps we should send him in your stead, Your Majesty, get him to do the wooing for you."

The room falls silent. I turn to stare at Culpepper, who has made the faux pas.

I raise an eyebrow.

"I didn't mean … I only meant…" He turns scarlet, his eyes swivelling round the room in search of support. Nobody looks at him. Since I favour Tom above all the other gentlemen and know his only crime was to let his tongue run away from him, I am not piqued. He is exuberant and overexcited, that is all.

In actual fact, the image of Will squiring the future queen to a feast is quite funny. I begin to laugh and slowly the others join in. Culpepper breathes more easily, rubs his kerchief across his brow, his laugh less hearty than the rest.

The corridor that leads to Anne's apartments is crowded as, followed by my gentlemen, I elbow a way along it. When we grow close, I halt and hold a finger to my lips before sending Browne ahead to warn the guard not to announce my arrival.

"Tell the lady I am a servant come with a New Year's gift from the king. Then I will enter as if I am Sir Nobodyinparticular," I instruct. "There must be no clue as to my true identity."

My companions nod and hustle into a casual group with me somewhere in the middle, no formality or heed given to rank. When we saunter into the chamber, nobody pays us much notice. I try to act as if I am there for no particular reason, but I cannot prevent my eye from straying to the group of women who are crowded about the open window.

They appear to be enthralled with something that is going on outside.

We saunter closer, still unheeded, as a roar of appreciation rises from the courtyard outside, and someone by the window gasps and exclaims in German. We move a few steps closer still, necessitating some of the women to shuffle aside. As the crowd parts, I am rewarded with my first glimpse of my future queen. My mouth drops open.

She is clad in the strangest garb. Her gown has stiff, rigid lines, and provides no hint of the body beneath, and every scrap of hair is hidden beneath the most unusual cap I have ever seen. She is still looking from the window, craning forward slightly the better to see what appears to be a bull-baiting taking place below. Unused to being ignored, the first stirrings of irritation induce me to clear my throat, to draw the attention of her women at least. One of them glances at me before making some remark to her mistress. Anne turns, her face petulant, ringed about the eyes with fatigue. But that is to be expected, for she has suffered a rigorous journey.

I clear my throat and speak loudly.

"Good morrow, Madam. We trust you slept well." Her gaze runs up and down my body and she nods dismissively and holds out her hand for me to kiss. I take it. Her fingers are short and stubby, her skin a little too warm, her palm clammy. As I place my lips on her knuckles, she turns her head toward the window again, and comments in harsh German accents. I don't know whether her remarks are aimed at me or the bull outside, but my temper is beginning to fray.

Determined to gain her attention, even if she is as plain as a pikestaff and nowhere near as young as I'd been led to believe, I tug gently at her hand.

"Good lady," I say, mouthing my words and speaking loudly and clearly in an effort to help her understand. "I am delighted to meet you."

Keeping hold of her hand, I move closer and slide my arm about her waist, which is not as narrow as it could be. Instead of yielding as I had imagined she would, she snatches back her hand and spins from my embrace, her face petrified into an expression I can only describe as disgust.

"Mein Gott, wie könnt ihr es wagen, Sir?"

For a long moment we stare aghast at each other. I don't know what she said but her women all look as horrified as she. I have clearly breached some misunderstood German rule of etiquette. Beside me, I suddenly notice Will Somer reach out to take hold of her gown. He lifts the skirt and rubs the fabric against his cheek, testing the softness. Anne slaps his hand away in horror, with a stream of what can only be furious curses. Her face is red and sweaty. I grab Will's collar and, scarlet-faced, I drag him away.

"I beg pardon, Lady."

With a perfunctory bow, I back away and, as soon as I can, I spin on my heel and head in humiliation toward the door. We gather in a small antechamber, staring at one another in stunned silence. I drop Will like a misbehaved puppy into the corner and turn grey-faced toward my companions.

"What in God's name was that?"

They are as aghast as I.

Denny shakes his head.

"She … she didn't seem to know who you were…"

"She could scarcely bother to drag her eyes from the bull-baiting!" Anthony Browne is indignant on my behalf.

I fumble for a kerchief and dab sweat from my forehead. I don't know when I have ever been so mortified. Somehow we must move forward from this. Somehow I must find the will and the courage to resume this ill-thought-out courtship of a woman I now know I can neither like nor desire.

I swallow, my throat dry, my heart shrivelled in disappointment.

"Was she … is she really as ugly as she seemed just now?"

"Not ugly, Sire, but … well, we've all seen the portrait, and she pales somewhat in comparison."

I frown darkly.

I will have Holbein's head on a platter for this.

"What was she wearing?" someone mutters.

"The women were all plain but … how can she not have known you?"

Tom scratches his head, perplexed at the way our plans have failed so completely. As anger bubbles up to replace my disappointment, I tear off my cap and cast it to the floor.

"She shall know me better hereafter."

I throw off my cloak, cuff Will about the ear and plump into a seat. Someone hands me a cup, but I do not drink. Morosely, I stare into the flames.

What in God's name is to be done about this?

I rake my fingers through my hair. My instinct is to run but I know my duty. I am not some peasant able to renege on a betrothal – there are policies and treaties to be considered. To reject her would invite war and, since my break with the heads of Europe, I am isolated.

Cromwell will handle it, I reassure myself, *it is his fault.* The alliance with the Hanseatic League was ever his plan. *He* is the one who must find a remedy. As close to disaster as I have ever been, I sigh and rub my hand across my face.

"I must go back."

"Back where, Sire?"

"Back in there. I must go to the lady as myself and let her recognise her great error and hope that we can move forward from this. Come, Tom, help me change into garments more fitting for a king."

This time when I enter the lady's chamber, I am clad in purple velvet and gold and there is no doubt as to my identity. I have no need of a crown to mark me as a king.

When my name is announced and I strut through the doors, the company pay me due homage and Anne, with an expression of horrified recognition, sinks into a curtsey.

Trying not to limp, nor to lean too heavily on my stick, I move toward her, take her clammy hand again and anoint her fingers with my lips. I rise and look into her face, which is pale, puddingy, and heavily ringed about the eyes. From the looks of it, a sore is developing at the corner of her mouth. She moistens her thin lips, stutters a few guttural words, and it is clear from her expression that she is attempting an apology.

I hold up a hand and she stops speaking.

Forcing a smile to my lips, I shake my head and laugh, dismissing our prior meeting as if it has no relevance. As if one day we will look back on it and laugh.

But we won't.

The disaster of our first encounter has enormous relevance. Throughout supper, I maintain an animated conversation with an imbecile who has no clue as to what I am saying. I watch her; noting her expression, her deportment, her strange foreign mannerisms, and with each passing second, I dislike her more. At closer quarters it becomes all the more evident that she is no beauty. Even when she is fully rested from the rigours of the journey she has taken, her features will be heavy, her nose will still be long and bumpy, and she will always be overly tall and stooped.

She is entirely lacking in grace. Of all the women he could have chosen, Cromwell seems to have selected the plainest, most gauche and unappealing female on Earth. I will never be able to get a child on this woman.

I can scarcely bear to hold her hand.

Cromwell should be here. While I suffer, he is sitting up in his sick bed, no doubt supping on dainties, waited on hand and foot while I, his king and master, must pretend delight in the beastly bride he has chosen for me. Damn the man to hell!

He should be made to marry her himself.

There must be a way out of this.

I pass a restless night during which I consider and dismiss a thousand remedies. Perhaps I can make reparation with Francis after all; a French alliance will remove the need of an alliance with the Hanseatic League. It wouldn't take much to bring the French king back in line, although … it goes against the grain. I have ever detested his oily, erroneous smile. But how can I ever bed Anne?

After the joys of Kate and the other one, and the gentle submission of Jane, how can I bring myself to … no, I cannot do it. There are limits and I am king; a remedy must be found, and it must be found soon.

In the morning, heavy-eyed, leaden-hearted and unable to face her, I send Sir Anthony Browne to the Lady Anne with a gift of furs. My companions and I return to Whitehall, but before we leave I send a messenger ahead to drag Cromwell from his sick bed so he can ready himself to explain his duplicity.

When I slide from the saddle and limp wearily up the steps to the hall, Cromwell is waiting. He steps from the shadows and straight away I notice his dark-ringed eyes, his drooping mouth, the shadow of stubble on his chin. His sickness wasn't a ruse, then.

I had suspected he'd made himself scarce so as to be out of the way when I discovered the truth of the peerless bride he'd chosen for me. More cheerless than peerless, as it turns out.

He executes a low bow and, after growling a greeting, I sweep past him, but I hear his quiet footstep following me along the corridor.

When the door to my privy chamber is opened, the spaniels emerge like demons from hell and I am engulfed in hair and tongues and tails.

My heart lifts just a little.

You can rely on dogs.

A servant comes forward to take my topcoat and another brings a tray of wine and refreshments. I do not offer Cromwell a cup or ask him to take a seat. He deserves no favours. My heart is sick with disappointment.

He clears his throat.

"H-how did Your Majesty find the Lady Anne? I hope she was well after the crossing."

I do not answer at once. As I sip my wine and ease my foot onto a stool, I think back on the disastrous meeting with my intended bride. Aspects of the disaster seem incredible now.

When I finally look at him, he flinches.

"It did not go well, Cromwell. It did not go well at all."

"I-in what way, Your Majesty?"

"I found her very plain, and more importantly I found her ill-mannered and offensive in almost every respect. In short, I do not like her."

His jaw drops, he spreads his hands, palm upward.

"I am sure that given time she will become accustomed to our ways. She has travelled far and is no doubt finding things strange."

"I cannot love her."

"Y-Your Majesty…?"

I put the cup, none too gently, on the table and wine slops across the board.

"I cannot love a woman like her. I cannot be expected to get a son on a woman like that. She is … I cannot do it."

At length he breaks the stunned silence.

"But, Your Majesty, the alliance, her brother … the lady will be shamed. I do not see what…"

"You *will* find a way out of this, Cromwell, or by God I will have your head for it."

His mouth opens and closes like that of a fish, but no words issue. Suddenly I see him for what he is. Norfolk is right. Cromwell is an upstart and every action he takes, and has ever taken, has been for his own benefit. He has never worked in my interest, only in that of himself.

I wonder what reward the Duke of Cleves promised him should he somehow manage to gull me into wedding his unmarriageable sister. I imagine he is laughing now. Well, he will laugh on the other side of his face when I refuse to take her. She can go back, discarded, tainted goods.

"Get out, Cromwell, and stay out of my sight until you have discovered a remedy for this."

But it isn't a head cold or a wounded knee, there can be no overnight cure. There is no immediate easement. The next day I must prepare myself to ride with Norfolk, Brandon and Cranmer to formally welcome Anne to our realm as the future queen.

"By Christ, Brandon," I mutter when we are alone in my chamber. "This is the worst fix I have ever found myself in."

"Is she as bad as you fear, Sire? I found her pleasant enough, once I accustomed myself to her manner of speech. I think, once she has mastered our tongue, you will find her better company."

Only Brandon would dare attempt to alter my opinion. I look him in the eye.

"Would you bed her then?"

He blusters and splutters, half laughing at the suggestion.

"I'd never dare contemplate such a thing, Sire."

"If you were me, then, would the prospect of bedding her please you? Honestly. I want a truthful answer."

"It is a difficult question, Sire. I am a happily married man, bedding strange women is not something I am familiar with. Therefore, I must decline to answer."

Despite my misery, I laugh aloud.

"Then you are both a scoundrel and a liar, Sir. You've bedded half the women in London, married or otherwise."

He holds out my coat while I shrug into it.

"Not quite half, Sire."

We are still laughing as we leave the chamber and encounter Norfolk and Cranmer halfway across the hall. Norfolk removes his cap, his face open and questioning.

"Your Majesty is feeling better? I am delighted to see it." In jest, he scans the floor around my feet. "And where is your hound, Sire? Is he not to accompany us?"

"Cromwell has matters to resolve. He will not be joining us today."

Judging by the throng that awaits us at Black Heath, Cromwell is the only soul in the whole of England who is not present to witness my official meeting with the Lady of Cleves. The cheers and well wishes waft toward us on the stiff breeze. I pull my cloak about my shoulders, duck my head into the wind and raise a lazy hand in response to their cries.

The sounds of adoration increase.

"By God, it's cold enough to freeze hell," Norfolk complains. "Let us hope the bride doesn't keep Your Majesty waiting long."

"If she tarries, it will be all I can do to stop myself from turning tail and riding away."

What a sight we must make, gathered on this frigid heath, everyone dressed in their finest, myself clad in cloth of gold and purple velvet and furs, bejewelled to the highest degree; and all for the sake of a woman with a face like a mule. How ridiculous it all is and how King Francis will laugh when he is told of it.

A clarion of trumpets announces the lady's arrival and I turn my head toward the approaching cavalcade. I force a smile to my lips, as if it is a joyous day, but as I wait interminably for the slow procession to arrive, the smile begins to ache. I dismount, remove my gloves and hand them to Brandon. With great ceremony, the lady is also helped from her horse. She pauses to allow her women to fuss with her clothes before she turns to face me.

"What on God's earth is she wearing today?" I mutter from the side of my mouth, and Brandon snorts, fighting to cover his amusement. It is all very well for him to find humour in it, and I hope that one day I will look back on this moment and laugh with him. But now, as my stiff, awkward bride is ushered toward me, all I want to do is weep.

I conceal my dismay and, giving no indication that I see anything amiss in her ugly clothing, I remove my cap and give her good greeting.

I am nothing if not polite.

"My Lady Anne, welcome to our realm. Welcome to England."

"Your Majesty, I am both honoured and joyful to be here."

Her words startle me, and I realise she has spoken in the English tongue. Somebody must have been coaching her. I wonder if she understands the words she has spoken. I move closer and kiss her cold fingers, and to the great rejoicing of the crowd, I embrace her.

Her gown of cloth of gold is stiff and unrelenting, her body resistant, and she smells … foreign. Maintaining hold of her hand, I move as far away as I am physically able. Of all the women I have ever met, she is the least attractive, and our wedding, such a short time away, is destined to be a failure.

What happens when a king fails to do his duty on a bride? The whole world is looking on and will soon know of it. She will tell her women of it, and they will whisper to their men folk, and the gossip will pass through the court, through the brothels and alehouses, to the meanest hovel in the country and beyond. The whole world will know that I, Henry of England, have failed in a king's most fundamental duty. It is the one task that cannot be delegated to another.

I wish to God it could.

I am grateful for the warmth of the pavilions set up to receive us after the ceremony. The braziers are hot, the wine is well spiced, and the repast goes some way to restoring my spirits. Anne, surrounded by the vanguard of her women, is speaking spiritedly to Cranmer, who has the fortune, or misfortune, to understand her tongue. He is laughing at something she has said, and I wonder if there is more to her than I have imagined. Perhaps she has hidden assets.

She glances my way and her smile dissolves; I wonder fleetingly whether she is as displeased with me as I am with her.

Could that be true? Could she too be disappointed? Was she deceived as I was with false images and descriptions? It is true I am not as lithe and agile as I once was. I can no longer joust, or dance long into the night as I once did but … I am still a desirable spouse.

I have the finest palaces, the richest, most fertile land. I write the best verse, compose the sweetest music, sing the finest songs. I still have vigour and, when my leg allows, I can hunt, at least for some part of the day. I am educated, interesting, and cut a fine figure; you have only to study my portrait to understand the man I am.

There is nothing she can complain of.

I smooth the fur collar of my coat; test the quality of my damask tunic. I'd defy any man to deny that I am the best-dressed king in Europe; my clothes enhance my physique. Anne's clothes, although of the finest cloth, are cut strangely. They have no allure; she has no allure.

I wish that she were dead.

The moment he next enters my privy chamber, I raise the matter with Cromwell again.

"What of her previous contract to the Duke of Lorraine? Can you find no impediment there, Cromwell? You must defer the marriage while the matter is investigated."

"We looked into it thoroughly during the initial arrangements, Your Majesty. You made sure that we did. I very much doubt we can find anything further."

His tone is nervous, almost wheedling. I have never seen him worry before.

"I need a way out, Cromwell. Find a way. I don't care what you have to do to achieve it but get me out of this!"

Desperate and lonely, I send for Mistress Bassett to come post haste from the country where I sent her just prior to the new queen's arrival. She comes to me, reluctant and pouting, and still irked that I have chosen another over her. I've convinced her she would be my choice if I wasn't at the mercy of my Council; I pretend I would wed her if I could but … I am king and all I do must be to the benefit of my country.

"Come," I say, "sit here, cheer me. What news have you?"

"News?" she says, as prickly as a hedgehog. "From the country where nothing ever happens? I think it is you who has been having all the adventures, Your Majesty. Don't think I haven't heard the gossip."

She helps herself to a grape, pops it defiantly into her mouth and sinks into the seat beside me. She smells of the outdoors, of earth and cold and there is still a tang of horseflesh clinging to her after her ride. All good English aromas. I draw her close, kiss her cheek just beside her ear, and she giggles, tries to shrug me away, but I know she likes it.

We tussle for a while, and then relax together on the seat, close to the fire. I pull off her cap and play with her silken hair, pick up a strand and tickle the end of her nose with it. She sneezes violently and laughs before leaning against me with a contented sigh. Quietly we watch the flames leap and dance in the grate.

"Are you going to tell me about her?" she asks at last, but I am reluctant to allow Anne into our idyll.

"I'd rather not. I want to forget all about her."

She sits up, turns and frowns at me.

"But I am eaten up with curiosity. If you tell me all about her now, I promise not to mention her again unless you do. Clearly, there is something wrong with her or you'd have left me rotting in the countryside. Is she not what Your Majesty expected?"

I sigh again; rest my head against the back of the seat, frowning at the memory of my encounter with the woman Cromwell has thrust upon me.

"I find her distasteful. She is rude and strange looking and there is a smell about her person, an alien scent I do not find charming. Unlike yourself…" I drag her close again, snuffle at her neck, inhaling her good English wholesomeness. After a moment she pulls away, frowning down at her hands, which are clasped tightly in her lap.

"But you are still going to wed her, aren't you?"

"I may have to, if Cromwell doesn't find me a way out but … Sweetheart, you need not worry, she is no rival for my affection."

Slowly her smile returns, her cheeks turn pink, and the dimples show on her cheeks again.

"So, I am to remain at court?"

"I will ensure you are given a place in her household, where you will be close at hand. In many ways it is better to be my mistress than my queen, and you will always be certain that when I seek your company it is because I desire it, not because of some marital constraint."

"But if she has a child, he will be named prince, whereas any child I bear out of wedlock will be nothing more than My Lord Bastard, should you even choose to acknowledge him."

My heart leaps at the image of her with my son in her arms; the likelihood of it happening is greater than that of me getting one with Anne of Cleves. I disentangle her hands and take one of them, enveloping it between my palms.

"Ahh, Anne, Anne, you think too much. Come with me to bed. I am tired of thinking."

6th January 1540

It is strange that, only hours after waking from a dream of my old mistress, they bring me the news of Bessie Blount's death. I knew she was ailing. Only last month I sent her tonics, mixed by my own hand, promising they would cure her but, apparently, they did little good.

"It was her lungs," I say, letting the letter drop. "There is little to be done once contagion reaches the lungs."

Bessie was a good woman. She gave me comfort when I needed it; she gave me my first son. I was so proud of Fitzroi. I often wondered if I should have married her, but ... she is gone now. There is nothing to be gained from regret. I rub my thigh, which is throbbing like the devil this morning, and sigh deeply. She was no age. I reach for Anne's hand, and she squeezes it.

"You must not take it to heart, Your Majesty. People die every day; we should not mourn their passing but celebrate the fact that they lived, the joys we shared. Be glad that you knew her and then concentrate on the here and now. Enjoy your own life while you still can."

She is right. I let my gaze travel the length of her body, knowing the delights hidden beneath her shift, and place my head against her shoulder while her skilled touch chases away my gloom.

Dallying with my mistress only defers the evil moment of my marriage day. Even though I threaten Cromwell with the Tower, there is little he can do to extricate me from the agreement.

"I swear, Your Majesty, I have been over and over the matter, there is no way out without giving offence. To refuse to marry her now would send her brother straight into an alliance with Spain and bring war upon our heads. England is vulnerable just now and we lack the finances for war. Your Grace, I am truly sorry but … I can find no remedy."

He seems smaller, his face thin, his expression like a cornered rat.

By God, he will regret the day he got me into this.

I have to go through with it. Two days later than originally planned, garbed in my finest, I stand beside the despised woman at the altar. My hands are cold, and the sweat on my brow is as slick as if I have taken the fever. Of all the marriages I have made so far, this is surely the worst. It is like offering myself up for sacrifice and I am unaccustomed to acting against my will. I hope the country appreciates what I do for them this day.

While every sinew of my body craves to break away, to run screaming from the ceremony, I hear myself give this woman my vow. I bestow upon her a ring which has the words *'God serve me well to keep'* engraved upon it, and she accepts it, red-faced and nervous, yet well-schooled and gracious.

Perhaps her pretence is as great as mine; perhaps she too would like to flee. Yet, why would she? There is nothing for her not to like. I am the finest catch in Christendom.

It is all I can do to defer to her as etiquette demands. I bow over her hand, lead her into the company and try to play the part of a proud bridegroom. I smile blithely as their cheers crash around our heads.

The rest of the day passes in a nightmare blur; the congratulations, the feasting, the jokes, our first Mass as man and wife, followed by a strained intimate supper. And then the bedding ceremony, which is, without doubt, the most humiliating experience of my life. I felt less a fool the time when my horse pitched me headfirst into a muddy ditch, and I had to be fished out by my companions.

It is not mud that besmirches me now, but I am just as contaminated, just as sick.

I enter the chamber, the great bed in the centre of the floor challenging me not to turn and run, the crowding attendants happily ignorant of my imminent horror. I cannot look at her, but I know she is there, upright in the bed, waiting to be deflowered. Bile gathers in my throat as my cloak is removed, leaving me in a furred bed gown, a warm winter cap. My heart is hammering, my palms sweaty.

I will kill Cromwell for this, I swear it!

At last, I raise my eyes to my *wife*.

Anne sits in the centre of the great mattress, her hair loose, her eyes dark, a rictus smile upon her face. I remember other wedding nights, other brides, women I adored, pure women whom I had long lusted for. They were fair, dainty, and my desire for them was all-consuming. I will never manage to do my duty with this one. The very thought of it sickens me.

Cranmer is readying himself to give a blessing and, grudgingly, I allow myself to be hustled toward the bed. When they turn back the sheets, I climb reluctantly in and pull the blankets to my chest like a coy virgin. Cranmer's voice drones, the cheers and lewd jokes crash around us. I scowl at the company. I want to fight someone. Punch and kick and scream.

Will Somer climbs onto the end of the bed, hangs on to the post and makes a bawdy gesture with his hips and shouts "Give her one for me" – and I scowl at him, glad for once that Anne has learned little English.

It seems to last an age as, one by one, they give us their good wishes and quit the room, leaving me alone with Anne.

Alone with our awkwardness.

I am almost afraid. Excepting whores, I have never bedded a stranger before, and even with them I was given the chance to carouse and drink a little before performing the act. When it comes to marriage, there has always been weeks of courtship; years, in the case of the other Anne. I was desperate to have *her*.

The blankets rustle as my new wife shifts her legs and clears her throat. Thinking she is about to speak, I turn to look at her and she grins and blinks.

I wonder if she is a little simple.

"Your women will have told you something of what is to happen?"

She nods obligingly but I am not certain she has understood. I slide lower in the bed and she does likewise, lies on her back, blankets clasped to her throat, staring at the canopy as if preparing to give herself up for sacrifice. I turn to face her, run my hand beneath the covers, and place a hand on her knee.

She leaps and gives a squeak of alarm.

"Sshh, ssshh." I calm her as if she were a skittish colt before touching her again. Her knee is cold and bony, a scar or something rough beneath my thumb. I slide my hand a little further up her thigh while she lies rigid, unbreathing, her eyes wide open.

I am limp. I turn away.

"I will extinguish the candle."

Rolling over, I put out the light and turn back to the matter in hand. She is better in the dark. She could be anyone. Thinking of Anne Bassett, I run a hand up her thigh again, skirting her nether region until I find her belly which is … slack, and her breasts, when I squeeze them, are likewise soft. I had expected them to be high and firm like Mistress Bassett's, as my other wives' were, as virgins *always* are, but Anne's are flaccid and have slid toward her armpits; armpits which give off a goatish scent.

My desire, which was already lacking, dwindles further. I roll onto my back, stare into the dark and groan silently. The quiet stretches on, broken only by the sound of her hoarse breathing.

"I find I have quite a headache," I say, even though she will not understand. "I shall just lie here quietly until it passes."

She does not speak or move again but I know she is awake. Her breath ticks in my ear, her heart beats rapidly against my arm, pounding like a rabbit in a snare. It seems many hours until her body relaxes, and her chest begins to rise and fall in the rhythm of sleep. When I am quite sure she is too deeply asleep to be disturbed, I slide from the bed and scurry like a thief from the chamber.

I lean back on the door of my privy chamber, panting from the unaccustomed speed with which I have travelled. "Oh God, what can be done?" I pray aloud, and almost squeal with fear when a figure rises in the corner.

"Cromwell? Is that you?"

I peer into the gloom but, to my great joy, it is not he. It is Anne Bassett, come to comfort me. I hold out my arms.

"Oh, Anne, Anne; how did you know I needed you? I am so glad you are here."

She moves into my outstretched arms, warm and fragrant and, instantly, I want her. Hungry for reassurance, I kiss her lips, her face, her hair. I tug at her clothes and push her back toward the bed. I sit her on the mattress and sink to my knees, raising her petticoats that I might discover her body, taste her skin, and lose myself in the perfection of her person. I may be shackled to the woman whom England must now call queen, but she shall never have my love.

The next morning there is a buzz of excitement in my private chambers; the conversation is full of innuendo, and bawdy jokes seem to be the order of the day. At first, reluctant to be seen as a failure, I allow them to continue. Let them think I am tired out from rutting their new queen until the first light of dawn. It will only add to the reputation of my virility, but … I remember, rather belatedly, that if I do not tell somebody that the marriage has not been consummated, the door to annulment will be closed. For good.

I will be stuck with her.

"Enough!" I yell and, in the silence that follows, startled faces turn toward me. My cheeks burn as I summon the courage to admit my failure. "Nothing happened. I - I … we did not consummate the marriage…"

Shamefaced, I slump into a chair. I cannot bear to look at the surprised, discomforted expressions on the faces of my companions, so I stare into the opposite corner. Thomas Heneage steps forward.

"Were you perhaps taken ill, Your Majesty … or the queen?"

"I – I…" I beckon him forward so I may speak quietly into his ear. "I did not find her … appetising, and found I was not up to the task. Keep that to yourself, Sir

Thomas. You'd better seek Cromwell so we can decide what is to be done. I am reluctant to return to her bed."

I do, however, attempt the thing again. After a few tortuous days when no obvious resolution presents itself, I commit to trying once more to bed my wife.

Obviously, somebody has been schooling her, for she now wears better clothes of a cut that is more flattering to her figure. And the pretty English bonnets are more pleasing than her ugly German cap. She has also added to her store of English words and attempts a stilted conversation. I find myself warming very slightly to her sense of humour, her loud raucous laugh and willing nature, if not her appearance.

If she were merely a court lady and not my queen I would no doubt seek her out, for her company is pleasant now her questionable hygiene has been dealt with. If only she were married to Charles, or Sir Anthony, I would probably make a favourite of her, but not a mistress, and never a wife.

If only she were not mine.

She sits beside me at supper, fiddling with her wide sleeves, which she complains are getting "in da vay." Anne Basset moves forward, curtseys before addressing her, and the queen laughs, places a hand on my mistress' arm and says something that makes Anne smile in return. She has an honest, unfeigned laugh, and I am glad to see no antipathy between them. God forsake their relationship should be like that of Kate and Anne Boleyn - I fear I could not stomach that again.

Of course, the queen is not yet aware of my relationship with Anne, but I doubt it will be long before someone informs her of it, or she works it out for herself. I am learning that, in her case, foreignness does not equate to lack of wit. She is sharp and, if our fortunes were reversed, I doubt I would do as well in a foreign country as she is doing here.

Someone lets the dogs in, and they bound across the hall to greet me, covering my hose with hair and slobber. I grope in my pocket for the treats I keep there and after I have slapped their rumps and scratched their ears, they abandon me and run to greet the queen. I watch open-mouthed at the snub.

Careless of her fine clothes, Anne encourages them onto her lap and lets them lick her face, squealing in delight. Her face is infused with pleasure as she lets forth an unintelligible stream of excited German, which I presume is a mark of enjoyment. And then she cranes her head above their writhing bodies and suddenly smiles at me. The breath stutters in my throat and, with a start of surprise, I recognise a friend, an ally.

Anybody who likes dogs cannot be bad, and the fact that they return her regard speaks volumes too. I stand up and hold out a hand. The dogs tumble from her lap, bounce barking around our feet.

"Walk with me," I say, and she stands up and comes quietly with me into the garden.

When the winter cold reaches her and she shrugs down into her wrap, I pause.

"Is it too cold for you, would you like to go back inside?" I gesture toward the door to help her understand my suggestion, but she shakes her head, beats her upper arms with her hands.

"No, Your Majesty. The cold make me…" she waves her hand around her head, as if summoning the words from the sky, "awake."

I frown, puzzled, but then I realise what she means.

"Alive? The cold makes you feel alive? Yes, it does me too. It chases all the megrims away."

Like a mummer in a play, I beat my chest and inhale deeply and she throws back her head and laughs. Her laughter pleases me, and as we stroll between the frozen flowerbeds, I do my best to amuse her again. By the time my leg is hurting too much to continue, and we turn back to the hall, we have discovered a sort of kinship. I still do not see her as an attractive bedmate, but there is some level of understanding now.

When we reach the door and are about to re-enter the company, I hold her back and take her hand. It is cold, and the fingertips are red, but I kiss it anyway.

"I will come to you again tonight, if I may. Perhaps we might do better together now that we are becoming friends."

She stares uncertainly into my eyes, a crease between her brows, and moistens her lips with her tongue. She frowns, looks at the sky, searching for words.

"You … visit … tonight?"

"Yes, yes." I step closer, nodding, relieved that she understands. "If that will please you."

Her frown is not altogether flattering. She licks her lips again and inclines her head.

"Verra well, Your Majesty."

When we re-enter the hall, it is clear from the sudden silence that the main topic has been the strange goings on between us. Will Somer springs onto the floor, bows low before the queen and offers her a bunch of turnips. Anne draws away, her face a sneer of disgust, but I cuff Somer around the ear in a friendly manner and he scampers away.

"He is joking. Harmless … funny…" I demonstrate by putting my hands to my belly and giving a false Ho ho ho! Anne frowns and shakes her head, making it clear that her love of dogs exceeds her fondness for fools. I will have to speak to Somer, forbid him to torment the queen, but I am puzzled. Surely they have fools in Cleves; they have them everywhere, do they not? What is there not to like?

This time when I visit Anne's chamber it is without ceremony and only a few gentlemen escort me to her. They leave us alone together and she sends her women away. Instead of climbing straight into bed together, we enjoy a drink before the fire. As our halting conversation becomes easier, I realise I am growing accustomed to her appearance and even grow used to her odd, guttural accent. But still, when the time comes for me to take her to bed, although I try my best, my body is unwilling.

This is a new experience for me. While we were drinking together and laughing at the strangeness of it all, I felt that perhaps this was the night I would find the wherewithal to take her. But now, now that she is naked in my arms, my ardour completely disappears. It is as if I am sleeping with my sister. I roll away, almost ready to weep at the horrible futility of it all.

Perhaps it is the expectation. She lies there, waiting, wanting me, offering me her maidenhead, but I lack the ability to take it from her. I sit up and, without looking at her, I pat her hand and fumble for my robe before making another ignoble retreat.

As I close the door, I think I hear her weeping.

Like a small child with night terrors, I run in search of my mistress. She helps me to bed, tucks the covers about me as if I am an ailing boy, then she sits on the edge of the bed, places a cup on the nightstand.

"I still couldn't do it, Anne," I say, greatly shaken by my repeated failure to perform. "Perhaps I am sick, perhaps I am cursed."

I throw back the covers, wrench up my night gown, and we both stare at my member curled in its gingery nest.

"Nothing wrong with him, Your Grace," she says, running a fingernail lightly along its length. At her touch, the mutinous fellow leaps and swells. She smiles with satisfaction. "And there is clearly nothing wrong with you either, my love. Shall I join you so we can put it to the test?"

The next day I consult my physicians. It offends me deeply to have to admit my lack of prowess in the marriage bed. I want to describe my later, very satisfactory, encounter with my mistress, but delicacy and a care for her reputation prohibits that. Instead, I invent a raunchy dream… "When I awoke in the morning, my sheets were still damp from my emissions," I boast. "Now, I ask you, gentlemen, if I were impotent would this have happened?"

They scratch their beards, shake their heads and agree that since the problem doesn't lie with me, the fault must clearly lie with the lady. If a woman cannot make herself attractive to her husband, then what can a man do?

Feeling better about the whole affair, I send for Cromwell and order him to put more effort into finding a clause to free me from the marriage.

"Invent something if you have to," I say, "you will be well rewarded for it."

It may well be the best service he has ever done, despite being the culprit who caused the problem in the first place.

I have not forgotten that.

A few days later, we leave for Westminster, travelling by river where a great pageant has been provided to welcome Anne into the city. The water is alive with craft, the royal party travelling in many barges. My household go before me, then me in my own barge, with Anne following along behind in hers. The roar of the onlooking crowd does much to restore my confidence; this is Anne's first taste of London and its people, and through her eyes, I see it all anew, and I wonder what she makes of it.

A surge of paternal pride ripples through me as I look on the throng; every bridge is adorned with flags, bunting flutters in the chill breeze, and people lean over to cheer us as we pass.

As we approach the ships that are moored along the banks, they fire their guns, sending clouds of birds up into the sky as if they are part of the planned celebration. The pennants flap and dance. I raise a hand and encourage the people to cry out louder, and can't help turning to peer back through the undulating curtains of the barge to see how Anne is enjoying it.

Her smile is wide, her head held high, her wave stolid and proud, as if she belongs here. My people call out her name, joyful at our apparent happiness, and for once I am not jealous to see their love for another. The pageantry complements her well and I feel a momentary pang of regret that we are so ill-suited. She would make someone a good queen, but not me, unfortunately, not me.

*

"Your Majesty, I do not ask for much, do I?" Mistress Bassett looks at me plaintively. I am instantly wary, anticipating a favour I cannot grant.

"No, my love, you do not." I wait for her to continue. She takes my fingers in her palm, pouting up at me like a five-year-old begging for sweetmeats.

"Well, you will recall my mother has applied to the queen for a position in her household for my sister."

"I have not been made aware of that, no."

"Oh." She frowns. "Mother has written to Cromwell."

"He has not mentioned it to me, such matters are not my concern, I merely approve his final selection."

"Oh, well…" She colours, and frowns, biting her lip. "I was going to ask you to refuse permission."

I had not expected that.

"Refuse it? Whatever for? That is a most unusual request."

"Well, you will think me foolish, but I have no wish to have her so close. She is a plain, unwise girl with very few graces. She will not understand the etiquette, or the delicacy of our situation, and I fear she will gossip or carry tales to my mother."

"Tales about us?"

She nods the affirmative.

"Hmm, we cannot have that. It might be common knowledge around the court, but most people have the discretion to pretend ignorance. I will tell Cromwell to refuse her application but to look out for a post in a lesser household."

She clasps my hand tighter.

"Oh, thank you, Your Majesty. I am most grateful. There is nothing worse than a younger sibling's judgement. She is envious and sometimes quite spiteful."

"It was wise of you to bring the matter up. I know we have been inundated with petitions to attend the queen, but none have been properly addressed yet … until matters are settled."

"Has Cromwell still not found a solution?"

"No, but I am confident he will, if he values his head. I am dangling the idea of an earldom in front of him, to speed him along."

She laughs deliciously.

"That should do it, Your Majesty. Like a sausage, an earldom would make any butcher's dog sit up and beg."

"His father was a blacksmith not a butcher."

She laughs. "Yes but blacksmiths lack the sausages to please a dog. I needed the butcher to complete my metaphor."

*

I am beginning to think Cromwell is avoiding me. When we do meet and I enquire as to his progress in freeing me from this marriage, he is evasive, and uncharacteristically nervous.

"It is not something that can be achieved overnight, Your Majesty, but rest assured I am doing my best to work it out."

A film of sweat glimmers on his brow, the lines about his eyes are deeper than before, the shadows beneath them darker.

"We must hope your best is good enough. Go, get about your business."

He is losing his efficacy. He used to be swift and efficient. He bows low, backs away and scuttles like a rat from my presence.

I shuffle the pile of letters I must attend to, sign one or two, place them in a separate pile. Outside a gale is blowing, setting the casements rattling so loudly that I almost miss the sound of a footstep. I look up from my task and find Anthony Denny halfway across the floor. My heart lifts a little. This fellow is good company, better than any of my gentlemen since Brandon has been absent from court.

"Ah, Denny," I say, welcoming him into my presence. "Pour us both a cup of wine and tell me your news. Hopefully, yours will be more cheering than mine own. At least, for your sake, I hope it is…"

My words dissolve into laughter, but it is shallow mirth, designed to disguise my increasing despondency.

While he brings me a cup and pulls up a stool, Somer apes his movements, copying his long-legged stride and the care with which he plants his feet. I ignore the fool and feign deep interest in what Denny has to say.

"I have no news of import, Your Majesty, although that new mare I was telling you about seems to be in foal at last."

"Oh, that is good news. Let us hope she produces a fine new colt to improve your bloodline."

Even trivial conversation is a trap, reminding me of my own failing. The royal nursery may hold a prince, but he is in dire need of a brother, and quickly too, for the years remaining to me, if not yet growing short, are not infinite.

Deftly Denny draws my thoughts away from my failings and we discuss the merits and drawbacks of horse husbandry. The afternoon is drawing in by the time Culpepper arrives with a bowl and bandages to re-dress the wounds on my leg. When he sees I am with Denny, he hesitates and makes to withdraw, but I summon him back. He too is good company, his wit and natural comedy guaranteed to lift my spirits. He kneels at my feet, arranges his equipment and begins to unwind the bandages. As the wrappings are unravelled, the stench permeates the room, and I notice Denny smother a grimace of distaste.

Sometimes, I think the physicians will never find a cure for these sores, or even a reason for them. Despite what the doctors say, it makes no difference whether I exercise or not, they refuse to heal, and sometimes the pain grows so severe that I am brought to tears.

I look away from the young man as he gently cleanses the suppurating sores. Somer pulls a face and falls sideways to the floor as if the sight has killed him. It may do yet. If he continues to mock my agony, I will have him whipped.

Only Culpepper shows no disgust at his task; he treats my limbs as if they are made of glass, but no matter how light his touch, the pain is always excruciating.

"Thank you, Tom," I say, when the torture is over, and he is tidying the soiled linen away. His beguiling smile puts me in mind of myself at that age. Oh, how it hurts to know that no matter how I fool myself, I will never be so handsome and young again.

"I don't know how much longer this can go on, Denny," I say when Culpepper has left. He looks up enquiringly.

"Do you refer to your leg pain, Your Majesty, or … or the other matter?"

I ease my leg off the stool, grope for my stick and heave myself from the chair.

"Both really," I reply with a wry smile. "But, in this instance I was referring to my marriage."

"Ah, things are no better then?" He has the grace to look embarrassed about quizzing his king on the matter of bed sport.

"I just cannot summon the will to do it, Denny. She is nice enough but that isn't all a man needs in a wife, is it? I need a little spice, a little sauciness … if you will."

Somer leaps up and begins to make obscene thrusting movements. Denny turns his back on the fool and stutters over his next words.

"I suppose Your Majesty has tried, erm … thinking of something else … someone else perhaps whom Your Majesty finds … um, alluring?"

I give a shout of laughter that has more to do with his discomfort in speaking of such things than the picture his words evoke of me pumping my unattractive wife while thinking lewd thoughts of another more nubile woman. I make a note to relate the incident to Anne Bassett when I see her next … which I hope won't be too long.

He accompanies me about the room. I lean heavily on his shoulder.

"Sometimes there is no joy in being king, Denny. A common man knows no such inconvenience. If he tires of a wife, or his fancy falls upon another, there is nobody to care if he deserts her and takes another or plays fast and loose with his marriage vows. Yet I, as king, must toe the line, one missed step and the whole world has something to say about it. If I were Jack the ironmonger and misliked my new wife, who would care or question it if she ended up in the river?"

His laugh is uncertain. "I am sure Cromwell will find a better remedy than that. He always has before."

I halt, throw back my head, amused by his dry humour.

"Yes, indeed, you are right."

My mind travels back upon the journey I have taken with Cromwell. I remember when I first became aware of him. It was during his early days at court when he was Wolsey's man. Had he not stepped in when Wolsey failed to find a way to free me from Kate, I'd like as not still be chained to her. If that were so, there would still be no royal prince in the nursery.

I recall our growing friendship, the wars we planned, the cunning he showed in bolstering my emptying coffers with monastic wealth. The late dinners, the conversations, the jugs of wine we shared, the intrigue…

He helped me win Anne Boleyn, and when she was untrue did not hesitate to tell me I had been made a cuckold. In freeing me from her and giving me Jane, he provided me with the means with which to beget my son, my heir… There is so much for which to thank him, yet now, now when I need him the most, he fails me.

I come to a halt at the hearth and stare into the fire, narrowing my eyes against the glare of the bright orange flames. If he does not find the answer soon, his career and perhaps even his life will be forfeit.

Norfolk will see to that.

It would go hard with me to see him die a commoner's death or languish too long in gaol. I've a mind to raise him up, give him status so at least he has the chance to die well. He deserves that much.

But first, I will give him the chance to redress his mistakes and without further risk of war, free me from this marriage.

May Day 1540

The morning of the annual May Day celebrations dawns bright and the whole court is merry. Culpepper arrives early, a little after dawn, to change my bandages before the gentlemen of the bedchamber arrive to help me dress. Already garbed in their finest, we will make a fine splash of colour when we enter the competition grounds. I am not competing today, since my leg continues to plague me, but Thomas Seymour and Richard Cromwell will be riding in my stead.

Before I have finished dressing, Will Somer appears, clad as usual in goose turd green with a jolly feather in his cap.

"I am ready," he announces grandly. "Are you wearing that, sweet king, are you sure that is wise?"

He regards my finery with a curled lip, which makes the gentlemen gasp, but I am confident I am looking my best. Somer is doing what he is paid to do. It is a shame more of my servants don't do the same. My companions may have missed the cheeky sparkle in his eye, but nothing evades me. I content myself with clouting the fool around the head and, when he ducks away laughing, I throw a jug at him.

It crashes at the feet of Culpepper who is just bringing my hat for approval. He stops in surprise, looks wide-eyed around the chamber.

"Is it safe to come in?" he asks with a grin before approaching and arranging my cap at a jaunty angle, and fluffing the wisps of feathers so that they float fetchingly about my head.

I put my hands on my hips, lift my chin and regard myself in the looking glass. One could almost mistake me for my younger self, the prince I used to be. I may be wider about the middle but that makes my figure even more imposing. My face is just as handsome as in my youth, only manlier, wiser; my clothes are equally as fine, if not finer. Any woman would be proud to call me husband. I release some flatulence, reach for my stick and limp toward the door with my finely clad gentlemen in tow.

By the time we reach the gardens, I am breathless and, with each step I take, pain shoots up my leg. It is not long before my conversation with Culpepper descends from gentle banter into short, barked replies. When we mount the stand, I sink gratefully onto the throne and rest my foot on the cushion provided.

Dear God in Heaven, it is more than a man should have to bear.

Somer settles himself at my feet and starts to play with the tassel on my cushion. A few moments later, the queen arrives, all smiles amid a throng of brightly coloured waiting women. After waving a greeting to the crowd, she curtseys, offers me her hand and chatters almost incomprehensively for a while, as if oblivious to the fact that, despite our nights spent together, I have not yet taken her virtue. I no longer even seek to do so.

Unable to face the humiliation of another failed attempt to be roused by her unappealing body, I just crave to be free of her. Yet still, despite all, Cromwell is dragging his feet and, all the while, Whitsuntide, when the queen's coronation is due to take place, grows closer.

I must be rid of her before then.

"Here comes the butcher," Somer says and, as if my thoughts have summoned him, Cromwell appears suddenly before me.

"Ah, my Lord of Essex, you have deigned to join us." I do not mention his new coat, or his finely wrought staff. "There are pressing matters we must discuss later. I trust your new title is pleasing. How are you finding it, my Lord Earl?"

He misses my curled lip and answers pompously.

"I like it very much, Your Majesty, and I am eternally in your debt."

I look away, sniffing disgustedly, as if someone has walked shit in on their shoe.

"See you don't forget it," I say as he backs away, head bowing, in a picture of servitude.

I will give him until June.

A roar of delight goes up as the first competitors enter the lists. I lean forward in my seat, the better to see, and wish I'd remembered to bring my spectacles. Sometimes I feel my whole body is betraying me; my legs are a constant trouble, my eyesight dims, my bowels give me discomfort, and even my libido is inconsistent. Once I would have been happy enough to hump the ugliest woman in Christendom, but now I have grown finicky and can perform only with the best company.

As always when I watch the joust, I remember that fateful day; I can never forget the crunch of wood against my skull, the bright flash of light as I lost consciousness. Neither can I help remembering the strange trance I fell into; hearing all, seeing all, yet unable to speak or move. I remember realising I was about to die, and I had no son. I had no HEIR! I shake the memory away and concentrate on the moment, glad for now not to be part of it.

A great thundering of hooves as the horse approaches, a crash of wood splintering on metal, the scream of a horse and the first contestant topples amid an uproar of applause. Dash it, my coin was on him. It seems I win at nothing today.

I give Somer a petulant kick and slump back on my cushions. If my next wager fails to bring in some coin, I will be considerably out of pocket.

So far, even my fool has made better gains than I.

The afternoon wanes, the cries of the crowd slacken, the excitement of the morning is replaced by yawns. Soon it will be time to retire to the palace, where I shall rest before the evening entertainments begin. Gone are the days when I could joust and feast and dance without pausing for breath. I sigh, thinking of the lengthy toilette required, the feigned goodwill, the false camaraderie. It is nothing like the old days. I wish Brandon were not away from court, we could ponder old times. In truth, I would rather take supper in my chambers away from the prying eyes, but May Day comes but once a year and even kings must mark it.

A short time spent reading before the fire and a considerably longer nap and I am soon revitalised. My clothes are laid out in readiness, and once more I am made ready for the world. When I enter the great hall, I find the queen has already taken her place at the table. She looks up when the trumpet sounds, raises a hand to greet me, and I bow before taking the seat beside her. The musicians begin to play, discordant at first, but soon easing into melodious unison. It is a song of my own composing; perhaps the evening will not be so unpleasant after all.

The queen says something, raising her voice above the music. She shakes her purse at me, the coin within chinking merrily, and I realise she is taunting me, boasting that her luck was better than mine. Somehow, with little knowledge of the competition, she placed her money unerringly on the victor almost every time. Inwardly scowling, I smile and wave a mummery of congratulations as if I am not smarting at the ignominy of such heavy losses. Soon, the tide will turn, and God will have me in His favour again. Soon, I tell myself, all these troubles will belong to yesterday. Soon, I will be happy again.

When Norfolk arrives and joins me at the table, the musicians begin to play a court favourite, and I am glad to recognise the first few bars of another of my own compositions. Gentlemen lead their chosen ladies on to the floor, and they form up for the dance while I look on glumly, wishing I could join them.

It is not so long since I was the nimblest dancer in the country. The men here are lacklustre in comparison. Their posture is wrong, their steps are clumsy, and when they reach the part where the gentleman is required to leap high in the air, their attempts are laughable. I am watching them, my despondency deepening with each moment, when suddenly, as if freshly descended from Heaven, a young woman spins onto the floor. She sinks into a deep curtsey before her young partner, who bows in return and offers her his hand.

I cannot take my eyes from her as they move away toward the back of the hall, following the directives of the dance. Then she spins on her heel and for the first time I look upon her face. And what a face it is!

She is laughing, her arms wide, her skirts swirling around her ankles, her red lips wide with joy. Her body moves as one with the music, lithe and vigorous. She is exquisite!

My heart leaps, my breath falters and I watch transfixed as she spins and skips, her mouth stretched into a smile. Beneath my gown, my lazy member stirs.

I lean toward Norfolk.

"Who is that girl, Norfolk? That one there, in the crimson gown. What is her name?"

He raises his spectacles and squints across the smoky hall.

"Ha!" He laughs. "Funnily enough, that's one of my nieces, Your Majesty. Katherine, my late brother Edmund's girl. She was lately in the dowager's household and has only recently come to court."

I cannot stop looking at her and, later, when I have retired for the night, her face swims in my mind, the sound of her laughter resounding in my ears. It is hard to believe she has been at court for an entire week without my noticing her.

I will never be unaware of her again.

"Katherine…" I murmur the name, as if it is unfamiliar, for it seems different somehow when applied to her … she is exotic, mesmerising, just as she is.

Over and over, I relive the first moment I saw her. I see again the instant she burst like sunshine onto the dance floor with her face alight with happiness, her cheeks dimpled with delight. Oh, to be young enough to… *That* is the sort of woman I need. As soon as I laid eyes on her, I felt young again, just looking, just witnessing her enthusiasm for life. She has no airs and graces, no false modesty, no posturing or posing – she is simply Katherine Howard.

When morning comes, I am so distracted by the thought of seeing her again that I hardly notice the pain in my legs as the bandages are changed and I am made ready for the day.

"I feel better today, Thomas," I say as Culpepper gathers the soiled linen. "Something has reinvigorated me. Are you using a new salve?"

"No, Your Majesty, I used the marigold infusion that you made up yourself."

I sit up, place a hand on each knee and beam at the gentlemen gathered in my chamber. "Well, I fancy a turn about the gardens and later perhaps, a trip across the river. I think I shall dine with Gardiner again; his offerings at table are always appetising. Norfolk, you will accompany me. Perhaps that pretty niece of yours isn't too busy to grace the company also."

"I will make sure of it, Your Majesty. We are honoured by your notice."

"And I will come too, sweet king, I have a new green tunic and a brave new feather for my cap."

Aping my pose, Somer claps his hands on his knees, and the dogs, who had been peacefully slumbering, think it a game and leap upon him, barking. He slides to the floor beneath a snarl of hounds.

I wave the other gentlemen out but Norfolk remains behind. I place a hand on his shoulder. "Your niece, Katherine … she's a good girl, is she, Norfolk? Not like the other..."

"I'd lay my life on it, Your Majesty. She is a good girl, not a thought in her head beyond shoes and jewels."

His face is open, assuring me that this young Howard girl is unblemished, untainted by the dishonour of her cousin, Anne.

"Good, good." I pat his shoulder and whistle for the dogs, who abandon Somer and come running, barging rudely past me to be first out the door.

The day seems long. I do not see her in the morning, and by the end of the afternoon I am bereft when she fails to appear. Long before it is time to depart for Winchester Palace, I retire to be made ready for the evening entertainments, insisting my finest clothes are laid out ready. I examine my reflection from all angles, confident that my face is as handsome as it ever was.

Time seems to stand still, every moment dragging before it is time to take the barge across the river. The closer we get, the faster my heart beats. I feel like the man I was of old, the virile prince enchanted by my brother's widow; the young king before his head was turned by the wiles of Anne Boleyn; there is nothing like love to rejuvenate a jaded soul.

As our craft nears the opposite shore, I try to remember her face and find I have almost forgotten it. I can see her eyes, remember the shape of her mouth, the soft hue of her cheek, but what shade are her eyes? And her hair, is it fair or dark, curled or straight?

The barge bumps against the wharf and the boatman springs out to secure the vessel. I am helped to stand, and assisted to shore. I cling to Culpepper's hand, stagger as the barge moves beneath me. Once, I would have leapt out before we were properly moored, but today I am less nimble and require the arm of a friend.

The steadiness of land is reassuring. Somer gambols on ahead while someone hands me my stick and we make our way toward the welcoming lights of Winchester Palace. I had hoped for a quiet meal among friends, but the hall is thronging with merriment. When I enter, the conversation abruptly ceases, and the company falls to its knees. I had not anticipated such formality. Gardiner comes bustling forward, bowing and urging me into his sanctum.

"Welcome, welcome, Your Majesty. I am honoured by your presence and have arranged a variety of entertainments for your pleasure."

His smile is wide, and I lack the heart to inform him I craved peace and privacy. It will prove difficult to improve my acquaintance with Norfolk's niece in this crowd.

We enter the hall to a blast of trumpets, and I take my seat at the top table, Norfolk at my side, Culpepper close at hand should I have need of him. I lower myself into the proffered chair and ease my leg onto a stool. When I look up, I realise the company is standing to attention, waiting for me to give them leave to sit. Casually, I raise my hand, and a babble of conversation and scraping of stools drowns the sound of the musicians, who are tuning their instruments in readiness. The torches flicker, the candles bob and dance, and the air seems to hum with expectation.

Had I wanted this, I could have had it at Westminster. All eyes will be upon me, my every move, every comment, bandied about Europe before the week is out.

The food is borne in upon trays and laid before me. It smells delicious, but it is not for the cuisine that I have come. Nevertheless, I pick up a pastry and gaze about the hall in search of the woman who has consumed both my heart and mind since yesterday.

Is it really so short a time? Putting down the pastry again, untasted, I lean toward Norfolk.

"Where the devil is your niece, Norfolk? I did not come all this way to look upon tumblers and minstrels."

A strain of girlish laughter takes me by surprise.

"I am here, Your Majesty."

A face peeps from behind Norfolk's broad back, a well-remembered face alight with merriment that makes my heart leap. At the very sight of her, my spirits are elevated to the heavens. How did I ever manage to forget her face?

"Why do you hide from us, my dear? Norfolk, swap places with your niece. I would get to know this lady better."

Mumbling apologies, Norfolk hauls his ageing body from the chair beside me and exchanges places with Katherine. Her presence engulfs me with gladness. I take her hand and raise it to my lips, lingering longer than is strictly necessary. I taste her skin, sweet like honey, inhale her scent, heady like roses and then, reluctantly, I release her. Our eyes meet and she laughs, as if as delighted by my company as I am with hers.

She leans over and peers at my plate.

"That looks tasty," she says, her eyes greedy. "My mouth is watering."

So is mine but not for the food.

"Have one, please. I should be honoured."

She colours but accepts the offering and, with mischief in her eyes, she sinks her pretty white teeth into it, a little honey oozing onto her chin.

"Oops, I am sorry," she says, wiping it up and placing the lucky fingertip between her lovely lips. "Mmm, it is delicious," she says. "I can never resist a pastry."

My heart is beating so rapidly I can feel it in my throat. I have not the slightest desire to eat but, to display unity, I take a huge bite from my own slice.

She laughs again. I wish she would never stop.

"You've crumbs in your beard, Your Majesty," she points out, and I thrust my chin toward her.

"Could you brush them away for me?"

Her eyes open in surprise but, quite unabashed by the familiarity, she reaches out and, with a gossamer touch, brushes my beard clean.

The moment lasts longer than most. I know this girl is going to prove significant in my life. She is not another Anne Basset or a Mary Boleyn. This woman has grasped my heart and my soul and while there is breath remaining in my body, I will be hers.

Silence falls, our eyes are locked and, after a while, she leans closer.

"Your Majesty, people are staring."

I pull away, look across the hall and see she is right but, as if tethered to her, I turn back.

"So they are. I do not really care. Tell me, what else do you like … besides confectionary?"

That laugh again, light like a fresh breeze. "I'm afraid I am greedy, Your Majesty. The women at my grandmother's house are always telling me I will grow as fat as a hog if I don't learn restraint."

"Well, if that comes to pass you will be the prettiest hog in the whole of Christendom."

I only say it to amuse her and this time her laughter is contagious, and although the company are unaware of the joke, they join in too.

At the back of the room, I see Will Somer grab one of the serving maids. She squeals when he tries to kiss her. The company grows uproarious, and the meal passes in a whirl. I am so deeply in Katherine's thrall that my plate is still half-full when it is taken away.

The musicians come forward and the dancing begins. I long to take the floor with her as I used to do in my youth. She watches the dancers, her foot tapping, her fingers performing a small secret dance of their own. I reach out for one, trap her hand in my own.

"I wish I could invite you to dance, my dear. There is nothing I'd like more."

She turns to me, her face flushed with happiness.

"Why don't we try, Your Majesty? This is not such a vigorous tune. You can stand still, if it please you, while I dance around you. It might amuse you."

And so, amid huge applause, I find myself limping beside her onto the floor and the company watches in amazement as I stand like an oak, an English oak clad in autumnal gold, while Katherine cavorts like a forest nymph around me.

She is just as agile as I remember. Her body is pliant, her step as light as air, dainty as a fairy and, when the music straggles to an end, I can wait no longer. I lean forward and, before all the court, I take her hand and anoint it with my lips.

June 1540

"I looked upon Cromwell as a friend once, you know, Norfolk. He led me to believe there was nothing he would not do for me, yet he cannot or will not free me from this hag."

"I tend to think it is a case of 'will not', Your Majesty…"

I look up sharply, my eyes narrowing in question.

"What makes you say so?"

He pulls a face, splays out his hands.

"May I speak frankly, without fear of repercussion?"

"Of course you may. Come on, man, spit it out."

He hawks, audibly swallows phlegm before replying.

"I … and others like me, suspect our 'Earl' of self-aggrandisement. He makes no secret of his Lutheran leanings. We know he plotted with – with the Boleyn woman to introduce the new learning. It was his agenda that led to the end of the monasteries…"

"But he was right, Norfolk, they were corrupt, all of them, living off the fat of the faithful. It was proven that most of their miracles were falsehoods, there was no blood of Christ, there were no finger bones of St Paul. It was all lies, the church deserved to come down!

He raises his hands in submission, closes his eyes against my tirade and, belatedly, I recall my promise that he might speak without consequence. I take a deep breath.

"Go on, have your say."

He inhales, gestures to a stool.

"May I, Your Majesty?" I wave him into the seat, and he lowers his body slowly, grunting with the effort.

"You may remember how toward the end of her … the - the days of the Boleyn woman, she and Cromwell, who had up until that moment been firm allies, fell into dispute?"

Suspicion stirs in the pit of my stomach, but I nod and wait for him to continue. He clears his throat again. Looks away.

"It is commonly acknowledged that there was some disagreement as to the nature of the monastic closures…" He waits for me to nod. I make him wait a few seconds before giving my assent. "Well, I and many others are of the same mind, wonder if he … embellished the charges he brought against the qu … against Anne."

My belly lurches so violently I almost vomit. My lips are tight against my teeth.

"What do you mean?"

He blows out his cheeks, looks me warily in the eye.

"I mean, Your Majesty, that I have long suspected she may after all have been innocent of some of the crimes against you."

"Which crimes?"

He holds out his arms, palms upward.

"Adultery? Treason? What would she have gained? Anne was no fool. And one has only to consider that the men who died with her were, every one of them, also enemies of Cromwell."

The silence that follows is so profound that I can hear the spaniels snoring by the hearth. I stare into a corner where the face of Anne Boleyn, so vital and bright, rises like smoke before me. *Was* she innocent? Not of everything … surely… I look at Norfolk, plunging my eyes deep into his soul.

"She was your niece; you are just seeking vindication."

He holds up his hands again.

"I swear before God, Your Majesty. I am your good subject. I would lay down my life for you, I have done, many times, and I would see my own mother go to the scaffold if I thought her guilty of even a small sin against you."

"Y - you are old school. You are trying to reinstate the old ways. Bring back the monks…"

Sorrowfully, he shakes his head.

"We all know it is too late for that, Your Majesty."

As I stare at him, his rheumy eyes fill with tears, and I realise he is speaking the truth … as he sees it. But if he is right, Anne's death, the death warrant I signed myself, was erroneous. It cannot be. Surely, it cannot be.

Sweat breaks out on my forehead. I run my hands through my hair and wish I had not allowed this conversation to begin. This is knowledge I cannot bear. I WILL not bear.

I fumble for answers.

"But the trial, Norfolk, the witnesses?"

He shrugs, turns his gaze away.

"Witnesses can be bought. It wouldn't be the first time such things have been rigged."

"But you yourself sat in judgement, and you deemed them all guilty."

And if she was innocent, so were those who died with her. My wife, my friends…

His eyes slide away, but not before I note a flash of shame … regret.

"Perhaps I was also fooled, Your Majesty…"

Silence. Black, dismal silence before the significance of this revelation rushes upon me in an angry, tortured tide.

"No, no, this cannot be. Her death was deserved, and so was that of … of my friends."

I see again their once beloved faces: Anne, George, Weston, Brereton, Norris … and that other fellow, the young one with the lute.

I stand suddenly, swaying, closing my eyes against the pain that shoots up my leg. I am going to be sick. I manage to limp a few steps before throwing up in the corner and, when my servants come running, I hold out a hand, fend them off without recourse to words.

Swiping sweat from my brow, I slowly straighten up; my head thunders, my heart bangs like a great hammer. Surely, *surely*, my skull will split in two. Slowly and painfully, I turn back to Norfolk, who has the grace to hang his head. As my equilibrium returns, I limp toward him, place my hand on his shoulder and speak quietly through my teeth.

"I need to think. You will speak of this to no one … *ever*. Not to me, not to others. Nobody must ever know of it. The whole thing must be forgotten. Buried!"

As *She* is.

But I can't get it out of my head. My concentration lapses during council, my mind drifting back to it. I bark at my companions, at the servants, even at my mistress. The court creeps fearfully around me, the conversation is muted, the atmosphere tight as if the world might implode at any moment.

Anne. Could it be true? Was I truly duped by Cromwell into destroying my own wife, my queen? For the first time in years, I allow myself to think of her as she really was. She tried my patience, she argued, she offended, she teased, but … I was never in all my life so astounded as the day Cromwell informed me of her infidelity.

She was fastidious in all things. Would she really have committed indiscretions with half my court? The moment of Cromwell's revelation is stuck fast in my memory. I will never forget how the news made my world spin, hitting me in the gut as hard as the impact of a charging bull.

It wasn't just a wife I was robbed of. I lost good friends too. Men I'd believed would lay down their lives for me. I feel again the rage, the sense of betrayal, the despair, and I remember the cold misery of the day she died, accused of treason, fornication … incest.

The horror and the shame of it washes over me again, as if it were yesterday.

George's face comes alive in my mind. He is laughing, shaking his head at my gullibility. *How can this be true?* I pride myself on my ability to judge a man, how to recognise an enemy on first sight, but Cromwell, the lowly blacksmith's son, has played me for a fool.

How he must be laughing from the safety of his great palace – everything he owns, from the horses he rides to the great houses he lives in; the very clothes on his back have been provided by me.

In a fever of uncertainty, I summon Cranmer, swear him to speak only the truth, but I can only bring myself to confide half of my suspicion. When it comes to it, I find it difficult to find the words. He clasps his hands, sits nervously in a chair before me and waits for me to begin.

"You're a good man, Cranmer. I have raised you high."

"You have indeed, Your Majesty, and my gratitude will be eternal."

I frown, considering my next words carefully.

"I know you lean toward the teachings of Luther." He opens his mouth to protest but I silence him with a raised hand. "But that is not my concern today. You are a good servant and that will suffice for now, but I would know who has the first call on your loyalty; myself or Cromwell?"

His eyebrows slide upward.

"My loyalty to Your Majesty goes without saying. Cromwell and I are friends and share many beliefs, many…"

"Enough to sit by as he betrays me? Enough to plot against my rule?"

His jaw drops, his head moves from side to side in slow denial.

"Never! I swear it. Cromwell's loyalty and my own is to you alone, Your Majesty. I would never … there is no … of what do you speak exactly, Sire?"

I inhale deeply and turn away to frown into the sulky fire.

"I suspect that in recent years, Cromwell's motives have been less than honest. I think he has been devious. He has worked with other agencies against my best interests, and against the best interests of England too."

Sweat oozes from Cranmer's brow, he swallows, his Adam's apple bobbing in his throat as if it will choke him.

"I would swear on the Bible that I am innocent of any such thing and I very much doubt that Cromwell has ever been anything other than your very good servant."

I see the truth in his eyes, or the truth as he sees it. That is the trouble with truth, it is variable. Cranmer is a good man. An innocent in a corrupt world. I have never really doubted him, but he is seemingly as gullible as I. Good men are easily fooled.

He shifts in his seat, clasps his hands between his knees and speaks earnestly into my face.

"Your Majesty will not forget that Cromwell and I have many enemies at court. Men who would seek to bring harm upon us, men who wish to snatch away the influence we enjoy, to enable them to further their own ambition."

"Of course I have not forgotten that. What king has ever been able to trust his closest companions? All men seek to rule us. They are intent on furthering themselves at our expense, keen to raise their families high but, when they believe they are powerful enough, they strike like a serpent strikes, when we are at our most vulnerable. I have it on very good authority that Cromwell is such a man and has been from the very beginning."

In the corner, Somer quietly sings a rhyme about a butcher who was hanged for stealing another butcher's sausages. Like many at court, he has always confused Cromwell's lowly beginnings as the son of a blacksmith with that of a butcher. I bark at him to be silent, and he subsides back among the dogs.

Cranmer's white face gleams in the gathering gloom. For a long moment, we stare at one another until at last his eyes drop away.

"I can only plead innocence in all of this, Your Majesty, and I beg you, please, do not act too swiftly. Be certain to identify your real foe before you act upon nefarious information."

I place my hand on his shoulder, and he relaxes slightly at the friendly gesture.

"I am no fool, Cranmer. There is very little that escapes me."

Yet even as I make the remark, I wonder at the truth of it.

When he has gone, I sit alone in the chamber until it is almost full dark, and a servant appears to light the torches. My mind is restless, my last words mocking me, for it is now apparent that I am wrong and there is much that slithers past my notice. My throne is like an island surrounded by a sea of snakes, and I stand alone in defence of it, armed only with my wits.

"May I get you anything, Your Majesty?"

The voice intrudes on my thoughts. I shake my head. He clears his throat again.

"Culpepper is without, wishing to tend to your leg."

"Eh?"

The man repeats it, speaking a little louder, enunciating his words as if I am a deaf fool. I realise that Tom Culpepper is just the company I need to rouse me from my megrim. I ease myself back in the chair.

"Yes, show Tom in."

The conversation of the young man who kneels at my feet and deals tenderly with my wounds is like a balm. There is no hint of intrigue, no mention of spies or betrayal. He speaks of dance steps, and jests, of wild rides across the countryside on half-broken horses. He talks of women, of music, and in his voice is the almost forgotten sound of youth, and optimism. He is invigorating, joyous, and hilarious in turn and, by the time he has rebound my leg and made me comfortable, I have almost forgotten my former melancholy.

When his task is done, he bows and takes his leave, turning at the last moment to bid me a restful night. I am sorry to be alone again with my thoughts, and my encroaching dotage.

And then, suddenly, Norfolk is there. I start in my seat, for a moment unsure where I am.

"I must have dropped off," I say, wiping drool from my chin. "Is something wrong?"

"I needed a word, Your Majesty, but your servants were reluctant to wake you. I hope you will forgive me."

"Only you dared?" I say, reaching for a cup and freshening my mouth. "What is it?"

I struggle to govern my slumbering wits, pull myself higher in the chair and smooth the front of my doublet that spreads like a green velvet meadow across my knees.

I suck in my belly.

"I wondered if you'd given any further thought to…"

"I've thought of little else," I snap, and he steps back, closes his eyes against my wrath. "What did you expect? That I'd forgotten all about it?"

"I am concerned that Cromwell may have got wind of our discussion. We have intercepted some letters he has written, and we have depositions from his servants – damning depositions. It is clear he works against Your Majesty's explicit desire. If we leave it too long, he may wriggle free, escape our shores and continue to undermine your rule from overseas."

Would he do that? Is this true? Or is it another lie, another underhanded move in the war between the factions that fracture my court? It is a risk I cannot ignore. Miserably, I nod.

"Very well. Have a warrant made up."

*

It is the end of the month before the attainder is brought against him. June, the month of roses, warm sun, and sudden freshening showers; a time when the court usually gathers in the gardens, when the minstrels stroll between the flowers, their songs rivalling the birds'. Yet this June is different. Cromwell is locked in the Tower on a charge of treason, and I too am imprisoned.

Alone in my chamber, I stare at the death warrant. I pick up my pen, hold it above the parchment and put it down again many times. Before I make my mark, I plunge it back into the ink bottle. The corner of another document peeks from beneath the first. I slide it toward me; force my eyes to absorb the painful words of his letter again.

And now, most gracious Prince, to the matter first whereas I have been accused to your Majesty of Treason. I never in all my life thought willingly to do anything that might or should displease your Majesty; and much less to do or say that thing which of itself is so high and abominable and offence as God knoweth (and who I doubt not shall reveal the truth to your Highness). Your Grace knows my accusers, God forgive them. For I ever always had love for your honour, person, life, prosperity, health, wealth, joy and comfort and also your most dear and entirely beloved Son the Prince, his Grace and your proceeding, God so help me in this my adversity, and confound me if ever I thought the contrary. What labours, pains and travails I have taken according to my most bounden duty, God also knoweth, for if it were in my power to make your Majesty to live ever young and prosperous, God knows I would; or if it had been or were in my power to make your Majesty so puissant that all the world should be compelled to obey you, Christ knows I would, for so I am of all others most bounden. For your Majesty hath been the most bountiful prince to me that ever was king to his subject, yea, and more like a dear father than a master. Such hath been your most grace and goodly counsels towards me at sundry times, that I ask your mercy where I have offended.

The letter is long and impassioned, and it gives me pause. I think long and hard, trying to root out the truth. What if, in condemning this man for disloyalty to the crown, I am, in fact, empowering his enemies? Norfolk and Gardiner have hated Cromwell since the day I first sought his counsel. They despise him for his lowly beginnings, seeing him as an upstart, a usurper of a court position that should rightly belong to noblemen alone. They hate his lowliness and his politics as much as they hate his religious views. What if, in severing Cromwell's hold on me, I am surrendering myself into the hands of a worse enemy?

I pick up the letter again. His outpouring of love and devotion lodges somewhere high up in my chest as I recall memories of late suppers, riverside walks, and quiet jokes. There were other times too; bitter quarrels, occasions when I clouted him around the head for overstepping the boundaries. He never seemed to resent my violence toward him, he always bounced back with a gracious smile on his face, and a jest to smooth the way forward and show that he held no grudge against me. Even when he insisted I was wrong, I always forgave him. But now, the violence I am considering will be final.

There is no coming back from the edge of the axe.

The sentiments of the letter hold little surprise. He makes the same noise as any other man pleading for his life. He declares himself innocent of all accusation; he states his intentions were always honourable, his love for me and his desire to serve me unchanged. Perhaps I should take Norfolk's head instead. I take up the letter again, skipping over the middle part.

Most gracious and most merciful sovereign lord, beseeching almighty God, whoever in all your causes has ever counselled perceived, opened, maintained, relieved and defended your highness so he now will save to counsel you, preserve you, maintain you, remedy you, relieve and defend you as may be most to your honour, wealth prosperity, health and comfort of your heart's desires. For the which, and for the long life and prosperous reign of your most royal Majesty, I shall, during my life and while I am here, pray to almighty God that He of his most abundant goodness, will help aid and comfort you, and after your continuance of Nestor's years, that that most noble Imp, the prince's grace, your most dear son, may succeed you to reign long, prosperously and felicitously to God's pleasure, beseeching most humbly, your Grace to pardon this, my rude writing, and to consider that I am a most woeful prisoner, ready to take the death when it shall please God and your Majesty. Yet the frail flesh incites me continually to call to your Grace for mercy and pardon for my offences and in this, Christ save, preserve, and keep you.

Written the Tower, this Wednesday the last of June, with the heavy heart and trembling hand of your highness' most heavy and most miserable prisoner and poor slave.

And he ends...

Most gracious prince, I cry for mercye, mercye, mercye

This last salutation almost breaks my resolve, but I think again of Anne. I can feel her presence. It is as if she is standing at my shoulder goading me, compelling my hand to pick up the pen again. If Anne was truly innocent and died at Cromwell's whim, then it is fitting that he too should die innocent.

I dip my pen and quickly make my mark.

July 1540

Condemning Cromwell seems to remove obstructions to the annulment of my marriage to Anne. Within weeks, an agreement has been reached that she accepts with unflattering readiness, that her precontract with the Duke of Lorraine is too great an impediment. She knows the legitimacy of royal children is vital, and accepts that her former contract may well have placed any children of our marriage in jeopardy.

She is happy to remain in England and, as Anne Basset points out, any woman would be ashamed to return to the land of their birth as a rejected bride. But that is not all she receives; she accepts generous settlements of plate and manors, palaces including Richmond and Hever, properties of which I am inordinately fond. There are other honours bestowed upon her too. She is to remain part of the royal household, with the title of the King's Beloved Sister, and barring my wife and daughters, will enjoy precedence over every woman at court. It is an amiable agreement, and she seems content.

Tired of the whole affair, I deliberately throw aside the blanket of gloom that has been smothering us and the court becomes gay again. I am free to woo Katherine openly now, and I shower her with gifts of land and costly fabric. With her at my side, we inject a bright and somewhat brittle gaiety into the summer of 1540.

And one fine evening after supper, pretty, diminutive Katherine Howard promises to become my fifth and final wife.

*

Word reaches me that it took three blows of the axe to remove Cromwell's head but, pushing away the horrid reality, I turn my full attention to my new bride. It is the future we must focus on. There is nothing to be done about the past.

Cromwell failed me; his death is justified.

At Oatlands, the palace I recently refurbished to house Anne of Cleves, Katherine graces every room she enters. Her gaiety invigorates even the dullest company. She is bright, energetic, vivacious, and I am gratified that nothing hinders our joining on the night of our wedding. I had feared the old problems would return, but there is none of the embarrassment I suffered with Anne in my bed. Katherine awakens the latent boy in me, and I manage to make love to her twice, once in the evening and then again on waking. She is delightful, as tight and sweet and fragrant as a rosebud.

On our first morning as man and wife, after breaking our fast we ride out across the park, enjoying the unprecedented warm weather. Insects are out in number, gallivanting among the flowers, the grass swaying in the warm breeze, the air buzzing with bees and butterflies, but by noon it will be oppressive.

"I will race you to the woods," Katherine calls over her shoulder, already halfway across the mead before I have even realised the race is on. Pain shoots up my leg as I forget myself and kick my mount into a gallop, but I ignore it and follow where she leads. I cannot help but remember other races with other women, other wives. Kate, Anne, and Jane. But my many disappointments are now in the past and God is finally smiling upon me. All I require now is that He send me a son ... and soon.

I allow her to reach the wood ahead of me, slowing my mount as she disappears into the cooler, green darkness. Barely out of breath, she turns in the saddle and laughs, beautiful in the dappled shade of the trees.

"I am the victor, Sire, now what is my prize?"

"You made no mention of a prize before the race began; in fact you kept it secret there was to be a race at all!"

She pouts prettily, flutters her lashes until I relent.

"Well, perhaps there is a small gift for you back at the palace. You can claim it later."

"Oh good, shall we go back now?"

"Not yet, my love, let us ride slowly here beneath the canopy so I might catch my ... so I can show you the swans on the lake that lies on the far side of the wood."

The music of her laughter merges with the birdsong.

"Very well, I suppose I can wait for the surprise." Surreptitiously, I ease my leg in the stirrup before we urge the horses into a slow walk.

There have been few instances of unadulterated happiness in my life, so few that even as it unfolds I recognise that this is such a moment. I shall keep the memory of it forever. The weather, the woodland, the company of my perfect bride, the certainty of another night with her, and another after that until I reach my dotage ... and soon, the prospect of a son. When she turns to look at me, her face is alight with joy, with love, and I know myself to be the happiest king alive ... the happiest of men.

Our marriage is as yet a secret. I want to keep her to myself, and even ten days into our idyll I am reluctant to announce our union to the world. However, I cannot tarry too long, for if she is already pregnant, there must be no question as to the legitimacy or the paternity of her child.

If the people are surprised by the swiftness of our marriage, they do not speak of it. Blessings and good wishes are showered upon us, gifts are sent from all over Christendom, and Katherine is in her element. I pick a careful path through the heaps of newly acquired finery that litter her chamber floor and lift a puppy from a nest he has made for himself in a fine length of sarcenet. I hold him up to my face. He opens his mouth and shows his pink tongue, his tiny pearl-like teeth. In less than a month, she already has more dogs than I do.

"Who is this little fellow?"

Clambering over the pile of clothing she is sorting, she comes close to me and ruffles the pup's ears.

"This is Brock, because he looks like a badger … see?" She holds back his ears and immediately his nose seems longer, the black and white face more badger-like.

"He does indeed, well named, my dear."

"And his sister…" she stoops and retrieves another puppy from beneath the bed, "is called Kitty."

My jaw drops in astonishment.

"Kitty? That's a peculiar name for a dog! How will she ever hold up her head?"

She laughs, expanding my heart as she plants a kiss on my cheek.

"I wanted something different, something I could be sure no other dog in the world was called."

Her cheeks dimple as she beams at me. I plump down on the bed and draw her onto my good knee.

"Ingenious, my sweet. Nobody else would think of such a thing."

"I know."

"It won't be possible to take all your dogs along when we leave for our progress in August. You will have to choose a favourite."

"But I love them all, Henry. They are all perfect in their own way, it isn't possible to pick which I love the best."

"But they are too young to enjoy travelling. It will be too much for them; we will be visiting Surrey, then on to Reading and down to Buckingham. The plan is to stay there a few days and then on to Ampthill by the end of the summer."

She tilts her head, rests it on my shoulder, and I can see down her bodice to the swell of her breasts. I watch fascinated at the rise and fall as she breathes, and I send up a fervent prayer of thanks for the possession of such a beautiful creature.

Kitty is wide awake now, chewing at Katherine's fingers, and my wife's laughter reverberates.

"How can something so pleasurable hurt so very much?" she wonders ingenuously. My eyes stray around the room to where her women are sorting through the new finery. I catch the eye of Lady Rochford, jerk my head to dismiss her, and she herds the women from the chamber, leaving us alone.

Katherine looks up from the pup.

"Where have they gone? Did you send them off?" Purposefully, I remove the dog from her hands and ease Katherine from my lap and turn her toward me, my hands bunching up her skirts so I might find her flesh.

"So many petticoats," I complain, and she laughs, catches her breath as I discover her skin. She wriggles her knees and my fingers rise higher, and to my delight, her thighs part obediently at my unspoken request.

Gently, I stroke the soft down of her quaint, lean forward to nuzzle between her breasts, while she throws back her head and gives herself up to the pleasure.

It is like the slow unwrapping of a parcel. The lacings slide from the eyelets, the stiff bodice peels away, revealing her kirtle. I turn her over and she watches me with dark serious eyes as I begin to loosen yet more lacing. Her shift is damp and creased, clinging to her body, her breasts clearly visible beneath. With a tortured moan of desire, I cast the clothing to the floor.

Afterwards, we lie together unspeaking in her dishevelled bed. Her hair is strewn across my chest, one long bare leg thrown across mine as she draws circles in the hair on my belly.

"If that doesn't get you with child, nothing will," I boast, and she shifts her leg, pulls herself upright.

"My ladies advise I should lie down with my legs raised after we've ... been together. That way your seed will have an easier route to my womb."

"Go on then, do so, do so." As she moves to obey, I slap her bare rump, making her squeal. "There should be laws against such beauty as you possess."

She makes a pile of pillows and reclines upon them, her hips higher than her head, her arms akimbo, her breasts pert and inviting, her hair flooding like water across the counterpane. I have noticed before that she is markedly immodest, but I take pleasure in it, rather than offence. It is part of her honesty, her unashamed acceptance of who she is. One of the things I like most about her is her lack of artifice.

"Once you are with child, I will give you anything you desire."

She turns her head, her eyes wide.

"Anything? I shall give it some thought. I am sure it won't be long before I have good news."

Hoping my promise isn't too rash, I roll reluctantly from the bed, wincing as my feet hit the floor and a shaft of pain slices up my leg.

"Oh," she frowns, "do you have to leave me already, Henry? I get so lonely when you are gone."

"I must. I have a consultation about the new fortifications we are building in the south, and there is further trouble from the Poles."

She sighs. "Poor Lady Margaret. She must be so afraid and lonely in the Tower."

"Then she should have better control over her family. Those damned Plantagenets have been nothing but trouble, even in my father's day. When will they accept that they've been beaten? England belongs to the Tudors now."

She rolls onto her belly, forgetting that she is supposed to be nurturing our son.

"But Lady Margaret didn't do anything, she wasn't involved…"

"Wasn't she? Sending letters to traitors, sheltering them? How long before she joined forces with them or started to send them funds? Money to be used against us."

It is the closest I have ever come to scolding her. She shrinks from me, her face crumpled in confusion, and I am instantly sorry. With my hose half on – half off, I clamber back on the bed and scoop her into my chest.

"I have no wish to fight with you, dear Kate, but you speak of things you do not understand. Come, lift your legs again and pray for a child to take root."

I help her into position. "There, stay there for an hour. That should do the trick."

Obediently, she does as I say.

*

Last winter was unusually dry and this year there has been little rain since February. As we approach the end of July and are making ready to leave on a progress into Surrey, the true seriousness of the matter is brought to my attention at the Privy Council meeting.

"It isn't just us, Your Majesty," Norfolk says, flapping his cap before his face in an effort to cool himself. "The whole of Europe is similarly affected. The Thames is now so low there are dangers of the incoming tide polluting the water supply."

I grunt, peer at the parchment he slides across the table toward me. It is unbearably hot in here, even with all the windows thrown wide. There is no air, every breath I take seems stale, a taint of disease to it that deepens my resolve to take my bride further into the countryside, away from the dangers of town.

"Farmers are complaining of crop failures, no fodder for the livestock. The cattle will start dying soon and then there's the risk of famine…"

"There is already flux and pestilence among the lower classes, and it won't stop there, soon it will be affecting us…"

While I imagine the horrors of pestilence, their voices increase to a babble, their faces, creased with worry, stare expectantly at me as if I have the answers, as if I can call upon God and order him to send the rain.

I throw up a hand and the clamour dwindles. I frown at the paper before me, the long list of catastrophes: hunger, ague, withered crops, heath fires, fish floundering in shallow streams that were once well-stocked rivers. I close my eyes and think hard, conjuring a myriad half-fledged remedies that shrivel before they have fully formed. This is beyond my power.

"We must pray," I say, ignoring the disappointed faces, the wary distrust that blooms in their eyes. "We shall send forth commissioners to the four corners of the realm, ordering prayers to be said in every parish. God will assist us. This is a test we must endure until He relents."

I stand amid a clatter of stools and, groping for my stick, I ignore the murmurings of disbelief and dissention, and go in search of my wife.

As I limp along the corridors toward her apartments, the troubles heaped on me by this morning's council meeting buzz like wasps in my mind. I can take action against most things that beset our nation. I can launch ships against foreign attack, I can send troops against enemies, I can and have protected my subjects from corruption and greed. The weather, however, is beyond my jurisdiction. It is God and only God who can govern the skies.

The door to the queen's apartments are ajar and I slip into the room unannounced. Kate is clad only in her shift; the sunlight that shines through the window reveals the shadow of her long, lovely limbs as she dances with her women. Some of her companions have likewise discarded their top gowns, but most are properly dressed. When she sees me, the queen stops dead, but her uncovered hair dances on, the curls at the ends continuing to sway and bounce for happy moments after her body has stopped moving.

"Henry! What a lovely surprise; I am so glad you have come. We are practising a new dance; it is the one we plan to perform for the ambassador's dinner next week."

I take her in my arms, kiss the top of her hair, her fragrance flooding my senses, making me stir.

"I hope, on that occasion, you will be wearing more than just your shift, my dear."

She laughs and spins away. I notice her women, abashed at appearing half garbed before their king, are struggling back into their gowns. It is only my pious side that is offended, the other half delights in being surrounded by semi-clad women. Anne Bassett, I notice, has remained fully dressed, as has her friend, Isabella Baynton, half-sister to Katherine. Their faces are wary, as if they are holding their breath, awaiting my displeasure. I turn my attention to the younger set, who have discarded their gowns to cavort with the queen. Lady Rochford, who is most definitely old enough to know better, is retying her sleeve, perhaps caught in the act of disrobing. As Kate dances by, I grab for her wrist and draw her back toward me, speak into her ear.

"You are a naughty girl who deserves a spanking."

She giggles and presses against me, confident that my displeasure is feigned. I can feel the heat of her body, my hand slides to her buttocks, naked beneath the thin linen shift.

"It is so hot, Henry. I don't know how you bear it in all those clothes. Why don't you take some off?"

"Take some off? I am not a plough boy!"

"We could pretend you are, and that I am your light o' love."

I am clad in my summer tunic, a light coat only and the finest of silk stockings. She tugs at my sleeve and reluctantly I let her have her way and remove my coat.

"There is no need to pretend you are my sweetheart. You are my sweetheart."

Her women retreat to the other end of the chamber as I pull her onto my good knee, surreptitiously squeezing her breast while she giggles and wriggles on my lap.

I let my gaze wander around the room, her women discreetly turned away, their heads down, eyes averted, but then I notice the company is not comprised only of women. Several of Katherine's musicians are present, tucked at the end of the chamber; one has a lute placed strategically across his knee. To my horror, I also spot Somer, curled up on the window seat, sound asleep with his head lolling. They too will have been witness to the queen's frolic; they will also have enjoyed the sight of her luscious legs outlined through her shift. Jealousy bites at my heart. I lurch to my feet, sending Katherine sprawling to the floor.

"Leave us, all of you!" I bellow, and they scuttle away like mice from a tom cat.

I look down at Katherine, my jaw tight, my eyes narrowed.

"You must learn decorum. It is not fitting for the Queen of England to cavort half naked before other men, do you hear me?"

Her face crumples, tears spout from her eyes. She rubs the back of her hand across her face, and I realise that, as usual, she has no kerchief. Reluctantly, I offer her mine, a huge square of lace-edged silk. As she mops her eyes and scrubs her cheeks, my frown eases.

My anger, so quickly roused, is as quickly quenched. I cannot stay cross with her for long. She is so sweet, so innocent, kneeling at my feet in her white linen, her hair flowing in a red river over her shoulders. I reach for a strand, the softness runs like silk between my fingers. She looks up and sniffs inelegantly. My gaze trickles down her body, enjoying her near nakedness, the tease of her taut breasts. She gives a tentative smile, which prompts me to reach out my hand.

"You can dance for me though, my queen, if you would."

My voice is husky with longing and, with much deliberation, she rises to her feet and moves to the window, where she begins to show me the steps of her new favourite dance.

I cannot recall when I have ever witnessed such beauty, such seductive innocence. As she sways, her arms perform a separate lazy dance to her body, which writhes and contorts. Like Salome, she keeps her eyes fastened on mine as she moves, eyes that are full of knowledge she rightly should not have, eyes that are ripe with invitation.

And as I watch her, my mouth grows dry.

October 1540 - Ampthill

The royal progress passes through Berkshire, and then north to Notley and Buckingham, where I attend a council meeting at the Old Castle House. Then, at the end of the month, we arrive at Grafton, the old home of my great grandmother, Elizabeth Woodville. Here, we hunt and feast, and each night I visit the bed of my queen. Although she shows no sign of being with child, yet the enjoyment of trying is comfort in itself.

There is time, I tell myself. *I must not give up the faith.*

As we ride on toward Ampthill, the heat starts to decrease, and we realise that summer is at last on the wane. On the first night there, the feasting is in full swing, the wine is flowing and the dancing frantic. The queen persuades me to join her on the floor and, to the delight of the company, I manage to perform a few steps. The refrain is a lively one and, after so long travelling, I would cope better with a slower melody, a dirge perhaps. It seems unfair that I should be tired to the bone while Katherine is still as lively as a kitten.

When the music finally ends and the dancing stops, applause thunders around us. I clasp my wife's hand, lift it high, and she jumps up and down, her hood crooked and her face slick with perspiration.

"Thank goodness that is over," I remark as we move toward our seats.

"What was that, Sire?" Katherine halts. "I didn't hear."

"Oh, nothing. I was just remarking on my love for that tune."

It will not do for her to realise how much she exhausts me. Nobody must guess that I cannot wait to take the weight from my aching feet, to rest my throbbing thigh. But just as we prepare to sit, Edward Baynton stands up, his cup held high.

"Your Majesty, I should like to raish a cup, a toasht to you and our grassious queen. A lovelier couple has never graced the throne…" He stumbles as if his knees have given out and clutches the edge of the table before sliding elegantly beneath it.

"Drunk as a lord," Katherine laughs as we return to our seats. "I never saw the like of that before," she giggles as she smoothes her skirts before sitting down.

"No." I frown.

It is not like Baynton to overstep the mark. He is a servant of many years, and was with me throughout the – the trial of my second queen. Anne … *was she really the faithless traitor of common belief?* I push the thought away and focus on the here and now. I have a new wife, a young, beautiful, politically ignorant and totally flawless rose.

The past is done with.

I shake my head, disapprovingly.

"I must speak to the Council about drunkenness. It is unseemly at court, and we must guard our reputation. Did you know that every little incident is reported overseas? I will have a word with Baynton when he is fit to heed me."

*

I wake in the depths of the night and know instantly that I have a fever. I grope on the nightstand, knock over a candle, and Culpepper, slumbering at the foot of the bed, leaps to his feet.

"Your Majesty?" He fumbles in the dark for a taper and reignites the flame.

"I am unwell."

My voice sounds alien, unlike my own. I haul myself up on the pillows but as I do so, pain like nothing I've felt before shoots up my leg. With a yelp of agony, I put both hands about my thigh, which is burning hot and swollen.

"My leg, my leg." I point at the wound, spew the words through gritted teeth. Culpepper stands stock still, his eyes fixed, the sight before him rendering him speechless. It is not until they bring the candle close that I understand why.

From knee to groin, my leg is twice its usual size, the skin is livid, the old scar stretched smooth and the flesh around it turned black and puckered.

"I will fetch the physician…"

Without waiting for my assent, he grabs his tunic and flees from the room, yelling as he goes. I fall back on the pillows, while other gentlemen emerge from the outer chamber. They fuss around, plumping pillows, pulling the covers to my chin, which I thrust rudely away.

I am so hot it feels as if a fire is burning beneath the bed. I lay back, prone upon the pillows, gasping like a landed fish. It seems an age before footsteps denote the arrival of the doctors. While the gentlemen fall back, the physicians move in, bend over the bed, and begin prodding and assessing, asking inane questions.

While they hum and harr, I hold my breath, grind my teeth.

When did Your Majesty last pass water? When did Your Majesty last vomit? What was the colour of Your Majesty's last stool?

I heave upward on my elbows and scream into their faces. "Give me something for the pain. NOW, or I will have your fucking heads!"

They fall back, cluster in a corner muttering and plotting against me, before nominating Culpepper to hold a cup to my lips while I sip from it.

I cling to his wrist.

"They are fools, Tom; I'd as soon trust you as any one of them."

His face swims before me. He murmurs something about honour and devotion before removing the cup and bringing a damp, cold cloth for my forehead. He turns to the physicians, his voice sounding as if he is a long way off.

"His Majesty is burning hot. Should we open a window?"

"Good God, man, are you mad?"

They throw up their hands, uttering warnings against the dangerous miasmas that linger in the night air.

"Beau, where is Beau, bring him to me..." I call out, hang my arm over the side of the bed and click my fingers, expecting to feel his hot wet tongue on my skin. "Where is Beau?"

I raise my head, daggers of pain shooting through my skull. "Who is Beau?" Culpepper asks.

"He had a dog of that name when he was a youngster." Norfolk wrinkles his brow, rubs his nose and looks away. *Norfolk?* Who sent for him? How long has he been here?

And then it seems I am in the great hall, still in my night rail, and the whole court is gathered around me. They are laughing at my state of undress, pointing at the ugly gash on my thigh, my white belly that undulates beneath my shift like a bowl of custard. Then Chapuys is there, turning up his nose, examining me with disgust before turning back to his comrades. "The King of Spain would never be so immoral," he sneers. And then I am no longer in the hall but back in my own bed.

I am sick.

I must not forget that.

"Beau?" My voice is small, like a whining child's.

"I could fetch one of His Majesty's hunting hounds," Tom suggests, but Norfolk's guffaw puts paid to that idea.

"Into the royal chamber? We cannot have that."

"He'd not know, not in this state." The tepid flannel on my forehead is exchanged for a colder one, someone lifts one of my eyelids, someone else dares to probe my thigh. I scream long and loud at the scalding touch.

I am in torture.

They speak in whispers, yet their voices resound in my head, echoing and loud now whereas before they were quiet. Great booming voices that reverberate about the room, rage in my ears like a clash of symbols. I put up both hands to muffle the din.

"The queen's dog, her pup. I could fetch that, His Majesty would not know the difference, not in this state, and it might bring him some comfort." Tom again, thinking beyond my pain to my spiritual need.

A rush of air as the door opens and closes again. The candles flicker, the smell of burning paper wafts toward the bed. Water trickles down my brow as they apply another flannel.

"We will have to cauterise the wound."

They are speaking to each other, not to me. I am their victim, they are my gaolers, and the rack they turn is tearing me in two. The voices clash, sword against sword in my brain.

"Do you dare?"

"Do you not dare? This could kill him. Would you stand before the court, before God, and admit you neglected to treat the king because you were afraid?"

Norfolk's bellow is the loudest of all, and then silence falls briefly. I lie there panting, present yet ignored, knowing I am ill, knowing this is not reality, it is nothing but a waking dream, a living nightmare.

Then a clattering of bowls and raised voices as they argue over who should wield the knife.

Is it not treason to draw the blood of an anointed king?

The door opens, a waft of welcome air engulfs me, and then the sound of pattering claws on the wooden floor, and a tongue, wet and warm on my hand, on my face, on my neck. Soft fur beneath my fingers, tiny teeth nibble at my ear lobe ... "ARGHHHHHHHH!"

The teeth bite deep, the piercing pain is all consuming. I scream for my mother, for it to stop. I scream for death, for mercy, and then something warm floods down my thigh, followed by the stench of rotting meat, rancid flesh.

Vomit surges in my throat and someone brings a bowl; my body wracks with unbearable pain as I spew vileness from my body. I clutch the puppy to my chest and feel its tiny frantic heart pulse quickly against me. As the pain recedes, relief rushes upon me in a cooling tide. My breath slows, my heartbeat decreases, chasing delirium away; my fingers move in soft, warm fur and a tiny tail thumps against my cheek.

Although the pain has lessened, it is still there. Recovery is slow and I am ill for days, but even though the crisis has passed I refuse to admit the queen to my presence. Instead, I send her a note and a precious ruby to thank her for the loan of her puppy. It eased me so.

Do not worry, I write. *I will soon be recovered. In the meantime, you must amuse yourself as you see fit. I will be back in your arms before long.*

But it is several weeks before I am fully recovered. Somer spends most of his time in my chamber, entertaining and annoying me in turn with his rude ditties, which he sings in a low off-key voice. I am glad he is there to help me through the darkness.

They tell me I have been overtaxing myself; over exertion caused the ulcer in my leg to fester and rupture.

"From now on, Your Majesty, I fear it must be drained regularly and kept open to prevent the fever from taking hold again."

I yearn for the physical perfection of my youth and rue how it was wasted, how briefly it lasted. I would give my soul to be that man again and able to love my sweet Katherine as she deserves to be loved.

Leaning heavily on my stick, I limp stiffly to the window, pain with every step, and look out across the garden to sigh with longing at the scene below. Life at court, it seems, has continued without its king.

A crowd of brightly clad courtiers are strolling between the autumn flowers and amid them is Katherine. My heart lifts to see her again. Her puppies scamper about her feet, she would be in danger of tripping were my favourite, Tom Culpepper, not at her side.

I watch as they walk together and smile when he says something so amusing that she throws back her head. There is nothing that pleases me more than hearing her laugh. I am glad that he is distracting her from my absence and I make a note to reward him for his loyalty that apparently knows no bounds.

October 1540 Dunstable

"I hope you weren't bored while I was ... indisposed?"

Katherine looks up from the hearth where she is grooming one of her dogs, combing him with great care and picking fleas from his coat with a grimace of distaste. She smiles, the dimples on her cheeks appearing like the sun from behind a cloud. The transformation to her features is sudden and completely enchanting. She abandons her dog and comes to perch on my knee, lowering herself gently for fear of causing me pain. My hand slides about her waist. Still trim, I notice, there is no hint that she carries a child. She flicks her veil aside and leans forward to kiss the end of my nose.

"I missed you, of course, but there were entertainments and things to keep me occupied. I ordered some new gowns and those new gloves arrived, the ones with the pearls…"

My leg, which has been much improved since they drained it, begins to throb but it is a pale shadow of the searing pain I suffered a few weeks since.

"We ride on to Dunstable in the morning, there's a council meeting I must attend, but after that we will spend a few days at The More, and then home, to Windsor … for some good hunting, I hope."

If I am up to it.

She smiles happily, kisses me again and slides from my knee. Apart from the misery of illness, it has been a successful progress. I have shown off my new wife to the people and avoided the pestilence that has been rife in the towns and cities this year. Now the hot summer weather is waning, it should be safe enough to return, although I had hoped Katherine would be pregnant by now.

What a joy it would have been to announce a forthcoming royal birth on our return to the capital. Not only would a child serve as proof of my continuing fertility, but it would also have shown those who questioned my choice of bride that the king is always right.

I watch the queen now. She is on her knees, her pup rolled onto his back, his tongue lolling, his legs obscenely splayed while he allows her to scratch his belly. I smile at the extraordinary dart of envy that enters my heart, but I push the sudden longing for her aside. There will be time for that later.

I must pace myself if I don't want to be ill again.

"I am going to take the pups outside," she says. "Why don't you come, it is still light enough?"

I reach for my stick, haul myself to my feet. Her women follow at a distance as we make our way to the gardens. The babble of their voices, the yapping of the dogs, the happy laughter of my queen follow us, and I enjoy a level of contentment that has evaded me of late. At last, I am in God's favour; in His mercy He has provided me with a young, fertile wife. I know a child will soon follow and on that day I think I might very well burst with joy.

The one blot that spoils my happiness is Mary. Our reunion while Jane was alive continued during my short alliance with Anne of Cleves, but now … she disapproves of Katherine. She does not say so outright, obviously she dare not, but her perpetual sneer makes it clear she thinks her too young, too undignified, and too ungoverned to be a queen. Even Katherine's Catholicism isn't enough to pacify Mary. No doubt she is jealous of my affection, for the queen is younger than Mary by some eight years.

I appreciate that it must be strange to have a mother younger than oneself, but you'd think, for my sake, she would be pleased. Why can she not just be happy for me?

When Katherine first complained of Mary's attitude, I took my daughter to task over it. The mulish expression she assumed while I scolded her was the exact replica of her mother's. The consequences with which I threatened her forced her compliance, but in a show of displeasure, she is less often at court, and has taken a step back from the entertainments.

I find I miss her. Mary is good company when she wishes to be, an asset to any gathering, with her effortless manners and poise - she would provide a regal balance to

Katherine's excesses. I wish they could be friends, as my youngest daughter is.

Elizabeth warmed to Katherine from their first meeting. Someone must have whispered of the blood connection between them because before they even met the child sewed the queen handkerchiefs, and embroidered a book cover to present to her. In exchange, the queen gave Elizabeth a jewel from her own collection, the value of which made my eyebrows rise. Katherine laughed it off when I reproached her for it.

"Oh, Henry, it is nothing but a trinket," she said, kissing my daughter and bidding her sit beside her.

Edward, of course, is too young to have preferences. He is happy to dribble over any bosom, but I was disappointed at their first meeting when Katherine passed him quickly back to the nurse and checked her gown for stains. I sometimes worry that she has little care for infants, but then I remind myself that it doesn't matter if she is not maternal, as long as she can bear me a son. There are others who can have the care of him.

Katherine's voice breaks into my reverie. I take her hand.

"I'm sorry, my dear, I was miles away."

The giggle that always precedes a sentence is like water over clear pebbles.

"I said, it is nice to feel the chill in the air and perhaps a hint of rain. It has been so long."

I look anxiously at the sky. Is it going to rain? I hope so. It will prove to everyone that God listens to me. When I sent out commissions for prayers to be read throughout the realm there were those who scoffed but, if it does rain, then God has answered and will prove that once again, I have made the right decision.

"The gardens are so dry. Even the lavender is suffering."

She stops, tilts her head questioningly.

"Which one is the lavender?"

"Oh, Katherine." I take her arm again. "What did your grandmother teach you?"

"Oh, very little. She left it to my ladies to coach me, although I … I did have a music master who taught me a little, and I can dance very well."

"You can indeed; you grace my court – our court – perfectly."

"There's a new one I've been learning that has quite intricate steps. My ladies say I will have it perfectly once I remember not to clamp my tongue between my teeth as I concentrate."

Somers takes the arm of one of the queen's female fools and they prance along the path before us as if they are quality folk. The queen laughs, high and loud, and even though they are out of earshot of our conversation, her women join in.

Katherine is like that. Her happiness is infectious. I have felt it myself. She brightens the darkest days. Apart from Mary, everyone loves her the instant they meet her. I have seen the crustiest members of the court melt beneath her notice. Even Cranmer is smitten, and he if anyone should disapprove of her Catholic leanings.

Our steps slow and I halt near an arbour, the leaves of the honeysuckle, long fallen during the drought, lie scattered about our feet.

"I have something for you." To contain her excitement, she clasps her hands while I grope in my pocket.

"Oh, do you? What is it? What is it?"

She grabs the package from me and tears the wrapping aside but, before opening the box, she glances up at me, her eyes alight with affection. "I love it before I even know what it is, because it is a gift from you."

Her voice is breathy, like a child's at Christmas. While her head is lowered I take the opportunity to dash away the emotion that has gathered on my cheeks. I send the Lord another prayer of thanks.

"Oh, Henry!"

She dangles the necklace before her eyes, drinking in the frigid beauty of the rubies and pearls. "It is lovely, thank you so much. Put it on for me!"

She drags the priceless necklace she is wearing from her neck and thrusts it into her pocket before turning away from me and lifting her veil so I can fasten it. Before I tie it in place, I pause to admire the way her hair grows at the nape of her long, elegant neck. I let my gaze trickle down, past her shoulders, to the neck of her bodice, glimpse the swell of her bosom, and remember the scent and taste of her. The need for her is sudden, and so demanding that my hands are trembling, obliging me to make several attempts to fasten the jewel.

December 1540

After a long dry year, the winter blows in wet and cold. We shun the outdoors and take refuge in our apartments where the fires are banked high and thick tapestries ward off the worst draughts. Each day, I escape from the duties of kingship as early as I can and head for the queen's apartments, where she is usually dancing with some of her household.

A group of musicians play in one corner while the women practise, and a few gentlemen are lounging by the hearth watching them. I regard the scene jealously. It doesn't seem right that while I am labouring for the good of the country, the underlings are at their leisure with my queen.

But then I recognise Culpepper's laugh and at my approach they stand and welcome me, stepping aside to allow me access to the comfort of the flames. The queen has not yet noticed my arrival, or at least she has not acknowledged it. I watch as, with dainty prowess, she steals the limelight from the other women.

Jane Rochford and Margaret Douglas make up the trio on the makeshift dance floor, while Isabella Baynton sits to one side, restraining Katherine's dogs, who are yapping and straining at their leashes. The trains of the women's gowns sweep the floor, the bells of their skirts undulating, and every so often, a small, slippered foot peeks from beneath. All goes well until Katherine mistimes a step and they collide inelegantly, and the dance descends to chaos.

"Oh, damnation, will I never get it right?"

I've never heard her curse before. Uncharacteristically, Katherine turns moodily away, pushes her women aside and emerges with her face clouded. She looks sulky and less pretty … until she notices me. Then, suddenly and dramatically, she is transformed.

She claps her hands, wreathes herself in smiles and comes to greet me. I drop my cane and stand shakily, my hands reaching for her.

"Henry! I didn't hear you come in. I suppose you saw how clumsy I am. I just cannot get the steps into my head. My mind wants to do one thing while my feet demand to do another!"

She slides her hands beneath my coat and around my waist, and lays her head against my chest. "I can hear your heart," she murmurs. My hands rest upon the back of her head and we stand for a while, just taking pleasure in each other, just being Henry and Kate.

The world seems to pause but after a while the silence in the chamber becomes strained. When I look up, the eyes of the courtiers are averted, all but one. My gaze clashes with that of Anne Bassett, who doesn't even try to keep the anguish from her face.

I draw back a little, and waving the company away, I nod for a servant to fetch wine. Placing a finger beneath her chin, I urge Katherine to look at me.

"What is the matter, Sweeting? It is not like you to be so cross."

As I look at her, the feigned happiness melts away, her eyes fill with tears, and her chin wobbles.

"Oh Henry," she sobs. "I am so sad."

"Why?"

I fend off her women and guide her through the crowd to a chair, sitting down with her on my knee. Drawing a kerchief from my sleeve, I hand it to her so she may mop her tears. When she has done so, she screws the silk into a ball.

"I – I thought … I was so looking forward to telling you I am with child…"

My heart leaps, my grip on her tightens, but she shakes her head, her chin drooping to her chest. "But I was mistaken, Henry. This morning I … I am so sorry, Henry, so very sad."

Her face crumples, tears rain down her cheeks, her shoulders juddering. I feel like joining her but, swallowing my own disappointment, I ease the kerchief from her fist and mop up her tears again, pretending it doesn't matter.

"There, there, do not take on so. There is time; you will give me a son by and by. I am sure of it."

But I am not sure.

Each month, my conviction that she will give me a son becomes less assured. She slumps against me, and we spend the rest of the afternoon in idleness. Every so often she groans, wriggles, presses a hand to her stomach, and each time she does so my disappointment deepens.

To cheer her, I give her a bracelet I'd been saving for a later date, and my ploy works so well she is soon busy planning the Christmas festivities. She bombards me with chatter about tumblers and players, musicians from Europe, and clothes for each feast, and our chambers are heaped high with gifts. It seems she has forgotten nobody, even the lowliest servant has some small offering from her.

"It will both warm and cheer him, Henry," she says, sitting back on her heels, twirling a fine knitted cap on her finger.

"Yes, my dear, but you could have instructed one of your women to arrange the gifts for the torch boys. The queen should have no need…"

"Oh, but I like buying presents. Look what I have for Kitty!" She holds out a jewelled collar, an eyewatering cost for a gift for anyone, let alone a dog. "And I have bought two similar for Anne's dogs and one for Mary's … as a peace offering."

"Anne's dogs?"

"Your loving sister. She is joining us for the Christmas feast, is she not?"

To my surprise, now that the demand for me to sleep with Anne is removed, I find my Beloved Sister to be pleasant company and am gratified that, after some initial distrust, she and Katherine have become friends.

"So she is. I just wasn't sure which 'Anne' you referred to. There are more than one at court."

She frowns and pouts.

"Well, *Anne Bassett* is never going to be among my favourites, is she? I don't know why I suffer that woman in my household."

"Katie, Katie, don't be silly. Since I laid eyes on you, it is as if no other women exist. Anne did me a service when I was low. I have no need of her now. She is no match for you."

She brightens and, with a rustle of silk, comes to sit beside me as if seeking reassurance. I put my arm about her shoulders, pull her closer and, as always, the very scent of her stirs me.

Surreptitiously, I count back the days in my head. It will soon be time for her monthly megrim again, it will be a good time to visit her bed this evening.

At the thought of her welcoming arms and pliant body, I grow warmer. I pull off my cap and glance at the window to see how long I must wait until nightfall. She will be fertile now; if I get her with child this night, by the spring the realm will be gay with hope again. By next Christmas, we could have a prince to shower yuletide gifts upon.

I feel it in my heart that 1541 is the year Katherine Howard shall give me a son and, when she does, I shall have her crowned.

No expense spared!

I wile away the afternoon dreaming of the birth of my son, a brother to Edward, the insurance my father always insisted was imperative. I picture Katherine abed, her hair flowing over her shoulders, my son cradled in her arms. She is strong, strong enough to survive what other women haven't … a pang of fear stabs me in the ribs, but I shake it off. It is a woman's role to risk her life in childbirth. They do not shirk from it; my mother gladly risked her life and went to God in her attempt to secure the Tudor dynasty, and so too did Jane.

But I would be loath to lose Katherine. It doesn't bear thinking of. *Oh, dear Father in Heaven*, I beg fervently, *spare me the grief of losing another wife.*

I deserve happiness in my twilight years.

But as the year 1540 draws to a close, my happiness continues to be marred by trouble. My niece, Margaret Douglas, not long released from the Tower after a contemptuous and unapproved marriage with Lord Thomas Howard, has now taken up with another Howard. This time she chooses the queen's half-brother, Charles. I don't know wherein Margaret's fascination for Howard men lies but their alliance is treason, whether he is family now or not.

Despite Kate's pleas, I put out an arrest warrant for her brother, but before it can be acted upon, I learn he has fled the country. Furiously, I send Margaret straight back to Syon House where she was on house arrest before I forgave her the last indiscretion. I am so consumed with rage I could suffocate. I seek out the comfort only Kate can give.

When I burst into the queen's apartment, several of her ladies and gentlemen bow from our presence, and I launch into a tirade.

"Why can she not keep her lowlier passions hidden, why can she not be discreet? She acts like a common trull, not a woman of royal blood. In God's name, she must know she is too close to the throne to risk the besmirching of her name…"

Katherine puts a finger against my lips.

"You are turning a funny colour, Henry," she says, pushing me into a chair. With great tenderness, she takes off my hat, strokes my hair while raining soft kisses on my beard. Gradually, I calm; my heartbeat slows, my breathing regulates.

I let out a sigh and close my eyes.

Damned woman! I think as my anger recedes. Katherine's ministrations replace ire with gratitude. I am blessed to have her. Like a mother bird with a chick, she fusses over my comfort, and I revel in it.

"There, that's better, my love," she says, pressing a cup into my hand. I take a deep gulp of wine.

"Margaret has always irked me, as much as her mother did. When my sister and I shared the nursery, we were always at odds. It was Mary who was my playmate, Margaret was aloof, carrying tales to our nurse and generally sneering at us 'children' as she called us, although she was only our senior by a few years. Once she knew she was going to be a queen there was no holding her. I doubt it would be any different were we to meet now. Her daughter is just as bad. I may leave her to rot indefinitely at Syon."

"It is over now. I am sorry my brother was so foolish as to take up with her. He should have known better…"

"The Howards' lust for power again. It is the same with all your kin and it's a great shame he slipped the net. His head would make a fine addition to those already adorning the bridge."

Her hand pauses in my hair and when I look up, her eyes are bright with unshed tears, her face bone white. I cover her fingers with mine.

"What is it?"

She smiles, shakes her head, dismissing her sadness.

"Nothing. You are right. Treason is treason but he is my brother, his death would bring … dishonour on me, on us and the child I will bear you."

"A child? Are you…?"

"No." She steps away, lowers her head. "I meant the child I will one day bear you. Very soon, my love. I- I sometimes think of those people lingering in the darkness of the Tower. I have never been inside, and have no wish to, but I imagine it is a drear place."

She looks toward the window, her eyes huge, full of fear, and I know she is thinking of her cousin, Anne, who entered the Tower one bright May morning, never to emerge.

The doubt that Anne's sentence was unjust returns; was her death due to Cromwell's ambition? But he was so convincing … if he *lied*, then my wife and my friends died at my order … for *nothing*.

On the whim of a blacksmith's son.

"I often think of how Margaret Pole must be suffering, her old bones will surely feel the cold and the damp worse than most … could I not write to her, Henry? To discover how she is faring?"

Her voice severs my thoughts of Anne. I shake my head to clear my mind.

"Write? To whom?"

"The Countess of Salisbury, Lady Margaret, she is old. My grandmother is of a similar age and I cannot imagine she would survive long in the Tower, and it isn't as if Lady Margaret was active in the plot against you. The thought of her suffering *hurts* me, Henry, it takes away my appetite. I am concerned that worry will make me weak. I need to be strong if I am to remain fertile..."

Her voice fades, her words trailing off as she realises I am not blind to her blatant attempt to manipulate me. "I am sorry, Your Majesty, I don't know what came over me."

She looks at her feet, her shoulders shudder, and I am aware that she has not yet abandoned her exploitation of my good nature. But I cannot be certain that too much worry will not affect her ability to conceive. I should consult the physician.

Is it a risk I am prepared to take?

I slap my hands on my knees.

"Very well, you may write to her, enquire of her needs, but you must not sympathise or in any way imply that you think her innocent."

"Oh, Henry!"

Her arms fly around my neck, her lips are hot on my cheek. "Thank you. Oh, I do *love* you."

I would grant a thousand pardons just to hear that; it is all the reward I need.

*

"I've a surprise for you, come!" I hold out my hand and Katherine leaps from her chair, grasps my fingers and accompanies me along the corridors. I am spending more and more time in my inner chambers recently, so the courtiers lounging outside in hopes of an audience straighten up expectantly. We ignore their blathering greetings and, while Katherine bombards me with questions, the courtiers bow like grass in the wind as we pass.

"Have you bought me a new mare, Henry? Or has your mare foaled, and you are going to give me her colt? Oh, do tell me. Have I guessed? Henry, am I close...?"

Her words tail off when we reach the courtyard, which is alive with men and carts, hoists and scaffolding. The coarse voices quieten when they notice our presence, the work ceases while caps are removed, and heads are lowered.

"What is happening?"

She spins around, taking in the scene, her forehead creased with puzzlement until, at last, her eyes fasten on the gatehouse. She tilts her head back, her mouth falling open.

"My goodness!"

Her voice is but a whisper and, when I follow her gaze, although I had ordered it myself, I am likewise awed.

A great clock, designed by Nicholas Crazter and manufactured by Nicholas Oursian, arrived a few days ago. Since then, the men have constructed scaffolding on the gatehouse that leads to the inner court and installation is underway. Even though I've examined the plans in detail, the clock face is bigger than I had expected, easily more than twice my height, with revolving dials which will provide information not only on the time of day, but the month and the day of the month. The twelve signs of the zodiac are featured, as is the position of the sun in the sky, and the phases of the moon.

"Goodness indeed…"

We drag our eyes from the clock and stare at one another.

"Is it for me?" Her lips stretch wide.

I grope for her hand.

"Well, it is installed in your honour, my love. A way of expressing gratitude that I have at last found a wife who makes me truly happy."

Her eyes are misty. "I had no idea it was coming. You are so good at surprises, Henry. I will never be able to match this."

I laugh and, as always, those looking on do the same. Somer weaves around us in a crazed dance.

"Oh, is it for me? Your worthy fool? Oh, I am honoured, Your Majesty. It is too much … too much!"

He rounds off his performance with a series of clumsy cartwheels, but no one is paying him the least attention. I squeeze Kate's hand tighter.

"It was supposed to be here sooner but there were so many delays. We shall be the envy of Europe now. Francis has nothing like this!"

"I've never seen anything like it. I didn't even know there was such a thing."

She turns to gaze at the clock again, and I do likewise; our hands still clasped, we stand and stare, every so often commenting on a newly noticed detail.

Christmas 1540

I am full of similar plans to make our palaces the finest anyone has ever seen. I order our portraits taken and plan the redecoration of the state and privy apartments. But before long, my own ideas are overtaken by Katherine's frantic arrangements for the festive season. I have tired of it long before Christmas Eve dawns.

Her excitement is wearing but I show her a good face and agree to almost all her ideas. I have learned that acquiescence is the most direct route to peace. Despite the constant nagging ache in my leg, the recurrent digestive complaints, I still thank God that I have her. When her natural exuberance overtires me, I just smile and nod, and pretend to be in good spirits.

While Mass is taken on Christmas morning, she constantly twists and turns in her seat, leaning closer to whisper some new snippet of the joys to come. She is not skilled at keeping secrets and I am already well aware of almost every gift she plans to present to me during the course of the holiday.

But I indulge her, it pleases me to do so.

She is clad in deep green velvet, a grey fur lining peeks from the neck of her bodice and the slashes in her sleeves and the crescent on her hood are edged in red and gold braid. She glows with a happiness that does nothing to disguise her impatience for prayers to be over so the festivities might begin.

As we parade back to the privy apartments, she clutches my arm, nodding happily to the courtiers as we pass.

"Slow down, my love, slow down…" I am reluctant to admit that her pace is so swift I can scarcely keep up.

"Softly, Sweetheart, let us proceed a little slower."

She cannot imagine the pain each step inflicts on me, and has no knowledge of the grinding cramps in my belly. I laugh indulgently and would gladly give up all I have just to be agile enough to be the husband she deserves.

She slows her pace, but I can feel her excitement. It reverberates from her as she tries to guess the gifts that are waiting for her. Once, and it wasn't so long ago, my lust for life matched hers. I remember leaping on the table during one such feast, whirling my doublet above my head and jumping before the queen … another Catherine … to present her with her New Years gifts. I recall how the whole court, enamoured of their potent king, looked on with as much admiration as my wife. But that wife grew old, her charms fading with her optimism as, one by one, our dead children were laid beneath the ground.

But *I* remained young and full of hope, and I continued to fight for the thing I desired the most; for the thing I knew made a king successful.

An heir, and another to follow.

I still nurture the small drying husk of hope that I may yet be granted another legitimate son. If anyone can provide one, it should be this woman.

My desire for her stirs, and I reach for her hand.

"I feel the need to rest before the feast begins. Come with me, Kate, you can sing to me and help me sleep."

She knows what I want but she hesitates and, for a moment, I think she will protest. She is pulled between the longing to join her young companions and the need to obey her husband but, in the end, she comes willingly, her face turning pink as we disappear into my privy apartments. My intentions must be clear to the court, but they bow to us as we depart, their faces blandly non-committal.

My chamber is silent, a place of peace. The servants have already remade my bed, the fire is newly laid, the flames warming the air, my slippers and a pile of furs have been placed close to the hearth. It is a domestic, homely scene.

I draw her to me, bury my nose in the softness of her neck and find her warm, fragrant and compliant.

"Come," I say, "help me."

She kneels and begins to untie my codpiece. With fumbling fingers, I unpin her placard and unlace her bodice, pull aside the neck of her shift so her breasts spring free.

My head pounds, my desire for her so strong I feel my heart will burst. Whereas once I would have thrown her on her back and taken her, I now require assistance to do my duty. I limp to the bed, and she helps me lie down upon the mattress. While her small nimble fingers and warm lips get to work, I close my eyes.

Pushing away reality, I imagine I am virile, in full health, and all women desire me. She shifts her position, kneels beside me, her breasts in my face while my left hand fumbles beneath her petticoats in search of her softness. It welcomes me, slick beneath my touch, but when I open my eyes her face is turned away to the wall. She bites her lip, frowning.

What is she thinking of? Do I not please her? I increase the pressure of my fingers until she groans in response and suddenly I am ready.

"Now, Katherine, now…"

Mutely, white-faced, she slides a leg across my torso, opens herself and allows me to enter Heaven. It is a merry Christmas indeed.

When we rejoin the company in the hall, I notice Katherine is quieter than she was this morning. It is as if her seasonal joy has dissipated. I outdo myself trying to restore her former gaiety, but it takes some while before her smile is restored. When I push a purse onto her hand and it clinks weightily in her palm, a dimple appears in her cheek.

"Thank you, *dear* Henry," she says, but when a herald arrives and presents her with a box crammed with jewels, she drops the purse. With a fist full of pearls, she dangles a ruby necklace before her eyes, then she springs from her seat and embraces me before the whole court. The foreign dignitaries shuffle their feet, rolling their eyes when, behind my chair, Somer makes loud kissing noises.

"Oh Henry, Henry, you are so … *rich*!" he cries, and the company pauses, holding their breath, unsure if I will laugh or roar. I have no choice but to laugh. Anger would make me petulant. Once I start to chuckle, they give vent to their own amusement.

"Oh, Henry, I do love you so!"

Ignoring the insolence of the fool, Kate's eyes shine with emotion, and I am well content to know how well she loves me. I will give her the world as long as she continues to say it.

When the dancing begins, I sit like an old man, watching in envy while my wife weaves in and out of the throng, partnered by men younger and more agile than I. Each smile she directs at them is a dagger in my heart.

I ease my bandaged leg, fart into my velvet cushion and rue becoming old. If only these damned useless physicians would discover a cure. It is not meet that I should be sat in the corner as if I am in my dotage. I am still virile enough; didn't I prove that this morning? Once she is with child, the world will realise that Henry of England is yet in his prime.

If only this damned leg would heal.

*

Anne joins us for supper. She enters the hall, clad in a gown as fine as the queen's, her deportment markedly better. My 'Beloved Sister' is looking well and I am bemused by the comparisons I note between them. While Katherine is vivacious, like a girl, Anne is regal, like a queen. When the remains of our feast have been cleared away and it is time to retire to the privy chambers, we request Anne to accompany us. Katherine plays with her pups while I accept Anne's challenge for a game of chess.

She plays with the enthusiasm of one new to the game, but Katherine thinks it a dull game and because she presents no challenge whatsoever, when I am matched with her, it usually is.

Anne, however, tutored by Brandon during her journey to England, is fast becoming a skilful player. It takes my full concentration to best her and, at the last minute, just when I think I have triumphed, she leans forward, places a finger on her knight and pushes it purposefully across the board.

She looks me in the eye and laughs as she takes my queen.

While she throws back her head, my eyes drift to her throat. Her neck is long, the skin paper white, and I wonder why, when I'd had the right to kiss it, I declined. Perhaps she had deserved more of a chance.

She rests her chin on her hands.

"What will you do now, Your Majesty? I have you in my grasp."

The accent that once seemed harsh is now exotic, and the displeasing lines of her face are softened by the candlelight. Interest kindles in my belly and when I lean closer, and our eyes lock, I see the undisguised attraction in hers. I wonder if she has been studying other skills as well as chess.

"I fear I am at your mercy, Madam, and I lack the will to fight you."

I can't seem to turn away; it is as if we are both under some enchantment. Too much wine. There is pleasure in the moment, an underlying danger, the thrill of discovery. I could go with the urge, make an excuse to the queen and summon Anne to my chamber later. I could show her my former impotence was merely a passing thing. Still trapped in the question of her eyes, I hold my breath, debating on which path to take, but then Kate squeals and I drag myself from the spell. Kate is screaming with laughter, holding aloft a pup while it piddles down her priceless gown.

"The little beast!" she cries as she shakes with laughter. Anne and I join in, the enchantment between us severed. I put down my cup and shake my head, while Anne clears her throat and goes to assist the queen who, her velvet gown damp and covered with dog hair, is making a futile attempt to wipe her skirts.

The queen looks up at me, her face still pink, and waves a puppy in my direction.

"I am going to call this one Harry, he reminds me of you, Henry, with his whiskery chin and cute little ears."

Anne straightens up and glances at me, her brows comically arched.

"So," she says, her lips twitching. "Your Majesty has cute little ears. I had never noticed before."

We break into laughter again. I hold my belly while tears gather on my cheeks, although the joke is not really that amusing. It is more from relief than amusement. How close I had come to entanglement with a woman the world views as my sister. I resolve to drink less.

"What?" Kate pouts. "What is so funny? Did I say something silly?"

"No, no, Sweetheart," I say, drawing her close and kissing her ear, "as if you would."

January 1541

As always, January is long and cold. We miss the jollity of the Christmas festivities, and the spring season is yet far away. It snows, the Thames freezes, the youngsters play outside my windows, snowballs and ice fairs followed by bowls of foaming frumenty before a roaring hearth. While they frolic, I remain inside, wrapped in furs, forbidden by my physicians to risk my health. By way of comfort, I eat and drink too much, and spend overlong watching and brooding while my wife goes about her frantic, gay life. Morosely, I realise that while her days are filled with dancing and merriment, my mornings are crammed with state matters, and regular bloodletting by the physician. Then later, after wearing myself out doing very little, I am forced to rest.

It is late in the day when I am woken from my doldrums by Brandon requesting an audience. With a dart of pleasure, I struggle to my feet so that I might greet my oldest, dearest friend. His duties in Lincoln have been keeping him from court, and it seems months since we met. The sight of his familiar face, the sound of his voice, his deep throaty laugh, are instantly cheering.

"We should spend more time together now I am happily wed," I say, pulling him in for a second embrace.

When he releases me, I fumble for the arm of my chair and sink gratefully back into it.

"Are you ailing, Sir? Nobody told me."

He offers his hand but I wave it away, dismissing his concern.

"No, no, I am well. It is just my leg troubling me. It is due to the cold weather; it is always worse at this time of year."

"I'm sorry to hear it."

His brow creases with concern. Once, he would have replied with banter, lifting my melancholy, taking my mind from my troubles with a joke. His serious face reinforces the sense that I am decrepit.

We both are.

He leans back in his chair, rubbing his thighs. I raise my eyebrows in question, wondering if he suffers a similar affliction to mine.

"Oh, it's nothing. I am fresh from the saddle and old bones always ache after such exertions."

"I don't think inactivity helps either. I am always better in the summer months. The cold weather wouldn't have stopped us once, would it? We'd have been out from dawn to dusk on the hunt and then off wenching all evening, taking a mere few hours of sleep before embarking on the same all over again the next day."

He leans back, and I glimpse the ghost of his old smile.

"Those were the days."

We fall silent while our minds drift back to our youth. The jousts, the fights, the women … *Anne.*

Everything comes back to Anne.

Brandon never trusted her, and neither did my sister. But I liked her, she made my blood sing, and I was young enough then to use her well. As always, I feel a pang of guilt at the manner of her death. Perhaps I should share with Brandon the suspicion that I had been misled about her, my fear I'd had her killed at another man's goading. But I find I cannot speak of it.

I shake my head and her vision dissipates.

"Remember how cross I was when you wed my sister without my leave? I misremember now why I was so irked … she couldn't have gone to a better man."

He laughs quietly.

"I still miss her. She kept me in check and curbed my darker tendencies."

"I bet she did. She tried to rein me in too. It was a crime she died so young. She was my first friend, you know … the only person I could rely on to tell me the truth. Everyone else just told me what I wanted to hear."

He sits forward, his clasped hands hanging limp between his knees.

"I hope I've always been honest, a true friend."

"Oh yes…" I nod slowly, "yet, you were always diplomatic. Mary spat the truth in my face whether I liked what she was telling me or not."

"She did that with me too, Sire." He laughs loudly, as he used to, opening his mouth wide. I notice a few missing teeth, and there is more than a glint of grey in his beard.

Age is cruel.

"How is your wife? Your family?"

He hesitates. "They are well, thank you. The children thrive."

If he were speaking to anyone else he'd have said 'sons', for he has been more fortunate than I and has a brace of strong boys. "I saw Prince Edward a sennight since, Sire. He is growing fast, and bright too."

My chest swells. "He is indeed. A brighter child I've never met, but he needs a brother. The queen and I have hopes of adding to the royal nursery soon."

The lie is involuntary, born of my need to match his prowess at begetting sons. It makes his smile widen.

"That is excellent news, Your Majesty. Have I your permission to congratulate the queen when I see her next?"

"No, no. Speak of it to no one. It is early days yet and we all know too well how easily they can slip away at this stage."

He sobers and sits back in his chair again.

"Indeed, we do, Sire. I shall pray for you, as I always do."

"Our plans for the northern progress are in hand. I – we will be travelling with a much heavier guard, for we must show them that the king is not to be trifled with."

"Indeed, Sire." Brandon hesitates. "The unrest isn't over for a few, the resentment of the people continues to simmer, I fear, despite my presence and the harsh penalties we issued."

"And all for the sake of a few monks, but how can the unwashed understand the niceties of the situation? They are like cattle, expecting everything to remain the same even when change is for the greater good. The corruption we uncovered was…"

"I know; I was never so shocked before. The stories that came out of the impropriety, the immorality…"

"Makes my blood boil when I think of it. The brothel keepers are more honest, at least they make no pretence of propriety. Yet all the simple folk see is the loss of the monasteries that provided them with jobs and cared for them in sickness. It makes no matter that behind the scenes they were fornicating and swindling, drunk at the altar most of the time…" I break off and frown into a corner, sickened by the lurid images of monks I once honoured as godly.

Groping for my cup, I take a deep draught and wave the vessel in the air between us. "Cromwell was right in one thing at least, Brandon. To scourge the poison, one must sometimes cut off the infected limb."

"Precisely, Sire."

"I am grateful to you for your service in the north, Brandon. There's not another man I could trust to do it."

"I live to serve you, Henry, you know that."

I do, but it is good to hear it confirmed. I find I am short of real friends these days. Most of them are dead; only Brandon and, to a lesser extent, Norfolk, remember the Henry of old.

During the uprising, Brandon held Lincolnshire virtually under siege. He and his vast army, his huge supplies of weaponry and stores of corn ensured our victory, and ever since he has been my mainstay in the north. His reputation in the county became so fearsome that the bards wrote songs about him. If it were anyone but my best friend, I'd be envious of his fame. I rewarded him well, with grants, many of them in Lincolnshire so he could keep an eye out for further insurrection. He is deserving of every reward.

"The queen and I will be visiting Grimsthorpe Castle on our way north. The hunting is so good there; I hope to be well enough to take advantage of it."

"I hope so too, Your Grace. It will be an honour to host you. We have made some vast improvements recently. I look forward to showing you the newly appointed hall."

He talks on, describing the extravagant furnishing, the new courtyard he has had installed, all in my honour it seems. He has excelled himself, becoming the biggest landowner in Lincolnshire, the most powerful of barons.

"It pleases me to see you prosper, Brandon. The troubles in the north would have been much worse but for you … and Norfolk, of course."

"Of course."

He looks away, pretending interest in the dogs, snoring close by. There is little love between Norfolk and Brandon. It often puzzles me why my closest companions cannot like one another more. I clear my throat to regain his attention and he smiles, claps his hands on his knees.

"My wife is very much looking forward to furthering her relationship with the queen."

"Katherine is in a fever of excitement about the coming summer. Mind you, she is usually in a fever about something. I had forgotten the enthusiasm of youth."

"Only you could keep up with it, Sire. I have trouble enough with my own Katheryn."

I had forgotten Brandon's wife is young too, not as young as Katherine, of course, but young enough to require an effort.

"Did you find motherhood slowed her down? I have hopes that the queen will be less … enthusiastic, shall we say, once she has a child to use up her energy. It is odd, is it not, that the very thing that enchants us initially is the first to pall?"

He leans forward, his forehead creased with concern.

"Surely you don't tire of her, Henry, I thought…?"

"Oh no, don't think that! I don't tire of her. I am her devoted lover but … my … it is exhausting sometimes. I find I have to take to my sickbed just to get some rest."

He grins. "She is over-demanding then?"

If anybody else had dared such a suggestion I'd have taken his head, but Brandon is different. He can speak and jest freely. Instead of taking umbrage, I laugh.

"She is very demanding, but don't you worry, I see she doesn't go to sleep disappointed."

When the light begins to fade, I order a private supper and instruct my servant to fetch the chessboard. A table is brought out and the board wiped. I watch as Brandon carefully sets out the pieces. I wonder idly how many matches we have had together over the years, how many times I have bested him.

"Oh, by the way!" I speak suddenly, making him jump and drop an ivory piece. It falls to the carpet, rolls beneath his chair. Brandon bends, groping for it, grunting as he retakes his seat.

"By the way … what, Sire?"

"I lost a game of chess to our 'Beloved Sister' Anne, and I am damned sure it was all your fault!"

"How did I have a part in that, Sire?"

He frowns, shakes his head, clearly puzzled.

"You taught her too well, Sir. She beat me at Christmas and cost me another fat purse."

He laughs, seeing now that I am in jest.

"Then I confess I am guilty, Sire, and beg forgiveness. Next time I see her I will make sure I work a few flaws into her game."

Our laughter merges, sobering as we both begin to contemplate the game ahead.

"It is good to see how Anne has settled down to her new role in England," Brandon says as he moves his first pawn. "I found her to be excellent company. My wife likes her too."

"So does mine, fortunately. Sometimes they conspire against me, and I become the bait for their teasing."

He lets go his piece and opens his mouth wide, lets forth a burst of laughter that rouses the dogs and brings Somer creeping from his hiding place.

"Who made a joke?" the fool demands. "That job, Sirrah, should be mine and mine alone." He looks at Brandon accusingly and I sense the opening of a lengthy battle of wits between the duke and my fool, and I am not in the mood for it.

"Here." I offer the fool a plate of his favourite pastries and, unable to resist the bribe, he takes it from me before skulking away again, wagging a warning finger at Brandon as he goes.

*

I'd never confess to anyone how nervous I am to ride into the realms of northern hostility. I am hurt that the populace rose up against me. I am injured that they took the part of the monks … the side of *Rome* … against me, their anointed king who has nothing but their good will at heart.

Before I depart, I tidy up business that cannot be allowed to lie fallow while we are away. I order one of my bitches that has failed to whelp successfully to be destroyed. I instruct the keeper of the wardrobe to distribute some of my unwanted clothing to family and friends. Mary gets some furs, Elizabeth a fine bolt of velvet that has been lying around unused for months. I visit Edward and lift him gingerly on my knee, and when he grabs my hat and tosses it at the slumbering hounds, I do not scold him. I quiz Lady Bryan as to his health.

"Oh, he is thriving, Your Majesty. But, as you can imagine, he is a handful. They are always full of mischief at this age."

She folds her hands across her stomach and smiles indulgently at her charge.

He is indeed a pretty child. His heart-shaped face reminds me of his mother, but his light golden hair is reminiscent of my own. When I was his age, I spent much of my time with my mother, the rest of it in the company of my sisters. This boy is alone, bar his half-sister, the bastard princess Elizabeth who plays with him more frequently than I do. He needs the company of boys, a brother or two to act as playmates and reinforce our dynasty. I sigh and rest my nose on his head, inhale the fragrance of his hair as I leave a surreptitious kiss.

"His food is still tasted, and his linen checked daily?"

"Oh yes, Your Majesty, everything is done to ensure his safety and well-being. One can never be too careful."

"Never," I affirm. "Not with a prince, not with my heir."

I hand him back to her and he goes happily into her arms. When I reach the door, I pause.

"Guard him with your life, Lady Bryan, for I am riding north and will be away until the autumn. It is the future king of England you hold in your arms."

There are felons in the Tower who are taking up space and victuals. I pardon some; others I order executed or hung as their status dictates and, at the last minute, I add the name of Margaret Pole to the list.

I do not do so lightly. I am aware that Katherine will be heartsore, for she has a gentle spot for the Duchess of Salisbury, as she insists on calling her. Truth be known, I do myself. She is my mother's cousin, she dandled me on her knee when I was an infant and was given the care of our daughter, Mary, when she was a babe in arms. But all that was before her traitorous family turned against the crown, it was before her sons sided against us, championing the church and decrying me as a heretic and worse.

I ordered the executions of her other sons, Exeter and Montagu, sometime ago, and if I cannot lay my hands on the traitor himself, Reginald Pole, then I will take his mother's head instead.

Early on the twenty-seventh day of May, without prior warning, Margaret Pole is taken from her cell and quietly executed.

"Why, Henry? Why?" Kate tugs at her hair; her face is besmirched with tears and twisted with grief. "She was your mother's cousin; how can you think of such a thing?"

I wrench my sleeve from her grip and, as I walk away, she slumps dramatically to the floor. I turn at the door, snarl at her like an angry hound.

"It is not your place to question me. It is my duty to rule. You have but one duty and that is to provide me with a son!"

I have never spoken so roughly to her before. Her face, that a moment ago was red, rapidly pales, her lips quivering as she plumps back on her heels. As I limp away from her, along the corridor, longing for the solitude of my chamber, I hear her give way to grief-filled sobs.

My heart twists.

*

This time I will be travelling further north than ever before, intending to go as far as York in a show of power to the people who revolted. I will make them rue the day they rose up against our rule. The other reason to venture so far is to meet with my nephew, James of Scotland. Despite the blood we share, there is little love between us, and this is a chance to cement an alliance, to join together against France.

I am uncertain how effective the meeting will be, but it is imperative that further strife is avoided. Since the break from Rome, England is isolated and vulnerable.

Recovered now from our recent dispute, Katherine is in a fever about the whole thing, every day she remembers something else that must be added to her baggage. New hoods and veils, riding gloves, a set of harness for her palfrey, new leashes for her dogs. Her list is endless.

As the winter and spring melt into summer, our preparations gather pace. The itinerary for our journey north is planned with vigilance. We will require a larger guard than usual, a show of force to deter any fresh violence against us. Each stop on our progress is organised well in advance to give the hosts time to make suitable preparation.

Sometimes I hear of muttered complaints that hosting the royal party has resulted in ruination for some men. It is not my fault if they undertake improvements that they can ill afford. I do not ask them to. More fool them if they empty their purses in return for our favour.

As my wife, Katherine will require only the best accommodation, and only the best entertainment en route. It is her first real public appearance as my queen, and part of me worries that she may lack the required decorum to impress the people. She has a tendency to be informal and impulsive, and although everyone seems to love her for it, it is unbecoming in a queen.

I summon Jane Rochford, and, as always when I see her, I am instantly reminded of Anne. She was once married to Anne's brother, an unhappy alliance that often brought down the queen's ... Anne's, I mean ... displeasure. Anne adored her brother; some say rather too much but ... I am unsure now of the truth of that rumour. I shake my head to dispel the image of her face and turn my thoughts back to the matter in hand.

"Lady Rochford, before we leave, we require you to school the queen in the niceties of etiquette while on progress. You, more than any, know the expectations of one in her position. Try to instil some decorum; tranquillity is to be encouraged."

She executes a deep curtsey.

"Leave it with me, Your Majesty. I will teach her the importance of restraint. If I make a game of it, she will comply readily enough."

I wave her from my presence and, as she bows her way from the room, her words resound in my head. There is something strange about them. How fitting is it that a queen should do the bidding of an underling? She speaks as if she holds Katherine on a leash, as if she is easily manipulated, as if the queen should obey Rochford's will rather than her own.

But my attention to the matter is stolen by the arrival of Paget, who has yet another list for me to peruse. As I make my mark against the tasks he has itemised, he details some of the arrangements that are already in place. I hope they omit nothing. The men who serve me now lack the skills of my former ministers. I recall the magnificence of the arrangements Wolsey made for the Field of the Cloth of Gold when I instructed him to do all he could to impress the King of France.

I need to make a similar, if not so extravagant, splash this time too. We will be a large entourage, half the court or more will join us, as well as their personal household servants and baggage. Not for the first time, I regret the loss of Cromwell. He may have been a villain, but he knew how to get things done and he never failed to arrange things just as I liked them … apart from the Cleves marriage, of course.

How I miss the days when I could leave everything to him and just enjoy life. Since his – his – departure, I am forced to attend council daily, and make decisions on matters of state. Oh, I have advisors of course, but I am never certain if their loyalty is to me, or themselves. I was sure of Cromwell until he was proved a villain.

30th June 1541

Somehow, by the end of June we are ready to embark on our progress. Clad in our finest riding clothes, the coats of our horses brushed to a high sheen and the carriages polished. The royal pennants snap, flying high in the welcome breeze as the entourage assembles and the first riders leave the palace gates.

Foot soldiers march ahead, pikes held aloft, followed by the mounted officers, while the royal party is somewhere in the middle, the lesser members of the household following on behind. I am pleased to see my daughter, Mary, making an effort to be pleasant to the queen.

She cannot hide her disapproval from me but at least she has ceased hostilities to please us. Although Mary looks pale and peaked, as if she has not slept properly, she smiles and waves to the gathering crowds. With a prick of envy, I hear the zeal in the people's voices when they call her name and throw flowers in her path. That adulation should by rights belong to Katherine, but I am gratified to see the commoners give her a hearty, if less exuberant, welcome, too.

As for myself, the cheers and cries of delight are as deafening as ever when I pass by. I whip their excitement to a frenzy, taking off my hat and waving it in the air as I did in my youth. I bear such love for my people! I feel my throat tighten, and my eyes grow moist as I realise they return my love in full measure. I should show myself to them more often; their adoration is a reminder as to why I suffer for them.

I am certain my father was never received with such gusto. From the day he set foot back on English soil to the day he died, he never received wholehearted support from the commoners. He was a stranger to most of them, raised overseas, a mythical exiled prince returning to claim his crown. But they've loved me from infancy. They've witnessed every stage of my life, seen me grow, shared every one of my joys and sorrows. They know everything about me, even the failures, and they adore me anyway. That is why I love them.

I bring out a bag of coin and, taking a handful, I hurl it into the crowd. The cheers rise ever higher.

We stop first at Enfield, then St Albans and Dunstable. All these places hold memories and ghosts of days gone by. Dunstable saw the annulment of my long marriage to the first Catherine, and Ampthill was where I housed her after I decided to put an end to our ungodly union.

As we journey on, the weather turns foul, and lashing rain and wind hampers our progress. The adventure begins to pall, our mood turning as dismal as the weather. When we reach Grafton, I take off my dripping hat in the hall and explain to Kate that this had once been the home of my grandmother, Elizabeth Woodville.

The house itself has been replaced, of course, and the gardens remodelled, but I still feel some sense of the past, the ties to my ancestors. As I tread through the rooms, pushing aside the ghostly memories, my spirits are doused further when I recall it was also the last place I saw Wolsey alive. I grow maudlin.

Was ever a man so cursed by faithless friends as I?

That night, I invite my favourites to dine in private. We pull the shutters closed against the rain and prepare for enjoyment. Brandon is not with us this night, having ridden ahead to make preparation for our stay with him at Grimsthorpe, but I am content with Katherine beside me, a few musicians, and her favourite ladies and my closest gentlemen. We grow merry, the youngest members of the party dancing into the early hours. The music rises and falls, the fire crackles, while I sit and eat and watch, with my foot resting on a stool.

When they form up for the next dance, Katherine is partnered by Culpepper, and they make an elegant pairing. I look on enviously as the steps of the dance take them close together. Their elbows hook, and then they part again, Katherine's hand reluctantly extended toward him as the dance dictates. Surrounded by the gaiety of the company, yet not part of it, I grow bored, longing for my bed. I've admitted to nobody how the journey is taking its toll, on both my health and my spirits. I close my eyes, rest my head on the back of my chair and thank God for the good company. The words of a song I wrote long ago jangle in my mind.

> *Pastime with good company*
> *I love and shall until I die;*
> *Grudge who will, but none deny*
> *So God be pleased thus live will I*
> *For my pastance*
> *Hunt, sing, and dance*
> *My heart is set:*
> *All goodly sport*
> *For my comfort*
> *Who shall me let?*
> *Youth must have some dalliance*
> *Of good or ill some pastance;*
> *Company methinks then best*
> *All thoughts and fancies to digest:*
> *For idleness*
> *Is chief mistress*
> *Of vices all*
> *Then who can say*
> *But mirth and play*
> *Is best of all?*

I can recall all the words, yet it was written so long ago, shortly after my first wedding when I was a different man, a very different man. I was young and full of optimism. I expect that, knowing so much of the world, if I wrote the song today, the result would read very differently.

I pass a restless night, pain in my thigh, the night temperature too warm for comfort yet not warm enough to throw off the covers. When I call for Culpepper, another comes in his place, claiming Tom is indisposed, so I have to make do with the administration of an unskilled hand. My loud complaints bring Somer crawling from his bed like a sleepy hound to curl up at the foot of mine. Before he lies down, he sits trancelike on my bed, his hair standing upright, and gazes about the chamber.

"Where's Tom?" he asks. "With his lady-love?"

In the morning, Mary sends a messenger apologising that she is indisposed and will not be joining us today. No doubt she has caught a chill in the relentless rain, but she promises to catch up with us on the road in a day or two. I suspect she won't. The queen's company is too gay for her.

Mary is sober-minded, pious like her mother, and has no time for mischief or late night carousing. I am beginning to see her point of view. Merriment is wearing. Too much wine of a night eats into one's morning when I'd far rather be clear-headed and well rested. I can think of nothing worse than crawling into a cold bed at dawn. That is why I am full of vigour this morning while the rest of them creep around me like nuns.

"I expect it is Mary's monthly megrim," Katherine says wisely. "She suffers with it, you know. Unlike I."

The queen's own 'megrim' as she calls it does little to deter her, and as far as I'm concerned, it occurs far too promptly and regularly. We've been married for nigh on a year, and I've visited her bed often enough for her to be well advanced in pregnancy by now, yet she is still as slim as a wand and shows no sign of pregnancy at all.

"It is gentile to suffer. Your constitution is inelegant," I growl, foraging through my pocket in search of a pouch of willow bark I carry there. I hold it out to her but before she takes it, I notice that she has taken my cross words to heart. I fumble for her hand, inadvertently making her drop the sachet.

"Forgive me, Katherine. I am in some pain this morning. It makes me snarl. I meant nothing by it."

She shows me a wavering smile, gropes on the floor for the willow bark, and goes in search of someone to prepare an infusion for my pain.

I did mean something by it, I think as she departs. I am growing impatient. The pleasure of her young body is becoming a chore. I had thought she'd be with child by now. I cannot rest until she is, and the nightly visits are taking their toll. It has crossed my mind more than once that the exertion of trying to beget a new life might well shorten my own.

She is undemanding, yet I want her to take pleasure in it. I had enough years with the first Catherine lying beneath me like a martyr to want to experience that again. With Anne, I met my match; she was wild, she showed me tricks I hadn't thought possible yet … *where did she learn such things?* She must have learned them somewhere. Was it at the French court? Was she Francis' whore as her sister had been? No; I swear she was a virgin when I first took her, so where, how, did she know such things? Her brother?

The unwelcome image of George Boleyn riding his sister like a mare in the hunt smears across my mind's eye and, with vomit in my throat, I shake my head to blot it out. I hawk and spit the filthy thought onto the floor.

I have Katherine now; sweet Katherine who loves me, who adores me. She will fall pregnant soon. I will focus on the wife I have now.

Anne is gone.

By lunchtime, the weather has brightened, and I am recovered enough to join the hunt after all. With several changes of horse, I manage to keep up, but I suspect them of slowing their pace to match mine. We return to the palace with a brace of hind, where a fine spread awaits us. Once again, the feast lasts long into the night. Ignoring my fatigue, I summon Kate to my bed, but she is listless and weepy, complaining of a headache. Mindful of her comfort, I keep the business short, hoping this time my seed will find its mark.

Shortly after sliding from my lap, she creeps away, back to her own bed. I'd have liked her to stay; I always take pleasure in lying beside her, playing with her hair, stroking her duckies until I fall asleep, but she said she felt so unwell she feared she might vomit, so I let her go.

August 1541

By early August, despite an unseasonal amount of rain that results in bogged down carts and horses mired to the knees, we arrive at Collyweston, once the home of my other grandmother, Margaret Beaufort. I have little doubt what her views would have been of a girl like Katherine sleeping in her state rooms, looking at her paintings, admiring her tapestries.

My grandmother had very particular ideas about what was seemly and what wasn't. *Henry*, I remember her voice as clear as yesterday, *princes never eat with their fingers! Henry, fasten your doublet. Henry, sit still, princes never fidget.*

I turn to share the memory with Katherine, but she is in close conversation with Lady Rochford. I snap my fingers and she looks up, her face tense, her skin pale. I wonder if she is pregnant.

She hurries toward me.

"Did you want me, Henry?"

She is all smiles as she slides her hand beneath the crook of my elbow. I cover her hand with my own.

"I was just thinking of my grandmother, this was her favourite home. Later, of course, my son resided here."

"Edward?"

"No, no: my son by Bessie Blount, Fitzroi ... he was a great loss to me…"

My voice breaks, she squeezes my arm.

"I am sure he was," she murmurs but I know she doesn't understand. How can a childless woman ever understand the impact of the loss of a son, so many sons, to a king?

What a bonus Fitzroi would have been to Edward. He would have stood fast beside him after I am gone. He would have supported him, been his right-hand man in times of war or strife. Perhaps he might have kept peace in the north; that requires a strong hand that a child king might lack.

Child king? I chide myself for speaking as if I might die tomorrow. There are many years left to me yet and by the time of my death, Edward will be grown and the queen will have provided him with brothers - long before then. Strong sons, like the sons of York my mother spoke of. Her father and uncles, Edmund, Edward, George, Richard … good men all, apart from the last, who stole the throne from my uncle, then murdered him and his brother in the Tower. Richard of Gloucester was a great strategist, but his death by my father's hand at Bosworth Field was fitting.

A loud bang brings me rudely from my reverie. Somer has found a drum from somewhere and is marching up and down the hall, beating a discordant tattoo. When I scowl at him, his head shrinks into his shoulders, and he grimaces the approximation of a smile, but the banging slows and eventually ceases.

"I like this place, oh king," he says, dropping his drum and gazing about. "I like the flowers and the fountains. So do the dogs!" He points across the lawn to where the queen's dogs have taken refuge from the hot sun in the shallow fountain. They are leaping and splashing, trying to snatch the cascade between their teeth.

"A shame we cannot join them," I remark idly, for it has turned very hot after the rain and the humid air is making everyone lethargic. But seemingly, the queen is unaffected and has no such constraints. Before I can stop her, she has lifted her skirts and is sprinting across the mead.

"Katherine!" I try to summon her back, but she is already kicking off her shoes and dipping her toes into the water. Bunching her skirts higher, showing off her long slim legs, she turns to me, her smile wide and infectious.

"Oh, Henry, it is so cool and lovely. Why don't you come in? There is nobody to see."

I look about the garden, where scores of courtiers are looking on, wide-eyed, alarmed, expectant. If I join her, they will need little encouragement to follow suit, for they are like sheep, or ducks in this instance.

For a moment I am tempted, just to see their reaction, but the idea dies as soon as it is born, as I recall the spies who dwell among us, ready to carry tales of any hint of scandal across the sea to foreign courts.

I imagine throwing off my coat as I would once have done, but when I reach the part where I'd have to roll down my hose and reveal the thick bandages that cover the open sores, the pleasure palls. Once, I would have resembled Neptune in the waves and been painted as such in the words of the witnesses, but now they would see just a crazed old man - a laughing-stock.

I take a few steps closer, hoping to lure her out without drawing further attention, but as I draw, near she kicks a spray of water at me. Her aim is true, and she strikes her mark first time. I am drenched, the feathers on my hat turning limp, dripping water all over my fine velvet topcoat. I stand aghast; a ripple of shock runs around the courtyard. I watch as her face freezes in terror.

Her fear injures me. *Does she not know me at all?*

Why is she regarding me as if I'm likely to send her to the Tower for mere mischief?

Silence falls and time ticks by while the courtiers hold their breath, waiting for my anger to crash down upon the queen. Even as it is acted out, I know this story will be carried across Europe, and my enemies will crow about my disrespectful bride. There is only one thing I can do, only one way I can possibly diffuse such a situation.

Tearing off my hat, I throw it toward her. It spins into the fountain, where the dogs leap up, barking as they vie with one another to catch it. Then, with my hands on my hips, I lean back and laugh aloud.

Our next stop is Grimsthorpe Castle, where Brandon and his wife are waiting in the courtyard when we arrive. I do not comment immediately on the improvements made to the frontage. I pretend I do not notice.

Breaking etiquette, he approaches my horse and helps me dismount and, as we walk away, he takes my arm in a mark of friendship. If his action also helps to disguise my stiffness after so long in the saddle, then no one remarks on it.

We climb the stairs to the hall together while the queen and her ladies are ushered along behind by Brandon's wife, Catherine Willoughby. I listen as they exchange pleasantries, pleased that she might be a steadying influence on the queen.

Culpepper follows close behind us, looking about the hall in anticipation of a good supper. Having been all day in the saddle, I am famished too, but I know Lady Brandon will have laid on a goodly spread. We couldn't wish for better hosts or finer company.

I jerk my head and, interpreting my unspoken order, Tom asks to be shown to my quarters that he may prepare for my comfort. He doesn't need to be reminded of the state the dressing on my leg will be in after the ride. He is quite aware of the build-up of pus that will need to be cleaned, the dead skin that will need to be cut away. Fresh bandages must be rolled in readiness, the salves and perfumes that anoint the wound will require unpacking.

I daresay he is reluctant to miss this sociable hour in the hall and I do not blame him, but I need him. It will take the best part of the afternoon to make me presentable for the evening entertainment.

I summon the queen to my presence, and when she enters she is pink-cheeked from the excitement of the day. As she crosses the room, she sees Culpepper bending over the table of salves and bowls of rose-scented water. Her step falters, and they exchange a cautious smile. Culpepper bows low.

"Katherine." I hold out my hand and she comes to me. I pull her on to my good knee, clasp her hands. "Now, don't take umbrage at what I am going to say. It is for the good of the realm."

She stares warily, as if afraid I am going to ask her to appear naked at the feast. I squeeze her hand comfortingly and shift her to the arm of the chair as she grows heavy.

"Do not worry. You are not in trouble. I just want to explain that there must be no further romping, no more impromptu baths in the castle fountain, no feeding the dogs from your lap at the table, no flirting with Cranmer, whose poor soul can't take it."

She giggles, withdraws a hand from mine to cover her mouth. "That was funny though, Henry, to hear him stutter and stammer, his face turned as red as a cardinal's hat!"

"Yes," I smother a laugh. "But it is disrespectful. People talk and gossip travels. You are a queen now. You must behave accordingly."

"Even with you, Henry?" She leans forward, like a temptress, her breasts an inch from my nose. I peer down her bodice, where her plump breasts nestle like a pair of white doves.

I feel a sudden longing. I moisten my lips, which are suddenly dry.

"No, not with me, not when we are alone, anyway." I sink my face into her chest, inhale the sweet scent of her skin and kiss the swell of her bosom. She holds tightly to my head, as if willing me to linger so, obligingly, I lick them too.

When she gasps, I look up to find her eyes fastened on Tom's, whose face is as scarlet as hers.

"You may leave us, Culpepper," I say and, grabbing an armful of things from the table, he flees our presence, dropping bandages and pots of salve as he goes.

Smiling, I reach for my wife. She is eager for me, insisting that we perform the whole act instead of simply cuddling and squeezing. Unlike the last few times when she has been almost reluctant, she bounces on me like an Amazon at full canter, squealing and gasping until I can hold back no more. Once we are done, instead of lingering in my arms, she climbs off and readjusts her clothing, while I lie back dazed and exhausted.

"I am sure I will soon be with child, Henry. Lady Rochford says the more we perform the act, the more likely it will happen. She says it is important to go the whole way…"

"Indeed, my dear. It is what I've been saying all along, so no more headaches!" I wink at her, and she flushes, smiles shyly.

"No more headaches." She nods assent and kisses me before skipping off to rejoin her companions. Once I am alone, I lie back, closing my eyes again.

Where did that surging insistent passion came from? It has left the blood surging through my body so I feel less like a king and more like a God!

The next afternoon, I call a meeting of the Privy Council, for even when I am rest, the business of the realm must continue. Norfolk is present, and Suffolk of course, a truce called in the hostilities between them. The Lord Privy Seal, the Earl of Southampton, also attends, as well as John, Lord Russell, and Tunstall, Wriothesley, and Richard Rich. It will be our last meeting before we reach Lincoln and York, the two foremost transgressors in the recent uprising. It is imperative that both towns make considerable reparation, both verbal and monetary, for their crimes.

I narrow my eyes and watch as the Council members wrangle and bend the truth to their will. They are self-serving knaves, save Brandon, who is the only one I wholly trust.

"They must be made to pay for their crimes," I say, thumping the table and making the cups jump. "It was treason, they are lucky I didn't hang them all! They are to pay for their liberty, make reparation for their infidelity to their king and they shall do so gladly. Tell them to sell their plate if they are short."

Brandon clears his throat, looks about the table as he speaks.

"Your Majesty, we are all agreed that the fines would be better given to you by way of a gift, an appreciation of yourself and your good lady's visit to their towns. Then, you will seem … generous and forgiving. We feel it is important that your visit should be seen as one of reconciliation rather than … retribution."

I stare at him for a long while. Norfolk shuffles his papers, Denny pours himself another cup of wine, and a fly buzzes irritatingly at my ear. I dash it away. I would like to seek vengeance on these northern traitors, yet I do see Brandon's point.

"Indeed," I say at last, and they emit a unified sigh of relief.

"I shall send word ahead as to what is expected." Denny runs a finger down his list of items to be discussed. "I think we have covered everything, Your Majesty, although, I've had nothing back from the Scottish court regarding your meeting with King James."

I stand up, waving a careless hand. "What can one expect? He is a shoddy king with a shoddy staff. You may leave me to look through these last few letters alone. I will send word if further action is required."

While they bow from my presence, I take a turn about the room to stretch my leg and bring the feeling back to my feet. Too much sitting causes numbness these days, an infuriating tingling sensation that should be preferable to the pain but somehow isn't. I have told the physicians of it, but they have as yet offered no remedy, not one that works.

Peace falls upon the chamber, the former hum of the Privy Council meeting has melted away. When I take my place at the desk again, my pen scratches, and the dogs snore at the hearth. In the corner, Will Somer plays with a ball that taps gently as he throws and catches it.

I put down my pen and draw the pile of letters closer.

"Henry, is it true?"

Katherine bursts into the chamber and I put down the document I am perusing.

"Is what true?"

"Do you have a secret plan to crown me in York? Am I to have a coronation?"

Her eyes are bright, her hands clasped expectantly beneath her chin, her whole body tensed with suppressed delight. To dash her hopes would be unkind and I am not a cruel man.

I hate to make her cry.

I place the letter back on top of the pile and remove my eyeglasses.

"There was some talk of it, but we decided York, after all their insurrection, was undeserving of the honour. The current plan is that your coronation should be held at Westminster … once you have birthed our child."

My father would be proud of my diplomacy. There is no such plan in place, but my lie seems to have worked. Although her face falls, her disappointment is a shade of what it might have been had I told her the idea of a coronation had been rejected. At least she has hope now and if she does indeed present England with a prince, then I will gladly coronate her with all honour and expense.

"I suppose you are right, and the ceremony will be far grander in the capital."

I beckon her closer and she perches beside me, although there is barely room for both of us.

"Our trip to York will still be remarkable. Have you had the final fittings for your gown?"

"Oh yes!"

She releases my hand and slips from the seat, spinning around as she holds out an imaginary skirt. "It is so pretty. I've never had a gown made with cloth of silver before. It shimmers and shines, and the fabric is so sleek it almost looks like water. I am to be the moon and you, my Henry, in your cloth of gold, will be the sun, and our ladies and gentlemen of the court will be like the constellations, shining around us. Oh, I can barely wait."

Silently, I congratulate myself on making her so quickly forget her disappointment at the coronation that is not to be.

"Well. It isn't very long now. A few more days hunting here at Grimsthorpe and we will be on our way to Lincoln. I will have to leave you to your own devices while we are there, for I have much business to discuss after the rebellion. I am expecting recompense, and a great deal of it too."

She picks up one of her dogs who has followed her into the room and begins to dance around with it. The poor fellow wags his tail in a valiant attempt to enjoy the ride, and sticks out his tongue, trying to lick her face. My own dogs, older and staider than Katherine's, wake up briefly but drop their noses back to their paws again. As she twirls and skips, she sings a discordant tune and I watch, distracted from my business by the litheness of her body, the lightness of her step.

It is not merely her agility I envy but her happiness too. A moment ago, she was disappointed, but now her joy is so buoyant she floats upon it like a lily on the surface of a pond. Not that I am *un*happy, how could I be with a wife like her, but I bear the weight of responsibility and knowledge. I am too aware of what could happen, what might happen, and the inevitability of life's end is always present.

I am so unprepared for death. To die and leave England with only a young prince to follow after would be disastrous. I know too well the fate of boy kings, but

Katherine, my little Katherine, is oblivious to life's ills. It is ignorance that makes her happy.

Who wouldn't be envious of that?

"You will join us at Lincoln?" I grasp Brandon's shoulders as we take our leave. "We have enjoyed our stay. I wish we could tarry longer but … Lincoln awaits."

"I will be following in a day or two, Your Majesty. Lady Brandon and I have one or two things to attend to before we depart. We wouldn't miss the spectacle of the citizens of both Lincoln and York paying recompense for their crimes."

"And you should be there. Without you and Norfolk, the outcome might have been very different."

He nods grudgingly and I wonder again at his dislike for the queen's uncle. I slap him on the back and turn my attention to his wife, who curtseys low and swears the pleasure of hosting us has been all hers.

"It was a very great honour to host you, Your Majesty," she says, the fine bones of her face shining with sincerity. "It is just a shame you cannot tarry longer."

If I stayed any longer it would put a strain even on Brandon's extensive coffers, but I do not say so. It is better that I appear oblivious to the expense my progresses place upon those I honour with my company. At least they can boast of the honour of our visit.

Southeast of the city by some seven miles, our royal pavilion is waiting at Temple Bruer, the camp casting a splash of colour against the fading hues of the summer landscape. Here, while our gowns are prepared, we enjoy an al fresco meal.

The countryside hereabouts is relatively flat and all but void of cover. I miss the vast oaks, the tang of bracken, the rich loamy scent of southern England, but the view is remarkable.

At our backs is the old Templar church, dissolved last year, with its straddle of tumbledown buildings huddled against the walls, while before us, the sun shimmers in the distance and Lincoln Cathedral looms like a great ship on the horizon.

Tomorrow, dressed in Lincoln green as a reminder that I am their supreme leader, the queen and I will enter the city so the citizens may grovel for our forgiveness.

It is a warm August afternoon; the streets leading to the Bishop's Palace are lined with people. Some call out lusty cries of good health and long life; others are less welcoming and watch us pass in sullen silence. I even detect one or two catcalls. My officers will track those men down and they will be punished. This is supposed to be a reconciliation, a chance for the city to seek my forgiveness. It is not their place to barrack me.

Usually, when I am out and about in public, I greet my people with joyful enthusiasm, but today I am reserved. I show them a face that is both proud and detached; they must understand the nature of their crime and the sort of man they have crossed. I am not a monarch to be trifled with.

Katherine, on the other hand, has forgotten my stricture that she show more decorum, and sits lightly on her mare, the gems on her hood sparkling in the sun, her rings winking as she waves and calls 'hello' to the children throwing flowers in her path.

She twists and turns in the saddle, taking everything in, commenting to Lady Rochford, pointing out the extravagance of the decoration. Her ladies follow a pace behind, and I notice how staid they are in comparison with the queen, how much more regal their manner. Isabella Baynton, her head high, her expression gracious, could give my wife a few lessons on deportment. But none can deny Katherine's beauty, and her infectious joy is certainly having an effect on the crowd. When she comes into view, their cheers increase and the hail of blossom grows thicker.

We pass into the shadow of the cathedral and the courtyard of the Bishop's Palace opens out before us. I glance at the lofty towers, assess the costs of building such a splendid edifice, and I am sure my estimate must fall far short. Such riches can only have been bred of corruption. Last year, we demolished the shrine of St Hugh of Avalon, who was canonised for his vision of this rebuilding of the old abbey. The work was testament to his own pride rather than to honour God. We removed over two and a half thousand ounces of gold and double the amount of silver. I also ordered the gold to be stripped from the shrine of Little Hugh, but I let his remains lie undisturbed. He deserves the honour of being allowed to rest in peace, but he would never have demanded a golden shrine. He was a simple lad.

As a boy, I was fascinated and saddened by the tales of the small English boy taken and murdered by Jews. I used to imagine him in my own image, but dressed in the ragged clothing favoured by the poor. I saw myself befriended by the Jewish boys, chasing pigs through the streets, knocking mischievously on doors and running off before they were opened. There were mangy dogs barking in our wake, small dark-eyed girls who giggled at our antics. We were happy for a short while but, as the day waned, the stage of my dreaming grew darker. Suddenly, there were men, bearded and foreign, with grasping hands and vindictive, prodding fingers. They spoke in a language I did not recognise and forced me along a path I did not wish to follow … my imaginings always stopped there. My infant self could not imagine the pain of a child dying at the hands of grown men, his anguish as he cried for his mother … I shied away from it.

I have not thought of Little Hugh for many years, but I think of him now I am here. I recall my mother shaking her head over the injustices that were heaped upon him. One of the few things the monks of Lincoln did right was to take in his broken body and let it lie for all eternity among the saints. King Henry III was right to hunt down and punish those who injured him. Poor murdered soul.

There have been rumours that it wasn't the Jews at all. Some say it was the work of the English to inflate the local hatred of foreigners. Well, whatever the facts, whoever the perpetrator, Little Hugh is dead and should continue to be honoured. I will not be the one to disturb him. Perhaps I will take Katherine to visit his shrine in the morning.

A sudden fanfare of trumpets blasts away my thoughts, and I realise I have been daydreaming. I turn my attention to a fellow who has taken his place on a rostrum and is making some kind of welcoming speech. His voice is thin and reedy, his words carried off by the wind, so I will never know the message he so feverishly imparts. I nod and smile, hoping it is the correct response. Then the grooms come forward and take hold of our bridles while we are helped to dismount.

Later, after we are refreshed and our garments changed, we set out again to let the populace look upon us. My servants fuss and rearrange the skirts of my golden tunic, repositioning my sword, fluffing up the feathers on my cap. From the corner of my eye, I can see the queen is receiving similar treatment.

She shimmers like a lithe fish, the silver of her gown flashing and dazzling all who look on her. But she needs no finery to dazzle me; she is radiant, her face glowing. She puts me in mind of Anne after a night of loving, an expression I have seen on none of my other wives.

Why must Anne always intrude, even on my most splendid moments? Why can I not forget her? Why do I continually use her as a gauge by which to measure all other women? I shake my head, dislodging my hat again, so that Culpepper is forced to straighten it.

The people are waiting to receive us. The gentry, the mayor, and citizens of Lincoln, and the clergy of the cathedral.

Traitors all, who should rightly be hanged for their crimes. I take my stand and look coldly above their heads.

One by one, the various groups come forward. The clergy is first; their chosen leader makes a hesitant speech, a speech full of regret, full of apology. A speech that begs my forgiveness.

I would like to draw my sword and strike off his head, but I have already spied the coffer that he means to bestow upon me by way of recompense. He hands me a rolled copy of his apology and I accept it and, without reading, I hand it to Norfolk. Everyone kneels; only the queen and I are left standing. I look across the bowed heads of the company to the sky where crows are circling, and the pennants of the city hang limp in the bright blue sky.

"Jesus save Your Grace!" they cry, while I look on dispassionately. A *te deum* begins, the voices of the choir soaring to the heavens. Katherine turns to look at me, and my eyes soften, as they always do when I look upon her. I was wrong to be displeased with her earlier. What does it matter if she is a little impetuous, a little lacking in discipline? She is young; it is all part of her charm. Too soon, she will grow up, and her passion for life will be dampened, her limbs will stiffen with ague, she will be old before she knows it. She should enjoy life while she is still young enough to dance.

The hunting and the ceremonies have wearied me, and I require a few days to recuperate, leaving the queen to her own devices. The next stage of our journey will take us on to York, where I will meet with my nephew, James, King of the Scots. It is vital that I am at the peak of my fitness for this meeting. It will not do to be compared unfavourably with another king.

It puts me in mind of my meeting with King Francis all those years ago, although we are not going to such extremes to impress, and I will be certain not to challenge James to a wrestling match. Amusement twitches at my lips. After all the years that have passed since then, all the joys and lows, the dead children, the wives … I can now smile at my old self who was so keen to prove himself equal, or superior, to his peers. I have no need to prove anything now, for only fools fail to acknowledge my superiority.

*

The chamber we are allocated might be the best they have on offer, but I miss the comfort of my own palace. Perhaps it is the inconveniences of too much time in the saddle, but my limbs ache, my buttocks are sore, and my leg is throbbing. I wince at a sudden sharp pain, and look down at Culpepper's lowered head.

"I am sorry, Your Majesty. I will try to be more careful."

I release my breath slowly through my teeth.

"No matter, boy, it can't be helped. We have felt worse pain."

"I remember, Your Grace; that time when the wound was so infected your face turned black."

"Yes."

"We must be sure to avoid such a thing happening again."

In truth, I have little memory of it, just some hazy recollection of surreal dreams, as if I were in another realm, ruled by demons.

"Have you ever been struck by a lance, Tom?"

"More than once, Your Majesty. I am unskilled on the tiltyard. It hurt like the devil."

I laugh absentmindedly as my memory floats down through the years.

"I've had some nasty dog bites over the years, and I was kicked by a horse once. That caused a stir."

"I can imagine!" He sits back on his heels, his eyes wide, his handsome face open, expecting me to continue my tale. "I am surprised any horse would dare!"

I chuckle, my mind wandering back along the years.

"It was before I was king, but there was panic among the courtiers. My grandmother wanted the animal destroyed, but I was fond of the mare and refused to let them do it."

"I suppose horses can't be expected to recognise you are different to any other man."

I frown, wondering if there is an insult veiled behind his words, but I find none. He dabs the wound dry with a piece of linen and gently applies a salve. It is cooling and pleasant after the probing procedure of the cleansing. The salve has little healing power, but it prevents the bandages from sticking to the congealing flesh.

I wonder if his job irks him. He never complains or shows the slightest revulsion at his task. Tom is a good servant, a fine friend. I often think it a shame we are not closer in age. What fun we could have had, hunting and carousing together, had he known me in my youth. How the women would have flocked to us, whether we had coin to spend or not.

"I almost drowned in a ditch once too, did you know that?"

"No, Your Majesty! How did you come to be in a ditch?"

I pause, recollecting the day when, finding our way blocked by a water-filled ditch, I decided to vault across it using a sturdy pole.

"They tried to stop me, but I was young and irresponsible, as most young men are. Anyway, the pole wasn't as sturdy as I and it snapped beneath my weight, suddenly plunging me into the filthy water. At first, so Brandon told me after, they all stood around laughing, not realising I was stuck head-first in the clay bottom…"

Culpepper's face is frozen into horrified lines.

"But, you could have been…!"

"Killed? Yes, I could! Then what would have become of the realm? I only had Mary then. Luckily, one fellow, more discerning than the rest, recognised my plight and leapt in to save me."

"Thank goodness for that, Your Majesty. Who was it who saved you?"

"One of the footmen, Moody, I think his name was. I rewarded him well, for the fellow was a hero. In an indirect manner, he saved England from another civil war."

Culpepper smoothes my hose and replaces my slipper.

"I hope that is more comfortable, Your Majesty."

"It is, thank you, Tom. I don't know what I'd do without you. Everyone else lacks your gentle touch. You are a good servant, a fine friend."

"And you are a fine king, Sire."

He flushes, bows low and, gathering up his equipment, leaves me to peruse the business of the day. There are piles of petitions to consider, grants to administer; in fact, it can hardly be called a rest at all. Perhaps I should walk the dogs, the gardens here are fine and the sun is less fierce today. But the physicians advised to me to rest and if I want to be in the finest fettle for my meeting with James, I must heed them.

I push aside the pile of papers and pick up my book of hours, idly turning the pages while Somer throws a ball back and forth for the dogs. A musician plays softly on his lute and a small fire crackles in the grate for, although it is August, the day is chilly.

I contemplate the bright illustrations, absorb the beauty of both the pictures and the words, but soon my eyes grow heavy, my head begins to nod. As I drift off, I acknowledge sadly that I am indeed growing old. I thought the day would never come when I'd prefer the comforts of my chamber to the thrill of the chase, the pull of the music, the allure of a temptress but ... here it is.

That day has come.

But, a few days later, I am recovered, both in body and spirit, and the entourage continues its progress toward York, stopping at Pontefract and Hull on the way. Pontefract played a large part in the uprising, the custodians of the castle surrendering far too easily to the demands of the 'pilgrims', as they speciously called themselves.

Lord Darcy pleaded that he was getting on in years, and the rebels had far outnumbered his men, but Cromwell always suspected his sympathies lay with the rebels. He resented the loss of the abbeys and the break from Rome, and was vocal in his views, even in the beginning, at the time of my marriage to Anne. Years may have passed since, but I have not forgotten the treachery of the people hereabouts, and seemingly, they have neither forgotten nor repented of it.

As we ride the lined streets, there is noticeably less joy in our arrival than there was at Lincoln. The adults stand sullen in the sudden squall of rain; only the children, who have neither the memory nor the resentments of their elders, cheer when we ride by.

Katherine, oblivious to the atmosphere, waves happily at them, scattering coin to the waifs, who scrabble in the dirt to retrieve as many as they can. I look neither right nor left. I do not wave. I do not smile.

Tomorrow, with great ceremony, these traitors of Yorkshire will make their submission, and I will receive further reparation for the rebellion. But they will never be forgiven.

Our apartments at Pontefract are well appointed. It is an impressive castle, largely regarded as one of the finest in our realm. While the servants scurry around, ensuring the queen and I have every need, I spend an hour with my wife in the rain-washed gardens.

"Oh, no, Button, stop that!"

One of her dogs is digging a hole in the finely mown mead, a pile of rich soil scattering across the path. The dog looks up unapologetic, his tongue lolling.

"Oh look, Henry, he is smiling at me. How can I be cross with him?"

She claps her hands and he comes to her unrepentantly, jumping up, leaving paw prints on her skirts.

"Oh Button, now look! You are such a naughty boy."

She lovingly ruffles his ears, kisses his nose and allows the wriggling beast to lick her face. The other dogs, eager for her attention, join in.

I feel a squirm of envy.

"Come," I say, "leave the dogs alone and walk with me."

I hold out my arm and she obediently takes my elbow. We stroll among roses and daisies, the lavender I notice does not grow so well here in the north as it does in our gardens in the south. It probably dislikes the constant rain and wind. My grandmother always said lavender preferred a poorer, lighter soil. As we walk, Katherine chatters about this and that, and how she passed her time during my recuperation at Lincoln.

"My day was very much as usual apart from the lack of your presence. I went early to Mass, I walked the dogs, received my dressmaker, danced and played, and ate too many pastries, just as always."

I laugh, obligingly.

"And … did you miss me?"

I hate the pathetic tone in my voice. I sound like a neglected old man, searching for reassurance, eager for love. It is not easy to be husband to such a bright, vigorous girl. I'd give ten years of my life to be able to match her energy.

"Of course I missed you, Henry. We all did."

She stops and reaches up to kiss my nose, run her hands down my cheeks. Her smile is so doting, so affectionate, yet it lacks the passion I long to see. She makes me feel like one of her pets. If I am truthful, I have never known her look on me with lust, as Anne did when I was in my prime.

Perhaps it is Katherine's lack of desire that reinforces the knowledge that I am ... past my youth. Maybe I should seek out Anne Basset; she is among our party somewhere. She always knew how to restore my flagging virility; it would take little effort on her part to make me feel a man.

I sigh and follow my wife as she skips ahead along the path.

The next day dawns bright, the dull damp mood of yesterday replaced with sunshine. My optimism rises as I am made ready to greet the public and I am in good spirits, exchanging jokes with Tom Culpepper while I break my fast.

The mood is infectious and the courtiers join in, laughing at my quips, gently mocking Tom, who is a favourite of everyone at court. I dab my lips, rise from the table and wait for my coat to be brought out. While it is fastened and the heavy bejewelled chain placed about my neck, I wonder what the day will bring. It can only be a better, brighter day than the last. The dismal weather made me maudlin yesterday, and I hope that feeling has passed for good now.

Life is too short for gloom.

The citizens are gathered; those who remained loyal during the insurrection are on the right, those who betrayed me are on the left. With great pomp, we file into the chamber with the sound of trumpets in our ears and take our place at the high table. I look coldly above the heads of the company while the announcement is made, then I turn to those on the right. These are the true men, who stood firm in support of their king. I assume my most loving expression as I thank them for their loyalty.

"You shall be rewarded well," I tell them. "We do not forget those who show fidelity."

Then I turn to the others, the false men on the left, and my smile degenerates to a scowl as my gaze encompasses those traitors who ranged against me. I make careful note of faces, acknowledging names of those who now show contrition and those who continue to ooze hostility. Keeping them on their knees, I launch into a tirade against falseness. A fug of fear rises as I lean forward across the table and make my displeasure clear.

"Have I not been a loyal, faithful king, concerned only with your well-being, and that of the realm? Is this how such dedication should be rewarded?"

I may have pardoned them but that does not mean they will *ever* know my favour. With my fury unleashed, I lash out my disgust that such men exist in the world.

A deathly silence follows. I can smell their terror. I sit down, lean back in my seat and let my cold eye sweep the room. One of the traitors steps forward, the paper he is holding trembling, marking the depths of his fear. He begins to speak, his voice shaky and unclear as he confesses their treason.

He thanks me for my great noblesse in pardoning them, begs my forgiveness and promises eternal future fidelity. It is a long speech, during which my mind wanders and my belly begins to rumble.

I wonder what is for dinner.

When he is done, he stumbles forward, offers one of my clerks a bulk of rolled parchments, one of which is handed to me. As the proceedings draw to a close, I stand up and leave the chamber without looking either right or left. Before I have even reached the top of the stairs, a great babble of voices issues from below.

Once I reach the privacy of my chambers, I take the time to peruse the submissions. I unroll the first and find it is writ in a fine hand, the letters curled and looped, like the work of a monkish scribe. I frown at it, fumble for my eyeglasses, and begin to read.

We, your humble servants, the inhabitants of this Your Grace's county of York, confess that we wretches ... have most grievously, heinously and wantonly offended your most gracious Majesty...

I let the letter fall, it is just more of the same, more grovelling acknowledgement of their lack of love. *Was ever a king so badly served?*

I sit and brood until the day grows dark and my servants come to make me ready for bed.

"Where is Tom?" I ask. "You fellows are too rough. Where is Tom?"

"He is nowhere to be found, Your Majesty. He was complaining of a headache earlier, so we are worried he may be ailing."

As always, the fear of contagion prompts me to accept his absence. It is good that he does not attend on me if he is ill. If he has not recovered by tomorrow, I will insist he keeps away until all fear of plague has passed.

Denny brings a tray of wine and wafers, places them on the nightstand and moves a candle closer to the bed. The thought of the long night ahead is unwelcome. I wish for company. I put down the book I had intended to read.

"I know it is late, but send for the queen, Denny. I could do with her company until I sleep."

He bows and leaves to do my bidding. I pick up the book again and turn the first page.

When I open my eyes, the sun is shining through a crack in the shutters. I blink into the dawn and pull myself up on the pillows. I have slept the whole night through. The room still slumbers, half in shadow, the candles burnt low, the fire almost out. At the hearth, the dogs are snoring, and Somer is curled up in a chair. I cough to attract the attention of my man and Denny appears, his hair in disarray, his tunic unlaced.

"Your Majesty, forgive me." He fumbles with the tails of his shirt before pouring and offering me a cup of ale.

"I must have been more tired than I imagined," I say after taking a deep draught. "I suppose I was asleep when the queen arrived, I hope she wasn't disappointed."

His face stills, a long pause before he replies.

"I could not rouse the queen, Your Majesty, nor her women. When I went to fetch her as you instructed, I found the door locked and all the women presumably asleep."

It is unlike Kate to retire so early. I frown into my cup, the amber liquid swirling.

"She must have been as exhausted by the events of the day as I was. It is as if we had all taken a sleeping draught, like an enchanted palace from the nursery tales. Still, I daresay we shall all be the fresher for it today."

Late summer 1541 - York

The summer months are almost over now, the nights are drawing in and I find myself longing for Hampton Court, for the familiar routines of winter. It is always so at the end of a long progress, and this is the longest and the most extravagant journey I have ever taken on home turf.

It has required more effort than before, my health has been troublesome, my good spirits intermittent. But before we return south, I must summon the enthusiasm to put on one last show to impress the King of Scotland.

One might think that with our family ties, James and I would be natural friends and allies, yet that is very far from the truth. He is a headstrong, self-obsessed individual who is so keen to protect the Catholic faith that he consistently snubs me and cosies up with France and Rome. Despite Ralph Sadler's best attempts to persuade him, James refuses to close the Scottish abbeys, claiming they have stood many years in God's service and will continue to do so. He is blind to the corruption, the greed, or at least pretends to be, because his financial gains outweigh his sense of moral outrage.

It has taken years to arrange this meeting between us. Our ambassadors have been back and forth, sometimes in agreement, more often in discord, but at last I have high hopes of reaching accord. It is vital that we awe him with our noblesse and power. He cannot fail to be impressed by the submission of York, and the monetary reparation that now fills my coffers.

I give orders that our best tapestries and furnishings be sent ahead, and the grandest clothing made ready; not just for the queen and I but for our households, servants, yeoman and archers too. I am determined that this will be the most splendid display of royal power seen outside the capital.

I sit at my desk, compiling a list of suitable food; swan, peacock and those tasty little quail, when Katherine's laughter intrudes on my thought. I put down my pen and limp to the window, look down on the garden where she is walking with some of her ladies. Among them I notice a few gentlemen in attendance, I try to name them but one or two are unknown to me.

I watch her. Her demeanour is different to that of Isabella Baynton, who walks decorously beside Lady Rochford. Even Anne Bassett, who follows a little behind, has more dignity in her step than Katherine, who skips and hops like a five-year-old, twisting and turning as she chatters and teases her gentlemen companions. Instead of keeping her hands clasped before her as her elders do, she waves them about, embellishing her words; and while her ladies titter gently behind their hands, she laughs aloud, her mouth wide, her lovely face alight with mischief. I wonder what impression she will make on the King of the Scots. *Will I look a fool with a child on my arm? Will he scoff in secret with his friends?*

I sigh and turn away. Lately, it seems I spend much of my time alone, dealing with matters of state while my wife romps with her friends. It isn't how I imagined it would be, but things seldom are.

The days pass. We hunt, we dine, we dance, or at least the others do. My leg is too troublesome, and I find the enthusiasm for life that returned full measure in the early days of our marriage is waning now. Now that I have discovered the secrets of her body and can enjoy it whenever I wish, the thrill of the chase has paled.

I am content to watch while she dances.

After a few weeks, the wait grows tedious. Each morning I ask if word has come from the Scottish court, or if they have given a date for the king's arrival.

"We've heard nothing, Your Majesty. I will send again to inquire."

I growl something unintelligible and get on with my breakfast. Even the food fails to satisfy. I am jaded with everything, everyone.

"I was hoping to wear my burgundy gown, but now I think I might change my mind. The yellow is nicer and suits my colouring better."

I stare blankly at the queen, who has her head on one side, waiting for my opinion. I don't give a damn what she wears. She could dance before the Scottish King in her night shift if only he'd arrive.

I am not used to being kept waiting. Most people rush to answer my summons, but James! He is an arrogant fellow, trying to prove himself above dancing to my tune. If I didn't desperately need the alliance, I'd return to Hampton Court now and deprive him of the pleasure of insulting me. It is a long time since I've been to war. *Has he forgotten Flodden? Does he not remember when his father perished on the battlefield by English hands?*

The longer I wait like a lackey for James to arrive, the more ridiculous I feel, and the more ridiculous I feel, the less inclined I am to let anyone know of it. If I march away in high dudgeon, they will laugh at me, but they will laugh all the louder if I quietly order our finery to be removed and sneak away like a thief in the night.

But I have to go. I cannot wait forever.

And then comes news that Prince Edward is ill of a fever. I send back a message, threatening dire consequences should he not recover. The next day passes with great consternation on my part, but before my messenger has time to deliver my orders, another missive arrives, assuring me of the prince's recovery.

I pray alone in the chapel, thanking God for His magnanimity in saving my son but, for future peace of mind, I order the prince to be moved to Ashridge, where the air is sweeter. I will not be assured of my son's recovery until I see if for myself, and at least the excuse prevents me from losing face over the failed meeting. It will now look as though I am the one snubbing the Scottish King.

Still simmering with anger over James' duplicity, we begin the long slow journey south. The further I get from York and its unpleasant associations with treachery and humiliation, the better I feel. As my impotent rage reduces, joy returns. Katherine seems like an asset again, especially when she attends to my needs as sweetly as she does.

I give her more jewels, feel a twist of pleasure when she squeals with joy as she tears off the wrapping. One evening while we are abed, I draw a box from beneath my pillow and empty precious stones onto the sheet. She sits up and allows me to adorn her naked body with rubies and pearls.

"You look like the Queen of Sheba," I tell her as I arrange the pearls so her breasts protrude through the ropes of jewels like the noses of spaniels through a curtain.

"I am the Queen of Sheba," Katherine says grandly, lifting her chin. "And you are my King Solomon!" She sits astride me, imprisoning me in her power and, warming to her game, I lie back, bewitched and blessed.

The further south we travel, the louder the cries of the populace as we pass through the towns and villages. Although the north had cheered us, I was not blind to the fact that their joy was fear driven. This is love. I am Henry their beloved king, and they love Katherine too. Whenever they see her, the crescendo of voices increase: 'God Save the King! God save the Queen!'

She waves happily back, delighting in their devotion.

I know where I am before I even open my eyes on the first morning back at Hampton Court. The temperature in the chamber is just right, the mattress is just the right softness. It even smells better than the apartments I used in the north. I am thankful for everything today.

I have forgotten the shame and fury over James' snub. I am grateful for my life, proud of my realm and delighted in my queen. At last, I am in God's favour. It matters not that He has not yet blessed me with a son, there is still time. The queen is young and I am in my prime. If last night is anything to go by, it won't be long until she is great with child.

All Saint's Day dawns fine and my spirits are high as I am made ready to take public communion in the chapel royal. After a good breakfast, clad in my finest, I make my way to the chapel of which Wolsey was always so proud. Above me is a gold-starred sky where hosts of carved golden angels trumpet in celebration of their triumphant king.

I am filled with contentment, satisfied that the years of striving for God's approval are at last over. It is as if I have reached the summit of a great mountain, and God is smiling on me. All across the realm, we hold special services giving most humble and hearty thanks for the most perfect jewel of a bride, the rose without a thorn, with which the Lord has blessed me.

The rest of All Saint's Day passes as every year, in an excess of merriment, feasting and dancing. After hearing Mass, there is a certain relief in more earthly delights. For once, my leg is not troubling me overmuch but, although I dance one or two less vigorous dances with my wife, for the larger part of the celebration I am content to watch her.

I obtain my joy through hers. She is nimble and lithe, and never happier than when dancing. I watch as she weaves in and out of her gentleman partners. Her constant practising has proved worthwhile for she stands out from the other women, as a queen should. Anne Basset tries to catch my eye, gliding like a swan through the throng to join the other women, but I keep my attention focused on the queen.

As I follow Katherine's progress, my attention is drawn by Jane Rochford, who is watching me, watching the queen and, as ever, I feel discomforted by her notice. She is one of the few who does not admire me, she doesn't even feign admiration. It is as if she sees into my inner soul, to the parts I would not want anyone to see. It is almost as if she is waiting for something, wanting me to fall. I return her scowl and she bobs a curtsey before looking away.

I turn my attention back to the queen, who is doing her best to dissuade Somer from dancing in circles about her. Each time she stops, he stops too and bows, asking her to partner him. In the end, she gives in and the court roars as Katherine and my fool skip hand in hand to the music. At the edge of the chamber, I see Culpepper joining the applause, his face stretched in smiles, his handsome head erect, his shoulders shaking with laughter.

Warmed by the unity of my court, the favour of my friends, but worn out by the day, I leave them all to dance on. I should have retired to my chambers an hour since. As I wend my happy way to bed, the music and laughter follows me, and as I am made ready for the night, I continue to watch them in my mind's eye.

November 1541 – Hampton Court

It is good to be home, and my spirits remain high. I jest with my gentlemen as my beard, greyer now than gold, is trimmed, my nails clipped. I select a doublet of black with silver thread embellishing the cuffs, the slashes across the sleeves and chest revealing a fine silk shirt beneath.

My looking glass reflects a king, a man in his prime, a wise and honest man. As my dress sword is arranged at my hip, I take the gloves Denny is offering and tuck them into my girdle.

"Where is my psalter?" I ask, and it is instantly produced. I tuck it beneath my arm and make my way to the chapel, wondering as I go if Katherine will make it to Mass so early.

My mind is not on prayer this morning. I am feeling spry enough to go for a ride. Brandon has returned to court this week, perhaps we can ride out together as we used to, if he is feeling up to it. I often forget that he too grows old.

The sound of the choir greets me, their voices ascending to the dizzy heights of the blue and gold ceiling. Immediately, I feel contrition that my mind had strayed to sport rather than giving thanks to God for another day. Before I enter and take my seat, I rearrange my face into a pious expression. But as I sit down, I notice a folded slip of paper. I pick it up, look about the chapel to discover the author of the note, but when no man meets my eye, I unfold the message and … the world around me crumbles.

Reality falls away. The ethereal voices are silenced. I am no longer in the company of my household, no longer in the presence of the Lord. I am spinning in an ugly black void, a hell where demons laugh and point and mock and bite. I am in a nightmare where I have become a laughingstock, and Katherine, my beautiful flawless Katherine, my rose without a thorn … is a *harlot*.

This cannot be true! I must get away. I must run before she arrives. I cannot bear to look upon her now. I stand abruptly, my hip gives way, and an unseen hand comes out to stop me falling.

"Let me help you…" Brandon is there. I cling to his arm.

"Get me out of here," I groan, and he assists me from the chapel. I flee from God, from the angels, from the prying eyes of my court. I flee from Katherine … my lovely Katherine.

It cannot be true.

Afterwards, I have no memory of how I arrived, but somehow I am in the privacy of my inner sanctum. I swear I will never leave it again. I slump into a chair, someone hands me a cup, but I dash it aside, wine spreading across my white hose.

I stare into the void, cling like a drowning man to Brandon's hand. I do not look at him. I hope he is not looking at me. I want never to be looked on again for I am a *fool.* I close my eyes, shut out the world, shut out the truth, shut out the nightmare my life has become. I long with all my heart for my mother.

She doesn't come.

I have never known such pain. I huddle alone in the dark; alone, although there are people in the chamber. Silent servants who creep like spirits around me, bringing wine and victuals, which I ignore.

I will never eat again.

My chest is tight, so tight I can scarcely draw breath. I am conscious that Brandon is still with me. I am aware that he has sent the others away. Although I make no acknowledgement, he and I sit in the dark together, neither one of us speaking, but his presence speaks volumes all the same.

After a time, I realise my face is wet. Tears, tears I cannot stop, gather on my face, in my beard, and sobs restrict my throat – pain, such pain. I cannot contain it. I thump my breast, rock back and forth like a great stricken ship foundered on the unfaithful schemes of a siren.

It cannot be true!

I try to speak but my tongue sticks to my teeth, to the inside of my mouth, like an alien presence, slowly choking me; it takes all my effort to control it. To form words.

"How?" I manage at last.

"Don't think of it, Henry."

Brandon struggles to his knees, clasps my hands tight, offering me his strength. "Do not dwell on the detail."

"But … but Norfolk said she was chaste … he said she was *untouched*!"

Anger seeps in, slowly replacing my sorrow. Anger and humiliation are stronger emotions than grief. As I think … as I consider … in painful, graphic detail the shameless way I have been treated, my body begins to tremble. Fury wells beneath my skin, a fury too great to contain. It *cannot* be true!

I struggle to my feet and roar like a great wounded lion, pulling at my clothes. The sound of ripping fabric mimics the tearing of my heart. More slowly, Brandon rises too; he grasps the collar of my coat as if to restrain the violence of my grief. He tries to embrace me but I am suffocating, my breath issuing in gasps, my heart racing, sweat pouring. I push him away, tug at my necktie, drag it from my throat and rip open the top of my fine black and silver tunic.

Priceless pearl buttons scatter like hail.

"People will suffer for this, Brandon. I will have their heads for this!"

It is hours before I can bring myself to look at the note again. I remain closeted away from the court, seeing no one. Brandon helps me prepare for bed, although it is not yet close to night. I crave the comfort of soft pillows, of warm blankets ... of a woman, of Katherine.

How can this be true?

I squint at the scrawled note. At the thought of her, knowing I have lost her, knowing I never really had her. The tears begin again. I am caught in an alternating nightmare of sorrow and rage. One minute I want to kill her, the next I want to beg her to tell me it isn't true.

"Is it true?"

Brandon stops what he is doing, raises his hands and lets them fall again. I know he will not lie to me, but some truths are difficult to voice. His silence tells me all I need to know.

"Who left the letter?"

"Cranmer, I believe."

"Cranmer. Am I so fearsome that he could not come to me privately? Am I the sort of king who kills the messenger?"

"I expect he was reluctant to injure you. We all know how…"

"How easily I was duped? She has made me a laughingstock."

"Nobody is laughing, Henry."

I rub my forehead, squeeze the bridge of my nose to prevent the pitying tears from starting up again.

"I suppose I must address the Council tomorrow. The queen … the harlot, is she in the Tower?"

"No - no, I believe she is confined to her chambers. We were unsure of Your Majesty's wishes."

He is using my formal title again. I preferred it when he called me Henry.

"What does Norfolk say?"

"I don't know, Sire. I have seen no one, I've been here with you."

"And I am grateful for that, Brandon. I will not forget it."

"Would you like me to leave you now? I could discover what is happening and bring you news of it. I could summon Norfolk."

I shake my head. If I were to see him now, I might take off his head myself.

"I will speak to him tomorrow but … yes, go and seek out the lay of the land. I will stay awake until you return."

He kisses my hand, bows low, re-establishing our role as king and subject.

Alone now, I am consumed by a torrent of grief, floored by disappointment, shock and misery.

But although I prayed for death, I wake in the morning. I have to carry on, as if all is well, as if everything is normal. I cannot let them see my breaking heart. My whole body is wracked with pain, I limp along the corridor to the chapel, lower myself painfully to my knees before God.

I misremember the words; I forget how to speak to Him. My mind is void of everything bar the knowledge of what she has done. The drone of the priest intrudes as he goes on and on, but I do not follow his words. Instead, I go over the past few months with Katherine, recalling every instance in which she could have been unfaithful.

And when I look, I find there are many.

A sob escapes me. I screw my eyes tight shut, lower my head to my clasped hands and hope nobody can see my shoulders juddering.

"Henry! Henry! Henry!"

My head jerks up. *Katherine!*

The anguish in her voice stabs through me, more wounding than her faithlessness. The longing to go to her, to hear her deny the allegations, is almost too strong. I want it all to be lies. *It must be lies.*

I turn my head, listening as the heavy footsteps of the guard carry her away. Her screams grow fainter, but I will hear them forever.

I can almost see it; the way she hangs limply in their arms, her white face, her stricken eyes. *Oh, Katherine, my Katherine* … she is begging for forgiveness, for a chance to explain. I blank it out, focus on her sin, her falseness, her callous lies, and coldness encompasses my heart.

I will never know joy again.

How Europe will laugh at me. The unsullied bride I took as my queen was impure after all. Other men, several so the whispers say, have known the delights of her body. Even before she came to me she was used, *soiled.* I might as well have taken a whore from the stews and made her my bride.

I send Cranmer to discover more. I order the arrest of those involved: a former music master, Manox, and her current secretary, Francis Dereham, a boastful, loudmouthed fellow by all accounts. I also lock up her grandmother, Agnes Tilney, who will be punished for her lack of care, her lack of guidance. Norfolk, summoned to my presence at last, falls to his rheumaticky knees, craving forgiveness, claiming ignorance of her sordid past.

"I swear before God, Your Majesty, that I have been tricked, just as you have. I thought she was a good girl, I thought she was honest. I too have been duped."

He clasps his hands, his face haggard and afraid. But I have no pity. I have half a mind to send him to the

Tower. It is only his past service that saves him, and the fact he may be of further use.

"Get up and get out, I don't want to see you," I say. "Have someone find Cranmer and send him to me."

He backs out, stammering gratitude, promising life-long fidelity to me and my heirs. I sit back in my chair and drum my fingers on the table. My heart is black with despair. I would not care if I did not wake up tomorrow. I can see no further ahead; the future is a blank wall.

I, Henry of England, have been destroyed by a faithless girl.

But I cannot remain here indefinitely. I will have to face the world sometime. I order Cranmer to continue his investigation, to keep the matter strictly quiet, but the court is on high alert, their suspicions roused by the sudden absence of the queen. For now, only the Lord Privy Seal, the Lord Admiral, Sir Anthony Browne, and Wriothesley are to be party to the truth.

But there are whispers in the corridors that can't be stopped, the queen's continuing absence giving rise to rumour and speculation. People creep about the dark corridors in fear, as if they were complicit, and some of them probably were.

As I leave Hampton Court quietly after dark and embark for London, I feel as if a thousand eyes are watching me go.

Does Katherine see me from her window as I hurry to the wharf and board the royal barge? Does she wonder at my destination, and weep with regret?

Tomorrow, she will know the reason why. In the morning, Cranmer, having interrogated former members of her grandmother's household, will question the queen herself.

Does it matter if her crimes took place before our marriage? I have not lived a chaste life. I have had wives and mistresses, whores and light o' loves; is it so different for Katherine?

But she *lied*. She came to me as a virgin. I took her to my bed on the condition that she was pure. As king, I must be certain that any child born to my wife is of my own making. There must be no doubt!

Anger surges again as I imagine the child-Katherine writhing beneath the touch of her music teacher. According to Cranmer, her erstwhile companion, Mary Lascelles, is taking great delight in defaming her former friend. She claims to have many times witnessed Katherine, naked belly to naked belly with that worm, Dereham. By God, treason or no treason, I will have his head; he will die for daring to touch the future queen.

The rhythm of the oars does not soothe me as it usually does. The intimate supper with friends does not distract me from the monstrous events that have overtaken me. When I retire to bed, I summon Anne Bassett to ease me, but before she has even bared her breasts, I turn away.

*

"How is she, Cranmer?" I cannot help but ask when he answers my summons. He sweeps off his hat and bows low.

"She is not well, Your Majesty, at first she denied everything but, as I related the evidence, the statements of her companions, she collapsed into hysteria."

My head droops but, mindful of the company, I raise it again and signal for him to continue.

"She begs Your Majesty's forgiveness, and pleads that youthful frailty made her vulnerable to the wickedness of young men. She says she had not considered how great a sin it was to conceal her former faults from Your Majesty."

"She made no denial?"

"N-no, not after the initial shock of discovery."

"She is young, fornication is a sin, but it is not a crime. Her only crime is deceit. We all tell tall tales from time to time."

I look hopefully at my companions, but the small hope is quickly dashed.

"Your Grace may be minded to leniency, but you must not forget that while we are all liable to tell 'tall tales', we never do so to our king."

He is right, of course. We must investigate the matter further.

"Have her sent to Syon while we discover more on this, Cranmer. See that she is comfortable but not cosseted. No fine tapestries or cushions. And remove her jewels and allow her no dogs."

She will hate that.

I do my best to present a good face to the court. When in company, I bluster and jest much as I have always done. At least there is no man living who dares make comment on the matter to my face. In my heart, though, I am sore. I know how the scandal will be muttered around the court so I seek my own company and, whenever I can, I wriggle out of state duties.

I am just learning to tolerate it, just starting to wake in the morning without wishing I'd died overnight of shame, when Cranmer begs an audience, claiming he has further news.

I know the tidings he brings are bad.

He enters my presence like a great spider afraid of being stepped on. He is sweating, pale-faced and wary, his fingers fidget with his papers. For a while, we speak of day-to-day things; the encroaching cold, the arrangements for Christmas, which is now not far away.

I pause to reflect what a sorry celebration it will be this year without my beloved queen, and have to force myself to remember that she is no longer my beloved. Very probably, she never has been. When the conversation palls, I wave a hand.

"Well, spit it out, man. What is your news?"

He shifts to his other foot, shuffles his papers again, and grimaces as he runs a finger along the inside of his collar. Then he takes a deep breath.

"I - it is hard to relate this, Your Majesty. The news I have is – is grim. I beg your indulgence."

"Out with it, man. I won't eat you."

But I am wary, fearful of what he is about to say. My heart beats harder, slower, and an imp is sitting on my shoulder, whispering the wicked truth before Cranmer can get his words out.

There have been other men, after. After we were pledged.

"Your Majesty, I have been questioning the queen's household and it seems there have been … erm … occasions when the queen has been absent from her chamber when she … perhaps should not have been."

His lips are dry and cracked, probably from sitting too close to the fire. He moistens them with his tongue and, although the chamber is not overly warm, he dabs his forehead with a lace-edged kerchief.

"Go on," I say, my voice dangerously quiet.

But as I speak the words, I glare at him, daring him to continue. His mouths moves, his voice far off as he issues a sentence of death.

"It seems she has not resumed her former relationship with Dereham. He claims her affections were, at the time of your progress to the north, engaged with another."

My skin crawls.

My throat tightens.

"Our progress? This summer past? With whom? How?"

I stand up. Cranmer cowers like a craven, and is slow to recover himself.

"C-Culpepper," he stammers, so quietly I can barely hear and have to urge him to repeat it.

"It seems she and Thomas Culpepper met on several occasions when Your Majesty was ... was indisposed."

Blood thunders in my ears. My muscles tense. My belly rolls. I want to rage, to scream, to roar like the lion I am, but when I speak, my voice is small and plaintive.

"Tom?"

I think I was doomed to fail from the moment of my birth. I was dragged from my mother's womb into the maelstrom of this world and instructed to perform miracles. Yet, from infancy, I've been battered by fate, by impossible expectation, burdened by a duty I never had a hope of fulfilling. I have been betrayed, cheated and unloved when all I have ever craved is a good woman who will give me a son.

Is that so much to ask?

This news, the betrayal not only of my beloved wife but also my favourite servant, will be the death of me. I know as I stand trembling from the blow Cranmer has delivered that I can never recover from it.

I have no wish to.

December 1541 – Hampton Court

Francis Dereham dies first. I stand at the balcony window of my chamber at Hampton Court, while the upstart traitor is dragged on a hurdle to Tyburn where, like all lowly traitors to the crown, he is hanged, castrated, disembowelled and beheaded, at my order. And I am glad of it.

His body is then cut into quarters and dispatched about the country as a warning to all would-be traitors. And I am glad of it.

My days of leniency are done.

But when it comes to it, I cannot use the full force of the law against Tom. Even now, the love I bore him will not allow it. For years, he soothed my pain and amused me, he cared for me, treated my leg as if it were made of glass. The least I can do for the love we shared is to offer him a speedy death. But when the day comes, it is not just Tom Culpepper who suffers at his execution. A part of me dies too. And I fear it is the best part.

Apart from Norfolk, whom I intend to pardon, the rest of the Howards and the duchess' household are to remain in the Tower at my pleasure. I may leave them there. I may release them. I am not yet decided.

Katherine's fate is inevitable, but I cannot bring myself to sign the warrant yet. While Cranmer and the Council work out an act of attainder to be used against all such traitors hereafter, I spend a miserable, lonely Christmas, and when I raise my cup to welcome in the glad New Year, it is a cup empty of optimism.

<u>February 1542 – Waltham</u>

I am weary beyond measure. I am old. My looking glass shows the wreckage of a man. My face is lined, my hair and beard almost totally grey, and my belly is vast. I have grown so large that I can hardly stand without help and require the arm of a servant to assist me from room to room. I miss Tom, I miss Katherine.

For months I have lived a doleful life. There are beggars on the streets more joyful than I am. I drink too much and overindulge at supper, finding comfort in my plate that I now lack in bed. Some brave fool suggested I seek another wife, but I am done with women. I am done with marriage, and must learn to be content with just one son.

Besides, Katherine still lives.

For now.

She will find no pleasure in the bright winter mornings, and never again will she ride out, rosy and full of life. Never again will she dance in the light of the fire, her hair loose and her arms bare. I droop my head to my chest and the damned tears fall again, as they do each time I think of that faithless girl.

Why was I so ill used? I poured all I had into her lap, opened my heart, loved her, *only her.* Yet all the time, they were laughing. I cringe, imagining the disparaging whispers, the mockery of my doting.

The attainder against her is secure. From this day, if any loose-living woman dare marry the king without plain declaration unto His Majesty of her former unchaste life, it shall be treason. Adultery by or with the queen or the wife of the Prince of Wales shall be treason. And the failure of witnesses to disclose such matters is now treason too.

I peruse the document once more. It is a tool that will end Kate's life, and that of the Rochford woman too.

I wonder now how she ever wriggled a way back into my favour. She knew what happened to Anne Boleyn; she cannot have forgotten, she knew full well that adultery against the king was treason. She witnessed firsthand the death of her husband with his sister, my other faithless queen, for similar crimes against me. Yet she had no pity.

What possessed her to encourage Katherine in sin? What did she seek to gain? Did she wish for death? Or was her spite aimed at me?

Well, she will not escape punishment a second time.

On the twelfth of February, they inform me that the queen has been transferred from Syon to the Tower, where she is to die the next day.

I get little sleep. I toss and turn, lost in terrifying dreams in which I wake in a blood-soaked bed beside headless Katherine, and when I turn in the bed, I find Anne on the other side of me, also headless and bloodied.

With a cry, I start up, crying out for Culpepper, but then I remember he is gone too.

I wrote his death on paper, as I have Katherine's.

My little loveless Katherine.

I throw myself back on the mattress, bury my head beneath downy pillows and weep again. When I sleep at last, I do not wake until almost midday. My servants creep around, not meeting my eye, not daring to make a sound. When I am at last ready for my toilette, I summon my gentlemen and they tell me that the queen died bravely at dawn.

While I was sleeping.

March 1542

It takes all my strength to carry on. When I am forced to appear in public, I hold myself proud, laugh loudly at Somer's antics, pay addresses to the court ladies … as if I am interested.

As if I am glad.

"I will never take another wife," I say darkly when the Council suggests I should consider matrimony again.

"Your Majesty, there is a petition from the Duke of Cleves suggesting that the union between you and the Lady Anne be…"

I look him firmly in the eye.

"That will never happen. Tell him that. The idea is out of the question."

He backs down, shuffles through his papers, and the matters of the morning move on to other things. But my mind does not rest.

Why should I remarry? When has marriage ever served me well? Five wives, three children, two of them girls, and bastards at that. Anyway, although I will admit it to nobody, I am unlikely to father any further heirs. I am jaded with life. I have no heart for marriage.

Women are faithless, feckless strumpets.

But I am lonely. Once the night candles are lit and the drapes pulled about my great bed, bleak solitude swamps me. I am beset by painful memories.

Day and night, I am surrounded by people. Every act I perform is witnessed. My toilette, my prayer, even when I am sleeping there is a servant close by should I need assistance in the night. My stools are taken away and examined by the physicians to ensure my health, my hair is cut, my beard trimmed, my spots squeezed and treated with salve … by others. My leg is tended several times a day. There is nothing I do for myself. Every task is done by servant and observed by strangers; the state of my mind and the vagaries of my health are discussed across Europe.

In short, although I am never alone, I am the loneliest man in Christendom.

When Katherine was alive and the curtains drawn about the bed, it was as if we were in our own little world, a private world. I miss it and I'm miserable. Even the coming of spring does nothing to alleviate it. How long I can keep up the pretence, I don't know, but I am weary of state matters. I am weary of fawning councillors, and as my patience with heretics and dissenters runs out, the punishments I inflict grow harsher.

To fill the void left by the late queen, I summon my daughter Mary to preside over feasts and court events. She fulfils the task remarkably well, reminding me of her mother. Her manner is gentle; warm yet dignified. She charms the foreign dignitaries with her ease of communication and grasp of many languages. For the first time since she was an infant, I find myself proud of her, but not for the first time, I rue the fact she is not a boy.

My heir, Edward, grows apace. He has recovered well from a recent bout of quartan fever and is proving a strong and lively child of ready wit who does as well at his lessons as either of his sisters.

He and Elizabeth share a schoolroom, under the tutelage of Richard Cox, John Cheke, and Roger Ascham, both children excelling at Latin and mathematics. I am inordinately proud of them, even of Elizabeth, despite her Boleyn eyes and ready wit that borders at times on impertinence.

She rules the roost in most company, even charming those members of court who despised her mother. But I keep my grudging admiration to myself for fear of encouraging her. Perhaps she does need a mother: a mother to guide her, teach her gentility and meekness so vital in a woman. She must be curbed if she is ever going to find a husband.

Although Mary is old enough to no longer require a mother figure, Elizabeth and Edward would both benefit, but still, I shy away from selecting another bride.

Thankfully, there are other matters to distract me from the question of marriage. The Scots continue to push the limits of my patience and I still have not forgotten the shame of being spurned by James at York.

Since our break with Rome, we have done all in our power to persuade James to follow suit, but he is stubborn and turns more and more toward France. In the end, still sore from the recent indignities I have suffered, I send an army north, with Robert Bowes, the warden of the East Marches at its head.

Fortune continues to withhold its favour however, and when the armies meet at a place called Haddon Rig, my force is soundly defeated. I am shamed again. A laughingstock again.

It would be different had I been there; with me at their head we would soon have sent James running with his tail tucked firmly between his legs.

My inner rage rumbles on in a subterranean river of unquenchable fire.

For comfort, I overindulge at table; too much wine, too much rich food, and my belly rebels, even my own body turning traitor.

I vomit copiously.

Sick and feverish, I send for a woman, but she does nothing to rouse me. I lie, vast and flaccid, beneath her endeavours to please and, in the end, I push her away, like a plate of tepid dinner.

"Read to me," I say, but then, looking at her more closely, I add, "You can read, can't you?"

"A little," she says, taking the book of hours from me. She frowns in the ill light and begins to stutter over the words, pronouncing them badly, missing the inflection and nuance necessary to good reading.

"I will sleep now," I interrupt her tortured endeavours. "My man will give you coin. Thank you for your time."

With red cheeks, she pulls on her gown and curtseys low. She has failed both as a woman and a scholar, but I do not ponder on her feelings. I roll over, bury my face in the pillow and wonder how much longer I must suffer.

In a vain quest for peace, I visit with a few close friends, where we feast and hunt, yet I remain unsated. The struggle to mount my horse, along with the pain involved in staying in the saddle, outweighs the brief satisfaction of the kill. But we return to the hall with two fine hinds and the feast that follows at least sates my craving for food for a short while.

Our recent defeat at Haddon Rig continues to smart and the Scots haven't heard the last from me. I summon a council of war to discuss strategy and assess the cost of another campaign.

Irritation becomes a permanent state. It is as if I am wearing a hair shirt - the situation with Scotland, the unacknowledged fear of failure both as a king and a husband, and now a military leader, chafe at me day and night. And that irritation is aggravated by continual pain.

For almost a year, I rage against ill fortune. I am so badly served, and sometimes I wonder if I have offended God.

But deep unhappiness never lasts. One becomes used to the pain, one ceases to mourn each passing second and finds distractions in small things. As the year nears its end, I find myself seeking the company of others more and more often.

One evening, I limp to attend a private function held in Mary's chambers. I dress informally, choosing fewer jewels than my usual habit, and my tunic has been selected for comfort rather than to impress. I would prefer to slip into the chamber unnoticed but, as ever, when I arrive the company pauses and sinks in unison into obeisance.

"Get up, get up." I wave them to their feet and hobble to greet Mary. She blushes as she always does in my presence and offers me the seat she has just vacated. I take it gratefully. Her guests stand stiffly about the chamber, their enjoyment of the evening spoiled by my arrival.

Do they imagine I am going to lay about them with my stick or order them to the Tower for some social indiscretion?

I flap my hand again. "Be at ease," I say. "Pretend I am not here."

Slowly, the conversation resumes, but I sense it flows less freely than before. I turn to Mary and her companion, a small, neat woman whom I recognise at once.

"Why, it's Lady Latimer!" I say, while she curtseys low. I admire the grace of her movement, the flushed curve of her cheek when she straightens up. "We are glad to see you returned to court. We were sad to hear of your husband's passing."

She looks away, embarrassment embellishing her cheek.

"Thank you." She glances at Tom Seymour, who is standing nearby, and I do not miss the hint of conspiracy in the look. I scowl at Seymour, and he bows and makes an excuse to leave us. Lady Latimer glances briefly into my eyes before looking away again.

"Would you care for a game of chess, Lady Latimer?"

Of course, she assents, and I assist her to a chair, allow her to set out the game. I watch her long fingers as she carefully arranges the pieces on the board; her nails are short and neat, and, although she is past the first flush of youth, her skin is smooth and unblemished.

I attempt to assess her age, but it is hard to tell. She is far younger than a twice-widowed woman has the right to be. She could be in her mid-twenties, or she could be past thirty. Intrigued, I make a note to ask Mary later.

As we play, I learn she is erudite without being a bore, and witty without resorting to cruelty. Sharp, I think. She is sharp, yet amusingly and gently so.

I am so taken with her company that the other courtiers in the room seem to drift away, their voices drop to a hum, their antics as important to me as the wasp that batters its head against the windowpane.

But I become so engrossed in the manner in which she plays that I forget to attend to my own strategy. Quite suddenly, I realise I am in danger of losing the game. I must concentrate. I frown at the board, trying to forget the charms of my opponent and, just as she is about to take my queen, I move my knight, preventing her escape.

"I have you trapped, Madam," I say, stroking my beard.

Someone stands up to recite a poem, the company falls silent as the words of my old friend, Tom Wyatt, infiltrate the room. We received news of his passing a few days ago; his death coming as a surprise to me since I saw him only recently. He sought audience and requested leave to retire from his duties overseas to spend his last years at his castle in Kent.

"I am weary, Your Majesty," he said. "I grow old and tired, my joints are stiff, and my heart is heavy."

I know the feeling well, but I will never be given leave to retire from court life.

"One more mission, this time on home soil, to Falmouth, and then you may take some time away from court."

I am reluctant to grant him permanent leave, but he accepts, as if he has a choice. A few days after that, news arrived that he had died en route, never having completed his mission.

I am saddened by his loss. There are few men left who can remember my younger days. He was hot for Anne once, brokenhearted when I wed her. I was jealous of his love for her, suspicious of her feelings for him. His early poetry consisted of little else but praise for some mysterious dark-eyed lady, who even a fool could see was clearly Anne.

She used to mock him, addressing him in an affectionate teasing manner reserved only for him. But now, of course, I know that she mocked me too.

She mocked everyone.

As the words of the poet evoke memories of the past, I ponder my next move. Lady Latimer's fingers fidget in her lap while she waits, drawing my attention from the board. A small dog, who has been sheltering unseen beneath her skirts, crawls out to snuffle at my shoes. I hope he doesn't intend to piss of them.

As the poet's voice dwindles, there is a hubbub at the door and a messenger arrives with a rolled parchment on a tray. He brings it to me, bends a knee and I sit up, abandon the game and break the seal. My heart leaps at the unfurling words. I struggle to stand, Mary's hand at my elbow.

"I have news!"

The conversation ceases, everyone turns to face me.

"Bring wine!" I cry. "Bring more wine, for the Duke of Norfolk has wrought a great victory over Scotland at Solway Moss!"

I expect Hertford played a part in it too, but I have been searching for a reason to bring Norfolk back into favour, and he has done well to quell the Scots.

"To Norfolk," I cry, raising my cup high. "This will show the arrogant King of Scotland who has the mastery of this island."

A great cheer echoes around the chamber and I look with real joy on the jubilant faces. Men are clapping one another on the back, the women embrace. I slide my arm around my daughter, plant a king-sized kiss on her lips and then, for good measure, I do the same to Lady Latimer.

"Oh, Your Majesty!"

She stumbles when I release her and puts a hand to her scarlet cheek, but I can tell she is not displeased. To steady her, I keep a firm hold of both arms, look down at her and acknowledge again what a fine-looking woman she is.

"Forgive me, Lady Latimer, I find myself quite overwhelmed, both by the joy of the occasion and the company I am in. Do forgive me."

She stammers something, a denial that there is anything to forgive. We both look down at the abandoned game, the scattered pieces.

"I'm not sure who won, Lady Latimer," I say, "we must play again tomorrow."

She opens her eyes wide, and with a brief glance past my shoulder, smiles her consent.

The victorious news from the north injects the joy that the court has been missing, and we are merrier than we have been since before … since our return from York.

I order jousts and picnics, hunts and feasts, and throw myself into the proceedings with as much enthusiasm as my body allows.

I find myself often seeking the company of Lady Latimer, who is learning I am not as fearsome as she thought.

"Only traitors need fear me, Lady Latimer. Traitors, or spies, or heretics. You are none of those, I suppose?"

She laughs, her eyes sliding from mine.

We play together often in the weeks that follow and I learn that she has a keen sense of humour. After a walk in the gardens and an intimate game of chess, followed by an evening of entertainments, I retire to my bed and find myself thinking of her in the quiet darkness.

I am almost eager to rise this morning and my spirits rise even higher at council when I am informed that the King of Scotland, who was ever such a thorn in my side, has died. This news is more than I hoped for!

Although only about thirty years old, I am informed he has always been a sickly man, not blessed with a hearty constitution such as mine.

"This is good news!" I exclaim. "He leaves no heir.

Scotland will be ours for the taking!"

Brandon rises to his feet.

"He does leave an heir, Sire. An infant girl of just a few weeks old, but she may not survive, and even if she does, a female child will be small hindrance to us."

A daughter, the curse of kings, but I show no sympathy in this case. A child will be easily manoeuvred to side with us against France. I have no doubt the tensions between our two realms is now at an end. As I beam my approval at the company, another thought strikes me.

"I have had the most excellent idea," I say, standing up and thumping the table with delight. "We shall marry the girl to our son, the Prince Edward, and unite the realm of England with Scotland. Such a union will surely put an end to years of strife."

Agreement eddies about the council table. Brandon raises a glass.

"A splendid remedy, Sire, it will bring peace to the realm and put coin in our coffers."

As one, the council raise their cups, and sing praises to their king.

<u>January – June 1543</u>

Christmas passes, the gaiety of court returns and entertainments fill our days. Once more we enjoy the favoured court dances that show the ladies to their best advantage, and the gentlemen delight in selecting which they will allow to steal their hearts.

As we did of old.

I notice that Lady Latimer has fewer dance partners than most of her companions, only my brother-in-law, Tom Seymour, invites her to join him on the floor. I expect it is because she has passed the first flush of youth.

I watch her accept Seymour's hand and they move through the steps of the dance; a frown mars my former joy. He is too handsome, too gallant, too lithe on his feet, and it seems she is not above relishing it all. I had thought better of her. I must find him a post overseas, remove him from my path.

I have no intention of being made a cuckold again.

My mood darkens as I acknowledge I can no longer hope to match his grace of movement, his elegance of dress. My clothes might be the finest and most costly in the realm but the body they adorn is well past its prime. Despite my status and power, he casts me into the shade. I am forced to acknowledge that fact each night when I am undressed.

As the garments are removed and my body emerges from the layers of silk and velvet, I am mortally offended every time. I am obese, diseased and broken, and I wish I could distance myself from it. If only I could be made young again. If only people could see beyond the limitations of my flesh to the prince beneath.

When February arrives, I do not allow myself to dwell on the fact it is a year since my heart was broken by Katherine's lack of faith. *How could I have been so deceived?* Blanking her face from my mind, I throw myself into matters of state; the dissent with Scotland that continues since the Earl of Arran took up the reins of government. I had imagined it would be easy to take control of the infant queen, but Arran quickly stepped in to take the post of Regent until she is of an age to rule.

But the new fancy I have developed helps leaven the disappointments of late. I watch Lady Latimer for weeks, assessing her, making up my mind as to her character and then, in July after a particularly tiring day, I invite her to dine with me privately.

She arrives a little after nine, her presence announced with far greater acclaim than her meek figure demands. She is dressed modestly; the swell of her bosom concealed beneath a gossamer fine partlet, and her gown is of moss-coloured velvet, with a French hood to match, a black veil covering her hair. The only embellishments are a single pearl necklace and an embroidered pocket.

I rise to greet her, take her by the elbows as I lean forward to kiss each cheek in the French manner. Her face is warm, her skin fragrant.

We draw apart and I escort her to the table, pull back her chair as if she is the queen, and I her humble subject. I summon a page to fill our glasses; she doesn't look at me as she samples it, but she smiles suddenly.

"Oh, that is very acceptable, Your Majesty," she says, dabbing her lips on a napkin. My heart does not bounce with delight as it once did with Anne or Katherine, but it grows warm.

I grow warm.

We talk idly, discussing the walk we took earlier, the antics of the dogs as they fought and frolicked on the lawn.

"I've ordered quail," I say. "It was a favourite of Queen Jane's."

"Oh, that is a good choice. It is my favourite too."

I am unsure if she speaks the truth or if she says so just to soothe me. I have the sense that she will do all in her power to please. I am king, after all, but I wish with all my heart she would see me as a man.

"You were away from court while Jane was alive?" I pose it as a question, but I know the answer. She was still married then, the wife of a suspected rebel, yet I am told her personal religious faith leans toward the new learning. Sometimes a man's faith has no bearing on his loyalty to me, the Catholics hate me for bringing down the monks, and the Lutherans hate me for favouring the traditional faith.

I really cannot win.

As a wife, Lady Latimer would have been forced to be loyal to her husband's wish.

"I wish I had been here," she says. "I've heard it was a merry time."

Was it? As I recall it, the court was still stunned by the execution of Anne Boleyn and the cream of the gentlemen of the court. I was filled with suspicion then, and feared every curtain hid an assassin, and every man had designs upon my wife. But I needn't have worried, the new queen, Jane, was timid and drew few admirers. I realised after just a few weeks that I had chosen a bride who was exceedingly dull after the heady wonders of Anne.

My own temper in those days, for all the outward show, fluctuated between rage and despair. But, having no wish to spoil our dinner, I say nothing of any of this.

"We will be merry again soon. The court was taken aback by the … the fall of the late queen but we are recovering now and looking for gaiety again. My court lacks but one thing…"

She breaks off the wing of a roasted quail and sucks flesh from the bone. Her lips shine with grease, her tongue emerges to remove a shred of meat.

"What is that, Your Majesty?" She looks up smiling as she rinses her fingers, but when her eyes meet mine and she reads what is writ there, the smile wavers. Her hand hovers above the bowl, water drips from her nails, her mouth is open, a pulse at her neck ticks. She swallows.

I reach for her other hand.

"A queen, Lady Latimer," I say urgently, "the country lacks a queen, and I lack a wife."

I had thought her eyes were blue but now they seem dark and blank, as if a screen has been drawn, shutting out the light and laughter.

Silence stretches.

Neither of us speaks for so long that I begin to wonder if she has misunderstood my meaning. I clear my throat, my grip tightening on her hand.

"What I am trying to say, my dear Lady Latimer, is that I would like you to be my wife, my queen ... you would want for nothing. You will have jewels, property, power, clothes, more jewels, more than you've ever dreamed of…"

I must sound like a shopkeeper promising his beloved that one day he will expand his empire to two shops. I should not have to sell myself. I stop speaking and watch as she fights a lengthy inner battle between desire and duty. Her lips are white, her jaw is tense. With lowered eyes, she pushes away the plate of quail and blinks the tears from her eyes.

I know she does not want me.

"I – I had thought I was not yet ready to marry again but, I – I think I would be honoured to accept, Your Majesty."

I stand up, my belly striking the table and spilling the wine. Taking her hand, I pull her to her feet.

"Henry, you must call me Henry now we are betrothed."

Before she has time to change her mind, I take her into my arms and anoint her mouth with mine. She tastes of sweetness, truth… When I release her, she gasps as if she has been holding her breath. Her face has turned very white, her eyes roll as if she is about to faint. I grab her arm, stop her from falling. She puts a hand to her head.

"Forgive me, Your Majesty, I am quite … overwhelmed."

I help her to a seat, perch as best I can at her side and watch her closely.

"It is I who should apologise. I am too hot, too ardent."

"Oh no, Your Maje-" she stops when I place my finger over her lips.

"Henry, my name is Henry and you…" I pause, my heart sinking as I remember her name, "… are called Katheryn."

"That's right, Your … Henry. I was named in honour of your first queen. My mother served her well for many years."

I knew that, of course, I knew her mother, Maud, but suddenly I feel old, as old as time itself.

Katheryn requests that we keep our proposed marriage secret for a while to allow her time to inform her family of the news. I am glad to grant her wish, for I know that once the announcement is made, our peace will be ended. Until now, apart from a little speculation here and there, the court has largely ignored my friendship with the lady, but once our plans are known she will not have a moment to herself.

I wonder if Seymour has told her of his appointment in Brussels; it would not take a genius to work out the reason for it. I just hope their relationship has not gone too far but, as long as she hasn't lain with him, I will let him live. It is a difficult question to pose so I set my spies on the matter, instruct them to discover the exact state of affairs between them. I cannot bear to be made a fool of again.

*

The tension at court between those who favour the old ways and those who prefer the new religion are stretched beyond measure. Daily, I have complaints from

Gardiner about Cranmer, and daily I have complaints from Cranmer regarding Gardiner's high-handed manner. It is no secret that Gardiner has his sights set firmly on the archbishop's hat; the see of Canterbury would suit him very well and he does all he can to oust Cranmer from the post. In return, Cranmer does all he can to hang on to it. It is like trying to relax with a cat and dog on your lap.

When I made the break from Rome, I expected there to be some dissent, but I had not realised it would be so violent, or as prolonged. Gardiner takes great delight in reporting Cranmer's keeping of an illicit wife, but it was not news to me. I pride myself in knowing most of what is happening at court, but often I choose to turn a blind eye. As long as a man is doing his job, I have little care what else he does, as long as his sins are small.

I do not see the harm in a cleric keeping a mistress, so what more harm is there in a wife? I toy with the pair for a month or so; one day I pretend I am going to charge him with the offence and the next I promise he can keep her. But in the end, when I am fed up with the squabbling bishops, I give Cranmer permission for her to stay, as long as he doesn't flaunt her. Gardiner accepts the news in empurpled silence but is quite unable to speak out further against my decision.

He is obsessed with heresy and reports to me almost daily on the activities and underhandedness of those with Protestant leanings. I grow weary of it. I want to enjoy my life and the prospect of my new bride, but they won't let me rest.

Gardiner disagrees with the idea of an English Bible.

"I fear it was better when the rabble only received the word of God through the medium of a priest. Especially women, whose brains are delicate. It is far better for them to be educated by their husbands in the home. Nowadays, too many female gatherings are veering toward theology, whereas before their conversation concerned the quality of one's best gown, or the skills of the local shoemaker."

I quirk my brow in his direction.

Pompous old fool.

"How many mothers' meetings do you attend, Gardiner, to have such extensive knowledge of them?"

He bridles, clasps his hands across his ribs as he archly replies.

"I have servants who make it their business to…"

"Spies, Gardiner, let's call them by their proper term."

It is really not his place to find fault with my decisions, and it has long been my desire to have the Bible printed in English. Allowing the public access to the word of God is not the problem; if they fail to understand what they are reading, then it is the fault of – of – the educators who have failed. They should have taught their flock to interpret the word correctly.

I soon tire of the whole matter.

I scowl at him, as the increasing irritation makes my head begin to throb. This is not how I planned things to be. I wanted to free my people from the yoke of Rome, not plunge the country into further dissent.

I wanted to help them. I wanted to make things better!

But my court is split in two. The traditionalists, Gardiner, Norfolk, and Wriothesley, snarl and snap at Denny, Paget and Rich, men who, despite their religious leanings, all do me good service and are usually in my favour.

Sometimes I wonder if it would be better if there were no religion; if we lived as beasts do, subject to instinct instead of the word of God.

The thought astounds me. I look anxiously to the heavens, cross myself fervently and silently plead forgiveness. I did not mean it. I am as religious as any man, but although I favour the old traditions of faith, a man's worth should not be judged on religion alone.

For myself, I find comfort in the old ways, there is a certain peace in the sonorous prayer, in the traditions that have passed down through generations. I never wanted to end the friendly practices of old, I simply wanted to be rid of the Pope, but it seems one cannot divorce Rome without in some part marrying with the new ways.

Loath to relinquish the gentle rhythms of prayer, I cling to them, making what I hope are imperceptible changes to the aspects of faith that do offend me. My intention is to die as I have lived, as a good Christian man, a Catholic king, but what comes after I am gone is beyond my control.

That will be in God's hands.

July 1543 – Hampton Court

The days before our wedding drag as slowly, reminding me of when I was a boy waiting for Christmas. But the day does come, and when Katheryn appears, clad in a pearl encrusted gown, it is as if the sun has emerged to shine bright and warm after a long, chill winter.

When I make my vow, I speak loudly, authoritatively, as if I am imploring God, reminding God that I have suffered enough and this time, please make this marriage a good one. If I seem to be ordering Him to smile on me at last, it must be remembered that He has shown me small favour when it comes to wives; it is high time I was blessed.

"I, Henry, take thee, Katherine, to my wedded wife, to have and to hold from this day forward, for better for worse, for richer, for poorer, in sickness and in health, till death us do part, and thereto I plight thee my troth."

I smile full in her face. She is nervous, her hands shaking, her voice tremulous as in return she gives me her vow before God.

"I, Katherine, take thee Henry to my wedded husband, to have and to hold from this day forward, for better for worse, for richer for poorer, in sickness and in health, to be bonair and buxom in bed and at board, till death us depart, and thereto I plight unto thee my troth."

Bonair and buxom in bed.

I lick my lips, imagining her naked in my arms, anticipating the night to come. It is many months since I took a woman into my bed, many long, difficult months, but now I have a wife to rectify that and put an end to my loneliness.

When I present her to the court as their new queen, they shout loudly with joy, hats fly into the air, and while they shower us with blossom, I grab Katheryn's hand and hold it high. Her nervous laughter sounds as if it may at any moment turn into tears. Women are like that, their emotions in perpetual turmoil, their humours as variable as the moon. And joy and sorrow are akin, as love is to hate, like birds on the same branch, and where one may fall, the other may fly.

Dignitaries have come from all over the Christian world to witness our joining. My daughter, Mary, whose friendship with Katheryn is in stark contrast to her dislike and disapproval of my last wife, comes forward with her blessing. She presses a small gift into the queen's hand, flashes her a knowing look, before the attention is stolen by Elizabeth.

At ten years old, my youngest daughter is already as pert and as beautiful as her mother was. I still find it disconcerting to be confronted with Anne's eyes each time I encounter her. The likeness unnerves me and, even though I am inordinately proud of her outstanding scholarly achievements, and her rude good health, I avoid her company as much as I can. She makes me uncomfortable. I always expect her to ask me inappropriate and precocious questions.

The queen bends down so their heads are level and I see Elizabeth whispering something into Katheryn's ear. A squirm of misgiving moves beneath my heart. She could be saying anything. I'd put nothing past her. She is forward and often speaks out of turn, her remarks raising eyebrows, and evoking hidden laughter.

As she listens to Elizabeth, Katheryn's eyes swivel toward me, her face stretching into a surprised smile. She laughs, straightens up, nodding as she scans the room, her hand lingering on the child's shoulder. My daughter remains possessively at the queen's side, flicks back the veil of her hood and, when Katheryn finds me, Elizabeth looks at me too. Her large brown eyes are full of knowledge, full of … hostility?

Is it hostility I see there? It is the look one might see on an opponent at cards, when they are holding trumps and about to empty your purse.

I push the question of my youngest daughter away as, one by one, they come forward to give Katheryn and I their blessing. John, Lord Russell, Keeper of the Privy Seal, bows low before us.

"Good health to Your Majesties," he says in his booming voice.

"May God bless you both," says Sir Anthony Browne.

The many voices blend, the faces alight with hope for the future. I make a mental note of those who seem happy for us: Thomas Heneage; Edward Seymour, Earl of Hertford; Henry Knyvet; Richard Long; Thomas Darcy; Edward Baynton; Thomas Speke; Anthony Denny; William Herbert. The list is long and there are few missing. I take note that my niece, Margaret Douglas, lately pardoned and allowed to return to court, is accompanied by Brandon's wife, and I am less pleased to see Anne Stanhope, Countess of Hertford, who is a woman I cannot abide. Jane Dudley, Viscountess Lisle, is also present and in deep conversation with Katheryn's sister, Anne Herbert.

I summon the latter two to greet me, and give them a warm welcome, hold out my arms and bless them with a royal kiss.

"We are family now," I tell Anne. "And Lady Lisle, how nice to see you. I have never forgotten how generous you were to our late queen, Jane."

She curtseys low, rises slowly.

"The late queen had a great liking for my quails, as I recall."

"They are a favourite of your present queen too," I say, insinuating Katheryn into the conversation. "We were dining on them the evening I proposed. Perhaps you will be of service again."

"It would be an honour to send you some, Your Majesty. It is not unusual for a woman to crave quails when she is with child."

Her eyes flick over the queen's body, Katheryn's smile wavers. She shakes her head.

"I am not - we haven't…"

To spare her blushes, I put my hands on my hips and lean back with a bellow of laughter, dispelling what could become an awkward conversation.

"We are only just wed, Lady Lisle, do you imagine we have pre-empted the priest? Ha ha, I am far too gentlemanly to suggest such a thing to a lady."

Our combined laughter draws the attention of people standing farther away, and they also start to laugh, although they were not party to the joke.

One glance at Katheryn and I see her face is scarlet, and she is clearly mortified. I cast about for a distraction, and see that Somer, distinctive by his favourite shade of green, is pushing his way through the crowd.

"*Oh Lord*," I think. "*What now?*"

He comes to a halt before us and makes a low sweeping bow.

"For your most gracious Majesty," he says with a wide smile. "I congratulate you on your marriage, and while I cannot offer gold, I offer the nearest thing I have."

The gathering push closer, craning their necks expectantly as he delves in his pocket and with great drama produces a bunch of withered carrots, which he offers to the queen as if they are indeed gold.

<u>August 1543</u>

I am sick abed again, but not so ill that I cannot sort through state papers from the comfort of my bed. I have decided to spare the expense of an entrée into the city for the queen. My purse has barely recovered from the costs of the misjudged celebration of the last queen. As ever when I think of her, I am assailed by a squirm of angry shame. I close my eyes and lock my jaw, swallowing the unpleasant taste her memory brings.

How can a woman lie so blatantly and still smile and be gay? Shouldn't all liars wear the crime of their deceit on their faces, so that we may see them for what they are?

I try to forget the times she fooled me with her wiles, distracted me with her lithe young body, her soft rosy – "A serpent!"

I do not realise I have shouted aloud until my attendant jumps so violently he spills water on the sheet.

"Your Majesty?" he asks, bewilderment on his brow. "Are you quite well?"

"Yes, yes. You may continue." To conceal my embarrassment I give a short laugh, wave a hand and instruct him to start re-dressing my leg. I look down at the top of his head, regretting he is not Tom. Sometimes I miss him more than I do Katherine. And, once more, their names bring the teeming thoughts crowding into my mind. I close my eyes, shake my head and try to breathe.

When he has made me comfortable, he covers my knees with a blanket.

"Have you finished with the papers?" he asks.

"Yes, yes; put them on the table for Denny to collect later." He bows after doing my bidding and takes his leave, but I do not miss the look in his eye. I have no doubt that when he joins his fellows in the outer chambers, he will tell them he fears the king is losing his mind.

I settle back on the pillows, drift off to sleep while I await the arrival of the queen. It has become habit for her to read to me of an evening and, afterwards, we discuss matters of state, those that concern her, and increasingly the topic turns to theology.

I knew before we wed that she was intelligent, it was one of the things I admired most about her, but I hadn't realised quite how fervently she supported the new learning. I hadn't appreciated that in marrying me, she may have had an eye toward increasing her own influence over matters of religion.

I am not altogether pleased.

If there was one thing I liked about my last queen, the lying cheating JADE! I thump the pillow, take a few deep breaths to calm myself as I force away the lewd image of her in Tom Culpepper's bed … it was her lack of interference in men's affairs. With Katherine, it was all gowns and dance steps and jewels, but with this Katheryn it is liturgy, politics, religion. The two women are as far removed as the moon is from the sun.

A few days ago, I noticed a coolness in Katheryn, a reluctance to look at me, a certain remoteness, but it was not until Gardiner sought audience that I realised the possible cause. Due to his long running crusade to put down any hint of Lutheranism, Gardiner recently brought to justice a trio of heretics – men of the new faith. The trial was long, as they probed into their minds and ultimately found them guilty. The penalty for their crime is burning, and the punishment was carried out accordingly. There was nothing underhand about it but Katheryn, it seems, believes that justice to have been flawed.

Of course, she does not raise the matter with me, but those who keep an eye on her movements inform me that the proof of it is there, in her flaming unspoken words.

I sigh, saddened that after so short a time she is already questioning my justice. She cannot see that the fault is with the perpetrators. Had they kept their beliefs hidden they'd still be free men, but instead they spoke out rudely against the six articles, and found fault with our methods, with our rule.

And she hasn't even examined the matter carefully. She completely overlooks the leniency I displayed! There were *five* men apprehended yet only *three* were burned. Surely, she must see the compassion in that. The due consideration that was given.

The door opens and the queen enters, a pattering of small dogs with her. They scamper toward me, leaping and yapping, jumping up, their paws on my hose, demanding that I rub their ears. I pick one up by the scruff of the neck and recognise it as once belonging to Katherine. It is a sweet, rough-coated little fellow. I quirk my brow in the queen's direction, and she answers my unasked query.

"Some of the late queen's dogs found a home with Lady Anne, but I took a fancy to this little one." She leans forward and ruffles his ears. His tongue lolls and, delighted with the attention, he rolls on his back, obliging us to scratch his belly.

"Another of her dogs went to my friend, Catherine Willoughby. It was so funny, Henry. She has named him Gardiner."

I snort with laughter, appreciating the sauce of Brandon's wife. I am still chuckling at the choice of name when Somer comes crawling from behind my chair and rolls on his back, kicking his feet in fair imitation of the pup on my lap, silently requesting the queen rub his belly too.

"I am not going to scratch your tummy, Will Somer," she says primly as she sits down, her hand to her mouth to contain her smiles. Ignoring the fool, she places a hand on my arm.

"It is so funny when she scolds the dog. 'Gardiner, go to your bed! Gardiner, get down! Gardiner, don't you dare shit on the carpet!'"

I give another snort of laughter as I imagine Gardiner himself coming learning of this. It seems a shame I cannot tell him, but he would not be amused. He has no humour, unlike my fool. Each time I sober, Somer makes another quip.

"Gardiner, stop licking your arse!"

"Gardiner, stop sniffing my balls!"

Soon, the three of us are rocking with laughter, the tone of the joke sinking so low that in the end I put up a hand, ashamed of myself. I frown at Somer.

"Stop it, now. Know your place!" and he promptly sits upright on his haunches, his arms stretched, his hands on the floor and barks several times before scampering away.

"Oh, my goodness, I don't know when I've laughed so much."

Katheryn settles down beside me, a hand to her ribs as she tries to get her breath. As she sobers, she wipes a stray tear from her eye. I grope for her hand and give it a squeeze.

"We will have to impress on Somer the importance of not repeating *any* of that. It would not please the bishop at all to think we mocked him."

"Oh, I agree," she says, her smiles tainted by a hint of fear. "Gardiner hates me enough as it is."

She picks up a book, flicks through the pages in search of the place she left off last evening. When she begins to read, I can still detect a tremor of laughter in her voice, but after a time her words drift over my head while my mind envisions my bishop reading his sermon, complete with fluffy ears and tail. I dare say the image will return to haunt me every time he seeks audience.

It is pleasant to see the queen settle so competently into her new role. It is as if she were born to it. The women she invites into her household are elegant yet erudite, their conversation scholarly, which is refreshing after the frivolity of Kate's short tenure as queen. In comparison, she is a restful wife, a companion rather than a bed mate. At last, I have found a woman whose intelligence and interests match my own, albeit that she seems to favour the new religion whereas I prefer the old.

But, as time passes, I find I can bear that.

We discuss theology often. Sometimes, after I have made love to her, instead of her returning to her own apartment she brings a tray from the night table, and behind the heavy curtains of my bed we talk of serious things.

"I may favour the new religion, Henry," she says, "but I would never try to convert you or use my position to influence your laws. I will always be obedient to you both as my husband and my king. I honour you as wife and subject. I am never going to set cuckold's horns upon your head, and I am no traitor either."

She doesn't look at me as she speaks, and I know she is aware of the dangers of her position. Every inch of my soul yearns to believe her. I pat her hand affectionately. It is good to hear her confirmation but I will watch her all the same. I have learned to my cost the changeability of women.

Inconstancy is part of their nature.

As the summer heat intensifies, the pestilence grows rife in the city. The rivers dry up, the lush meadows become parched, and the Thames turns into a slow-moving sewer. I shut down the court, bar all entry to the palace from the city, and take Katheryn into the countryside.

The change of air does me good. Suddenly, I am refreshed and discover I do, after all, have the energy to take time to hunt as we travel through the West Country. At every stop we make, we are given the best chambers, and feast at the expense of our hosts. The household excel themselves at entertaining us, and Somer, who has accompanied us, grows sulky when I laugh at the jokes of other fools and tries to outdo them, jealous of his position of royal fool.

Katheryn takes pity on him and remains indifferent when the other entertainers perform, but claps so hard when Somer rolls his humour across the floor that her palms must surely sting. It is moments like this, moments that seem to pause in time, that give me the chance to relish the happiness I feel.

Often, we do not recognise contentment until it has passed, and these late summer months are little different, they drift by in a haze of hunting, picnics and feasts and autumn arrives before we know it.

"The summer went by so quickly," Kate says, as we ride back to Hampton Court.

"If only kings had the power to stop time," I say. "I would do so now."

A child sticks out his head from a hedge, his mouth falls open when he sees us, his eyes as round as pennies. Kate waves at him but he is too astounded to return her greeting.

"I will lay odds his friends don't believe him when he tells them about it later," I laugh. I sit easy in the saddle, the reins loosely in one hand, and look with pride about the countryside. The meadows we pass were parched in summer, but the world is quickly turning from yellow to golden brown. It smells of decay, rotting vegetation, and the air, which is chill both night and morning, grows so warm that by midday we are forced to remove our cloaks as we sweat beneath the fickle sun.

Not all men are as fortunate as I to escape the plague-ridden cities in the hottest months, and on our return we learn that our favourite painter, a long-time member of our court, has died in our absence. Holbein will be missed. He leaves behind a huge archive of paintings, portraits of court members both past and present. He painted me many times, always seeing the best in me, discovering the most flattering aspect, the most favourable pose.

I will miss him.

Katheryn comes upon me as I am staring at the portrait he made of Jane. Her pale plain face is unreproachful, a hint of worry in her eyes, but her fine velvet gown and splendid sleeves make a queen of the unprepossessing woman concealed beneath. Yet her image continues to radiate peace and I suppose it always will. I now realise that it was her tranquil nature that attracted me. I was so jaded after the wild gallop through Anne's affections that I had just wanted time to recuperate.

Katheryn comes to stand beside me, her hand slipping into mine. I jump, startled by her sudden silent arrival. She examines her predecessor without any apparent rancour.

"Did you love her best, Henry? I – I won't mind if you did."

I look down at her earnest face, the light lines upon it softened by the torches.

"Love her best?"

I turn back to the portrait, examine the planes and shadows of my dead wife's face and realise I can barely recall her voice, let alone her conversation.

"No, I don't think so but … she gave me a son. I cannot help but have gentle feelings for the wife who gave me my heart's desire."

Katheryn smiles, satisfied that she has my heart, and we slowly return to my chamber. As we walk, I lean heavily on my stick while she relates small details of her day that she thinks might amuse me.

Most of her time is taken up with her women, making bonnets for infant orphans, the mundanity of the task leavened by theological discussion. It holds little interest for me and I interrupt her as she relates the minutiae of her day.

"Holbein died before he could finish his most recent portrait of me. We must find another court painter to replace him."

"Mmm, I was thinking that too. I admire the work of Master John; he studied under Holbein, you know. I am sure he would portray you very well."

I lay my hand over her fingers that peek through the crook of my elbow.

"We must have him paint you too, my dear. You deserve your place in the royal gallery," I say, and she flushes with pleasure.

"Well, if we do, I insist that he paints Mary and Elizabeth at the same time … perhaps we could pose for a group portrait?"

"We mustn't forget Edward. As the next king, he must be recorded for posterity too."

There are already far more portraits of Edward than of his sisters, but that reflects his status, nothing else.

"Oh, of course, we won't forget Edward."

I beam at her, glad that she shares my love for the boy and often instigates visits with him, or buys him presents, writing messages of love, sending him books and playthings.

Yesterday, she showed me a fine lawn shirt she is making for him. It gives me a twist of pleasure to see her mothering my poor motherless son.

"I have been considering Edward's education," I say. "I've interviewed only the best tutors and have come to the conclusion that Dr Cox will provide the most appropriate instruction."

"Richard Cox? Yes, I agree. He is a good choice."

"He will, of course, be taught language and scripture, all the sciences, and philosophy."

"How …? Will … will he be made aware of the new learning, Henry? As future king, he should be well versed in all matters…" Her voice trails off.

"He will be schooled in everything, including theology. As you say, as king he must be master of all knowledge, aware of the changing world around him, just as I am. He must also excel at sports, so we will engage men to coach him in tennis, archery, fencing and horsemanship."

I frown as I inwardly acknowledge that Edward is showing none of the physical attributes required to be a great sportsman. When I was his age, I was already master of my pony and badgering my father for a horse so I might be allowed to hunt and joust. I understand now why he was so adamant that I wait. But Edward prefers the comforts of the library.

"And music and dancing are important too." Katheryn's face grows animated. "Perhaps I could teach him some rudimentary steps, although, of course, I could never replace a music master."

"Yes, yes, of course, occasionally, but most of Edward's time will be spent away from court. I have arranged a school where he may be educated in the company of other boys – Brandon's son, Surrey's heir and one of the Dudley boys … among others. I feel he is too serious; he needs to learn how to play, how to have fun. Companions of his own age should keep him out of trouble, or rather more likely, lead him into some."

I laugh and she laughs with me, although there is nothing remotely funny in an obedient prince. The son I dreamed of was made in my image, rebellious, outrageous, troublesome. I am not sure a mind of one's own is something that can be taught.

"Will he be joining us at Greenwich for the Christmas feast?"

"Who? Edward? He is a little young yet."

"Oh, surely not. It might do him good to experience the jollity of the Christmas season at court. We could ask Mary and Elizabeth to join us too. Think how perfect it would be to have all the children together. They see each other so rarely. The courtiers will love it."

I think about it. Imagining scenes of my obedient offspring displaying their love and gratitude to their father before the whole court. I consider the stories that would be carried throughout Europe by visiting ambassadors. The grace and kindness of Mary – such exposure might even get her a husband. The wit and intelligence of Elizabeth, the healthy vitality of my son, my heir. It has been a long time since positive observations of our court were carried abroad. Of late, all the tales emerging from this court have been of gloom, betrayal, sickness, unrest and death. It will make a change to show off the present marital harmony, the family security, the love that surrounds the throne of England now.

"That, my dear, is an excellent suggestion. I wonder I did not think of it myself. We shall invite all three to Greenwich, and while they are here we will have likenesses taken by masters John and Scrots to prepare for their portraits."

The months grow gradually cooler until December when the Thames starts to freeze and I am obliged to wear a fur-lined doublet beneath my heavy padded coat. The fires in my privy chambers are kept roaring and the meals are larger, warmer; thick seasoned pottage with chunks of English beef, followed by hot fruity pies.

While the court prepares pageants and plays, and the musicians practise new pieces with which to entertain us, Gardiner continues his crusade against Lutheranism, even going as far as to probe into the dealings of members of my own household.

Katheryn is ever at my elbow, working diligently, pushing her books away when I join her and regaling me with her plans for Christmas. The words 'when the children arrive' are constantly on her lips and I laugh at her each time she uses the phrase.

"Mary is not a *child*; she is but two years your junior," I tease.

"Oh, yes I know, but she is your child, Henry, and I sometimes feel she has…"

I do not miss the hint of criticism that douses my former humour.

"Feel she has what?"

My words are clipped. I peer at my wife, watch as she reddens and flounders for an explanation.

"Well. She has … you cannot deny she has experienced some troublesome times. I would like to make up for the years she missed at court."

Troublesome times. Mary has experienced troublesome times? What of me? If her mother had acquiesced and confessed the truth of the matter, and had Mary not been so stubborn in support of her, she would never have left my side. I would have happily allowed her to live on at court as my honoured bastard daughter. There was never any need for the tantrums, the feigned illnesses, the stubborn refusal to see sense, the constant favouring of her mother against me.

Against ME, the king!

"She should have learned obedience sooner," I say without warmth. "Had she only done as she was told, none of it would have happened. Do you think I wanted her sent away in disgrace? Do you think I applauded the way she showed me up before the whole of Christendom? She acted like a stubborn brat and deserved every moment of her exile."

Katheryn's face turns white, her colourless lips gape like a fish deprived of water as she flounders for a reply. Her throat moves in an attempt to rediscover her voice.

"I only meant…" She swallows, tries again. "I only meant that she must have missed you … and you her. I merely wish to make amends, to instigate a lasting peace between you. A healing."

I reach out, pluck an apple from the bowl, and take a large bite, chewing as I contemplate the matter. At length, I nod.

"Very well, as long as you are not taking her part."

"Oh no, Henry. I would never take anybody's part if it was against you."

I smile at her suddenly and she almost collapses in relief. Her shoulders sag, her eyes close, and her right hand creeps to her breast. When she opens her eyes, they are misty. She reaches for my hand.

"I am so sorry, Henry."

"You are forgiven. It was just a misunderstanding."

For a while, our conversation is stilted, the atmosphere awkward. I am aware that she is watching her words, carefully considering each comment she makes for fear of re-offending. And I, for the first time, wonder how far removed her words really are from her inner thoughts.

As Christmas approaches, the palace ripens into festive gaiety. Garlands of greenery appear in the hall, the scent of spices permeates the air, and the sound of music pours from the windows. During the afternoons, the entertainers gather in the great hall to practise, musicians run through their music, the tumblers and fools go through their paces. Every afternoon, Will Somers strays from our side to join them, his green coat adorned with a sprig of holly, a matching piece fastened to his cap.

Katheryn is full of whispered secrets. She tells me excitedly of gifts she has for the children. She has chosen a fine illuminated book for Mary, a set of embroidery silks for Elizabeth, and a fine new saddle for Edward. To please the queen, I have created her brother William, Earl of Essex, and her uncle becomes Lord Parr of Horton. As an extra surprise, I have invited them and other family members to join us for the festivities.

The jollity is due to begin on the twenty-third but, right up until the last moment, I am kept busy with matters of state; there are always charters to peruse, warrants to sign. I insist that minor matters are put aside until after the New Year, but the more serious affairs must be dealt with forthwith.

The main matter occupying us currently is Scotland, as ever a thorn in my side. At the last moment, their parliament refuses to ratify the treaty made in July, and the proposed marriage between my son, Edward, and their infant queen, Mary, is now broken. It has been done purely to insult me; the inference that my heir is not good enough for their queen is the last straw.

"God blast them all!" I cry, thumping the table so hard that pain shoots up my arm. A cup topples over, wine spills across the board and trickles from the edge of the table. Gardiner leaps from the stream of liquid and tries to staunch the flow with his kerchief. The other members of the Privy Council seem to be too in awe of my temper to react. They sit frozen to their seats as my rage thunders about the chamber.

"They shall rue this decision. From this day forward, Arran will never know a moment of peace. We shall unite with Spain against them, and then where will our Scottish neighbours be? If there is to be no marriage between Edward and Mary, and no marriage between Arran's son and Elizabeth, well, we shall take hold of their infant queen by force and keep the crown of Scotland for ourselves. Once Scotland is mine, all their ancient laws and liberties shall be blasted from existence."

The faces before me are tense and white. I retake my seat, and try to calm the hammering of my heart, cool the sweat of fury from my brow. When I look up, I read fear and apprehension on some, and undisguised admiration on others. Puffing out my cheeks, I place my hands on the table and haul myself to my feet, grope for my stick, but before I leave, I turn once more.

"Mark me, gentlemen, war with Scotland is inevitable. I shall lead the army myself and if any of you here be spies, let it be known to your Scottish masters that Henry VIII is coming. England is coming."

At Katheryn's insistence, I throw off the gloom of impending war long enough to enjoy the festivities, and after a while enjoyment does indeed supersede anger. It is good to see my children, gathered together for a celebration, rather than reproof. Edward and Elizabeth know each other well. They are close, and exchange their

New Years' gifts sweetly, and after supper, when the dancing begins, I applaud as my son leads his sister onto the floor. I watch the two small people I have created with a mixture of suspicion and awe. They put me in mind of my sister Mary and myself at a similar age. I recall us dancing to impress ambassadors to my father's court. What will these two become, I wonder, where will life take them?

It is strange to see them together, Edward in his mother's image, Elizabeth so like Anne that she sends shivers up my spine. No two women have hated each other as much as their two mothers did, unless, of course, it be Elizabeth's and Mary's, yet here they are, friends. These three Tudor children are my reward for decades of marital discord, and it warms my heart to see my offspring reconciled.

The court looks on dotingly, clapping and tapping their feet in time with the music, and it is some time before I become aware that Mary lacks a partner. She is sitting beside Katheryn, giving no sign that she minds being left out. She claps and smiles just as gaily as the rest.

I do not smile, however. It is wrong. She is a Tudor princess of England and, as my daughter, should never lack a partner. Men should be falling over themselves to lead her out. I scan the hall in search of a suitable gentleman who is likewise alone. Most of the young men are already partnered; Francis Bryan leans drunkenly against a pillar, but he will never do. Then I catch the eye of Kathryn's brother and jerk my head in Mary's direction. He follows my directive and, after a moment, the newly created earl comprehends my meaning. He hesitates just a moment before approaching the princess and bowing low before her. I pretend not to notice but watch them from the corner of one eye.

It is like a mummer's play. I see her surprise, her initial confusion melting into embarrassment. I watch as he makes his earnest request that she join him in the dance. For a moment, I think she will refuse him but, with a blush and a fluster of shy reluctance, she accepts his proffered hand. He bows low while she stands, and places her fingers in his palm.

They are both pink-faced as they move elegantly across the floor, and I realise that perhaps they have never been formally introduced. It is my habit to think that everyone is as well connected as myself. I know every man in the room and am aware of most of their activities. Parr and Mary are roughly of the same age, it had not occurred to me they would be strangers. I had overlooked the fact that Mary has only recently begun to appear regularly at court. They may well have never met as adults. But I suppose it matters little, I only intend him as a dance partner; I want nothing more to come of it.

But I hope nobody reads anything more into the dance, because Parr has recently managed to free himself from an inconvenient marriage. I wonder if I have blundered. My daughter is volatile when it comes to men; she has passed the age when most girls are married and is ripe for a union. Even as my bastard, Mary is far above a match with Parr, however loyal and fond a subject he may be. I hope she realises that.

A gentle laugh at my side draws my attention and I turn to find Katheryn's eyes upon me.

"You look worried, Henry. Do you think you may have stirred a hornet's nest?" she says, with a nod toward my blushing daughter. "Let us hope they are not in love before the dance has ended."

"Oh, I hope not. I would have to send him on an extended mission overseas."

Her breath catches momentarily, a slight frown blooms on her brow, her eyes are narrowed with questions. Her thoughts are with Thomas Seymour, I can see it in her face. Seymour is still absent on his enforced mission; to keep him from her reach I have refused to allow him home. As if a spell has been cast over us, I cannot draw my eyes away. If she asks me why I sent him abroad, and I answer truthfully, it may sever the narrow thread that keeps us in accord. But, in the end, it is she who first looks away.

"Fear not," she says, with a casual shrug. "I believe my brother's sights are already set elsewhere."

"Your brother is a fine match for any woman, just not…"

"Just not your daughter. I quite agree. They're poles apart, both in breeding and interests. Mary needs a man she can be the mistress of; William would never stand to be governed by a wife, but it is high time a firm match was found for Mary. She has long been ripe to be a bride and has scarcely lived yet."

"She is close in years to you…"

She swivels toward me, her brow creased with exasperation.

"And I am three times married, Henry. I have seen something of the world. Mary is…"

"A prisoner?" I scowl at her, my temper rising. She laughs, touches my hand lightly.

"I was going to say lonely, my love, but if you think her a prisoner, then it is you who holds the key."

She thinks me a gaoler.

My blood is stirring beneath my skin, irritating, warming into an anger that evokes cruel words, but before I can retort, she kisses me on the lips, strokes my cheek.

"Please, Henry. I meant no harm. I think only of Mary. Come, let us stop this bickering now before we fall out. Let us be merry as we planned. Oh, how I wish we could dance together."

She turns back to the dance floor, where women twirl, the colours of their gowns merging with the popinjay hues of the men's tunics. I think longingly of other feasts in days gone by, when I led the dance, moving like a honeybee from one lovely lady to the next. I couldn't do it now, not unless I was bewitched, but the sight of my queen's wistful face spurs me on to one more try. I am not dead yet. I tug at her sleeve, and she turns back toward me, her lips parted.

"Tell them to play a stately dance and I will do my best to keep up."

I am proud to manage two dances with the queen. Not the abandoned leaping performance of my youth, but I keep up with the steps. The storm of applause that follows is more than gratifying and I am so buoyed up by my prowess on the dance floor that I excel in bed that night. For the third time since our marriage, we fully consummate the union. Afterwards, as Katheryn is making ready to slip away to her own apartments, I ask her to stay.

She hesitates, removes her outer robe again, and climbs back in beside me. "Come," I say, brooking no refusal. "Lay your head on my shoulder."

I hold out my arm and she enters my embrace, places her cheek a little way above my heart. I heave a sigh of contentment. I have all I need; a loving wife, a trio of strong healthy children, I am relatively healthy, and my country is at peace.

Once I have conquered Scotland and made my mark in France, I will have all I have wished for. It is true that a trio of sons would be better than one, but Edward is strong and clever. With an honest council to guide him, he will make a good king – perhaps even as good a monarch as myself.

Katheryn moves her legs further down the bed and pulls the sheet higher up her shoulders.

"I fear I might fall asleep, Henry. I am so tired after all the excitement."

"Then sleep, my love," I say, kissing her hair. She does not reply and for a long time we are silent in the darkness. The chamber is lit only by the glow of the fire, and the night torches on the far wall. I breathe long and deep, my eyelids droop, my body relaxes, and the cares of state melt away as I match my breath to Katheryn's and slide slowly into sleep.

March – July 1544 - Whitehall

"Are you sure you are well enough to go, Henry? I would not stand it if anything were to happen…"

"Do not fuss so, my dear. My leg has healed, the fever I suffered in February is long past. I should have followed Dr Butts' advice to keep to a lowering diet long ago."

"You have made a remarkable recovery, but I worry you may relapse without me to keep an eye on you. All the exertion of war may well set you back again."

I may not have recovered at all had it not been for her. During the darkest hours, when my life was endangered, the accumulation of black humours was so intense that she ordered her bed moved into my chamber so that she might nurse me herself. I have a faint memory of her cool hands on my fevered skin, her soft voice soothing my agonised tears. It is possible that I owe her my life but … we rarely speak of it.

"I am not some child to be pampered. I am not a woman with a recurring malady. I am a king and a warrior, and my enemies will not wait because you fear I am infirm. Now, dry your eyes, Katheryn, and let me go."

She climbs reluctantly to her feet, her face crumpled with doubt. I pause, tuck a finger beneath her chin and force her to look at me.

"Is this the face of a Regent of England?"

Her worry turns to pride, a smile wavers at the corners of her mouth, she braces her shoulders and looks me in the eye. Hers are red from weeping, and I am so touched by her care for me that I have to blink away my own tears.

"All shall be well," I say. "Sir John Wallop has already joined forces with the emperor and my presence in the northern territories will split the military force of the French king. It will be a two-pronged attack and we shall swiftly put the French armies to flight. I will win back Paris, which is rightfully ours, and be back before you know it."

She grabs my hand, kisses it passionately.

"I shall govern England in your absence, Henry, and care for your children, but we and the country will never be wholly complete until you have returned, safe and well."

I cup her cheek, pull her toward me and kiss the top of her head.

It has been a busy six months preparing for war. The problem of taxes has been overcome, the sullen resentment of the populace, who never understand the importance of foreign wars, ignored. The armies I sent north to quell the Scots quickly took Edinburgh and, with my kilted kin deftly quelled, I now turn my attention to their allies. France.

Although I make light of Katheryn's fears, the possibility of my own death has never been far away. On her advice, I recently restored the line of succession. Should anything happen to me while I am away, Edward will follow as king, with Katheryn as regent until he reaches his majority. God forbid, should he not live until then, Mary is to follow. Then, should Mary also die without issue, it will be Elizabeth's turn. The possibility of the termination of the Tudor line is horrifying, and even Tudor bastards on the throne is better than a return to civil war. Of course, our line will never end. Edward will marry a fertile queen ... and Mary and Elizabeth will provide his son with loyal cousins, to fight for him and forge strong family ties. I wince just contemplating my bright Edward, the heir I longed for, failing to fulfil his promise.

The Tudor line *must* prevail. Of course it will.

"I am leaving all in good hands," I say, summoning my page to bring my cloak and hat. "My barge is waiting."

The moment of leave-taking is awkward, the strange relationship that has never fully been understood by either of us making us tongue-tied.

"Take care," she says.

"I will."

I kiss her fingers for the umpteenth time and turn toward the door. The discomfort caused by walking is less troublesome than it was this time last year and, almost ceremoniously, I leave my stick behind.

At the wharf, I turn for one last look at the women who have gathered to see me off. Katheryn, Mary, even my Beloved Sister, the Lady Anne, have come to bid us farewell. Elizabeth is twisting and turning, her mind on other things, until her governess grabs her arm and bids her be still. She stands erect and waves at me gaily; she has no clue that I might be riding to my death. I smile at her naughtiness; she reminds me of myself. I sweep off my hat and hold it aloft.

"I leave all in your care, Katheryn," I call. "Remember, Hertford is ordered to *assist* you, not instruct you. I shall write before we set sail for Calais."

Like a good wife, she clutches a kerchief to her chest, bites her lip and waves me goodbye. The barge shifts beneath my feet, the stench of the river rises, and a dog barks furiously at me from the far bank. The oars lift and dip, a spray of water splashes my boots.

I have promised to return. I have sworn myself fit enough for war but, now the time has come, I suffer a twist of worry that I am making the wrong decision. But be it right or wrong, there is no turning back now.

Was I always such a worrier? I have no memory of fear in my youth. The last time I sailed for war with France, I was filled with valour, and certain of victory. I suspect it is experience that affects me now; the possibility of failure just never occurred to me before. But now…

The ship might sink, I might drown en route, I might be killed in battle, or die of the bloody flux, but at least, having come so far, my reign has been remarkable, ensuring my name will never be forgotten. I can only trust in God.

As the river bears us south toward Gravesend, the people line the banks to wish me luck. I wave languidly. They have been starved of my presence of late. Ill health has kept me from them and for more than a year I have kept to the relative privacy of my inner sanctum. Whereas once I welcomed courtiers into my private apartments, these days I prefer to be left in peace.

As I grow older, I find too much stimulation depletes my health, and there is nothing surer to rouse my temper than tiredness. The company of my physician, Dr Butts, my wife, and Will Somer is enough to satisfy.

I lie back on cushions and half close my eyes, and before long, sleep takes me. In a strange half-dream, I am aware of the movement of the barge, the dip and splash of the oars, the aroma of weed and mud.

I could be anyone.

A belch bubbles from my belly, the taste of frumenty a memory on my tongue. My mind retraces the years that led to this moment. It is not my first experience of war. It is not the first time I have sailed for France in search of glory, leaving a queen behind as regent over England. That queen was also named Catherine, although she was a proud Spaniard, fiercely protective of our union with her kin against their ancient enemy. A cloud passes over my rosy dreaming when I recall how she put my own small glory overseas in the shade during my absence by vanquishing the Scots at Flodden. But it was long ago, I can think of it now without rancour. A smile trembles in my cheek at the memory of her outrage when Norfolk refused to send me the head of King James IV as a trophy of war.

Not for one moment do I imagine the present queen being so savage in victory, for she was not raised in war-torn Spain by Isabella of Castile. But I often think it strange how things have come full circle, so many similarities, if you ignore the differences. It is almost as if nothing has changed. The same countries involved in an age-old war, the same catalyst, the same prize; but the result will not be the same.

This time, the glory will be all mine.

Brandon has been in Calais for weeks, organising the troops, preparing the camp, ordering the supplies and the erection of the royal pavilion. I'd have been with them earlier in the year if it hadn't been for my leg corrupting and near killing me.

My campaign tent may be large and luxurious compared with the canvas billets of the ordinary soldier, but I still wonder how I will cope. It was all very well in my youth when my body was strong. In those days, I could sleep wherever I laid my head, for I slept the sleep of the blessed.

These days, I am likely to wake at dawn and regret the whole thing, crave the comforts of Hampton Court. I have not left England for many years now but, as we set sail across the sea, it seems like just yesterday I was here before.

I stand at the rail, watch the surging grey waves, turn my face up to the wind-tossed gulls, and sneer at the landlubbers who are stumbling green-faced about the deck. I laugh when they throw up their supper, scoffing at their weakness, for I feel I was born to be a sailor. I revel in the swell of the sea, the roar of the wind, the flap and creak of the rigging, the wheeling gulls.

The brief homesickness I felt last night dissipates rapidly as the invigorating sea crossing awakens the latent hero within. Almost as soon as land is sighted, I am straining my eyes to be the first to see Brandon, who I know will be looking seaward in search of his king.

We might be old men and our beards might be grey, but our hearts are as ferocious as boys'. We are hungry for the fight, thirsty for French blood, but first we need ale, and a willing maid.

"Brandon," I cry as my old friend limps toward me. "Here we are again! By Christ, I have missed this. I can feel the blood-lust roaring in my veins again."

"Well met, Sire. I am relieved you've arrived safely; the wind was strong overnight."

"The channel was like a pond, man. There was no cause for worry."

"Oh, it is good to see you, Sire. I never imagined we'd ride to war together again. I thought those days were long behind us."

He grins at me, genuinely pleased, and I slap him on the back.

"Let us get the praying over with first, then you can show me to my tent."

We give our thanks to God for a safe crossing and beg for good fortune in the forthcoming battle. He cannot fail to be on our side of course, for Boulogne belongs to us.

It always has.

<u>August - September 1544   Boulogne</u>

Camp is set up a mile or so north of the town. Behind me is the sea and, in the other direction, I can just about see the outskirts of the settlement. The helmets of the Frenchmen line the walls with a bristling of pikes, the barrel of small cannon thrust rudely toward us. The tower that rises high above the other buildings flies the French colours - well, we shall soon change that.

Brandon draws my attention from our target, pointing out our vantage points as he runs through the proposed strategy for a swift end to the matter. As I envision it, a surge of conviction runs through me. We will have the victory, even if we have to hold them captive in the town for a year.

I had expected the weather to be debilitating. I had expected dust and sweat and sunstroke, but I had not expected a torrent of relentless rain. Rapidly, the defensive ditches fill with water, forming a quagmire underfoot, and it collects in great puddles on top of the tent so my men have to periodically push from beneath so it cascades from the roof, turning the already muddy ground into a pig wallow. Outside, men slip and slide through sludge like boys on ice. Straw is scattered at the entrance to my pavilion, where it quickly becomes a dirty, stinking mat that clings to men's boots and gets walked into my quarters.

"It's like a stable in here!" I bellow and my squire scurries to sweep it away, even though it will just as quickly return. My shoulders are perpetually damp, my hair sticking to my skull like a cap. If it goes on much longer, the ague will creep into my bones, and I am sure I feel the beginnings of a cold.

Perhaps Kate was right, perhaps I am too old.

It is fortunate I had the foresight to ensure that adequate supplies of medicinal remedies were included in my baggage; I instruct that some is made up in readiness and dispensed to any man who needs it. At the back of my mind lurks the knowledge that if the situation is prolonged, the cold won't be our only concern; there will be fever, hunger … pestilence.

As the days and weeks pass, my men report a shortage not only of food but of supplies of gunpowder and shot, but with the ships bearing rations delayed in the channel by the weather, there is little I can do. Norfolk sends word by messenger from Montreuil complaining that his men are forced to drink water instead of ale.

"They are hungry, growing weaker by the day." His words are written so clearly, I can hear him roaring.

"We must have faith," I write in reply. "The rain cannot last forever, and God is with us. The ships will be here soon."

And I am right; eventually, my prayers are answered. My ships manage to fight their way through the storms, bringing respite just in time, and also missives from Katheryn, proving she has written to me daily as she promised.

With a twinge of guilt, I retire to my tent and sit with a blanket draped about my shoulders, a bowl of steaming frumenty at my elbow, and read the queen's reports. She is playing the part of Regent well; it is good practise for her should the worst ever happen to me. Edward could not wish for a better or wiser guide than his stepmother.

She writes of her concern for the increasing numbers of Scottish prisoners who require housing and feeding, of reported imminent invasions, of a captured Scottish ship. She promises that the monies I requested are on their way to us and says she has a further four thousand soldiers standing by, ready to embark and join us in Calais.

As fast as my men fall, they need to be replaced. It is vital. The French lack the luxury of fresh recruits and while their numbers lessen within the besieged town, ours remain strong.

It is a long and bloody road to victory and the queen's letter evokes the sights and smells of home. Katheryn ends her letter with the words, '*The prince and the rest of the children are well.*'

I picture her at my desk, seated in my chair, my pen in her hand. I daresay she has taken my likeness from her pocket and placed it close at hand so she might look upon my face as she writes to me.

I rub my chin, realise how thick my beard has become, for it has not been trimmed for several days. I grow lax in my habits. Ruefully, I recall my promise to my wife that I would write to her from Dover, before I embarked for Calais, but events and time have overtaken me.

I should have written weeks ago.

A further letter from Katheryn dated a few days after the others reads:

The want of your presence so beloved and desired by me, makes me that I cannot quietly enjoy anything unless I hear from your Majesty.'

A sudden rush of guilt prompts me to pick up my own pen and send her a reply. I do not mention the damp, or the threat of approaching pestilence. I do not speak of the ache in my bones or the constant stench of the mud. Instead, I write of the glory of adventure, the battle songs, the campfires, the brightness of my new armour, the smell of gunpowder in the air, the camaraderie of war. She will not understand but I hope she will comprehend that my enjoyment is overshadowing any discomfort I might be suffering.

We have set our men at building an artificial hill. It is heavy work in the rain, but it keeps their spirits up. Once it reaches adequate height, the plan is to set guns upon it so we may bombard the town at our will.

And soon, I promise her, ending on a gentler note, *when the deed is done, the battle won and the town taken, I will return to you and together we shall relive my triumph from the warmth of the castle on those long winter evenings that lie ahead.*

Although my words are unblemished by too much truth, they are not exactly lies. I write to comfort her, to keep her from worry; she needs to rest peacefully at night if she is to run the country efficiently. My grandmother believed that trouble-free sleep ensured a trouble-free mind and body; sleep helps a body to function well, and I agree. A woman in charge of England is one thing, but a woman wrung out with worry is another matter entirely.

A few days later, I write again:

The castle with the dyke is at our commandment and not like to be recovered by the Frenchmen. Castle and town are like to follow the same trade for this day we begin three batteries and have three mines going; besides one which has shaken and torn one of the greatest bulwarks.

For six weeks, the sound of cannon fire devastates the peace. On the day of our victory, I stand atop the hill and watch as Boulogne is blasted. When a thunderous explosion rocks the ground beneath my feet, I grab at the man nearest to me. Instinctively, we cling to each other as the smoke clears, revealing devastation the like of which I've never seen. The church steeple has tumbled, and the defensive tower, that a few short weeks ago threatened to destroy us, is now itself destroyed. The buildings that on my arrival boasted of prosperity and strength are now crumbled into ruin.

Silence rings in my ears as the stench of smoke and powder rolls toward me, soundlessly engulfs me. The birds have ceased their song, there is not a breath of wind to stir the pennants above our heads. No man speaks as we stand together and look upon what we have wrought.

And then there is a clank of armour as someone stirs, and as if we are waking from an enchantment, we release the breath we have been holding and look at each another.

Brandon chuckles. His face is filthy and his beard as ragged as a pirate's. I expect I look the same. I slap him on the back and laugh aloud as the sound of our victory cheer echoes about the hillside, as thunderous as the recent gunfire.

And now, I think, as I look at the devastation around me, I must turn my attention to Paris.

We celebrate long into the night, the ordinary soldiers mingling with the officers. We make a great din, as only fighting men can, we sit on hard stools at ale-drenched tables and each man relates his own favourite story of the siege. It has been a long, hard six weeks in which we have all bonded, united by the shared experience – the highs and the lows. I feel like one of them now, a part of a great event, when usually I am detached, kept apart from the commoners, closeted away in my chambers. It is like the days of my youth when my companions and I would sneak across the river to sample the sins of Southwark.

Brandon struggles to his feet and, to prevent himself from sliding beneath it, keeps one hand on the ale-sloshed table. His words are slurred, his face a rosy ring of sentiment. He lifts his cup, slops wine over the rim.

"I'd like to offer up a cup to my friend," he says, peering at me blurrily. "And this man ish not jusht my friend, but my lord, and my king."

Fifty smiling faces turn toward me, and they too raise their cups.

"Good health to King Henry!" they cry, and I find I cannot make reply because my throat is closed, and my eyes are pricking with tears. But I raise my cup and drink with them.

"To England!"

"And St George!" someone adds, although he had little to do with it.

There is a kerfuffle at the entrance and a messenger ducks beneath the door into our presence. He is mired from the road, his face red, his hair plastered to his head, his cloak dripping puddles onto the carpet.

"Your Majesty. I h-have news…"

I nod to Brandon, who totters across the floor and relieves the boy of his message. He takes it with a mock bow, and sways as he stumbles slowly back to the table. He frowns at the words…

"Oh, for Heaven's sake!" I snatch the letter away and begin to read while Brandon stutters a drunken apology.

My head suddenly clears.

"God's teeth!"

Everyone starts at my uncharacteristic blasphemy.

"What is it, Your Majesty? There is nothing amiss at home…?"

Brandon runs his hands down his face, seeking sobriety, and waits patiently for me to show him the letter. Silently, I read the words once more, hoping I misread it the first time, then I tear off my cap and rake my fingers through my hair.

"He's done it again," I growl. "The fucking emperor has done it again."

"Done what?"

I toss Brandon the letter, his curses matching mine as his befuddled brain absorbs the news.

"He has betrayed us. Instead of waiting as was outlined in our plan, he has ridden on Paris ahead of schedule and when his army could not win, he came to an agreement … with the *French*."

Brandon describes the Emperor Charles using a foul expletive, with which I entirely concur.

"Now what, Sire?"

I lean back in my seat, grip tightly to my cup.

"Now the French king is free to unleash the entirety of his forces upon us."

"He will attack Montreuil first."

"No doubt, and Norfolk is still there, awaiting supplies. What do we do, bid the duke to retreat or do we ride in support?"

"We must secure Boulogne first. My advice is to order Norfolk to join us here so that we may regroup, recover ourselves for whatever comes after."

My heart is heavy. My spirits that a few moments ago were soaring are now grounded. I close my eyes, aware that the men are watching me for signs of weakness, signs of defeat. Katheryn's face floats before me. I wish she were here. She would know what to do, and what to say. She always helps me to see things clearly. If I could just rest my head on her breast a moment … the thought of Kate reminds me of another, more imminent threat.

I jerk my head, thump the table, immediately regretting it when my sleeve comes away dripping with ale.

"The Scots may not be as defeated as we had hoped," I cry, the realisation of the fresh danger to my realm chilling my blood. "The French are now free to retaliate from our own border. I must return home immediately so I can deal with matters there. See to it! Make ready my ship!"

I click my fingers and a man scurries off to begin preparation for my departure.

"You must remain here, Brandon. Wait for Norfolk and offer him whatever assistance he needs to get here."

I stand up, address the gathering directly.

"Speak of this to nobody. We have no wish to undermine morale, and Boulogne is yet to be properly defended. You must secure it and make arrangements for the prisoners, and those remaining in the town. There will be sick and wounded to attend to. We are not monsters."

So, less than two months after I quit the shores of England in search of victory, I return, having only briefly tasted glory. I put aside my disappointment at having to postpone the capture of Paris. It was a taste I would have liked to savour. The emperor's betrayal has cost me, not only the French territories I craved, but a proper celebration of our victorious siege.

I had imagined flags flying above crowded streets, I envisaged wine flowing, cries of triumph, cheers of joy, pretty girls hanging garlands of flowers about my neck. I imagined a hero's welcome, and I am damned if I will let the feckless emperor deprive me of it. I send word ahead to Katheryn to order up every vestige of pageantry she can muster and bring it to the streets of England. The years remaining to me are necessarily few and if I am to ever earn the title of warrior king, it must be now.

On our return, Dover greets us with passion. I am gratified to receive the accolade I had imagined, pleased beyond measure to be hailed as a returning hero. It makes it all worthwhile and tempers my disappointment at the emperor's betrayal. I forget the disappointments I left in France and focus entirely on the small triumph.

How many times have I ridden through the crowd-thronged streets of England? More times than I can count, yet the joy never palls. My father used to say that the crowd will cheer for anyone.

'Dress a pig in a silk gown and give it a sceptre and they will cheer for it,' he used to sneer. But he was ever curmudgeonly. The reason he never won the wholehearted love of the people was because he didn't love them.

Perhaps it was because he could not forget how those cheering citizens had so recently cheered just as loudly for crook-backed Dick.

But the people have always loved me. I was little more than an infant when I first experienced the love of the English. I feasted on their adoring cries as I cavorted, milking the crowd for more cheers. Not even the disapproving glances from my father and grandmother could stem my joy then, and they are not here to spoil my triumph today.

Would they be satisfied now? I wonder. I have ticked off almost every criterion on their list of things necessary to a king. I have a good queen, I have a fine son, I have taken back a piece of our lost territory in France. I have not failed.

Not *entirely*.

I shake off the shadow of their memory. I will embrace this moment and carry it with me forever: the din of their cries, the sombre pallid colours of their clothes against the brightness of the sky, the garlands, the showering flower petals that settle on the road, on our tunic, on my hands.

My mount sidesteps, tosses his head and whinnies, as strung up by the excitement as I. Keeping him easily in check, I ride with one hand, hold my hat aloft and wave it, whipping my people into a frenzy.

I am happy for a while.

I am so pleased to see Katheryn's healthy, shining face when she rides out to meet me en route, and the evident joy with which she greets me that I slide clumsily from my horse and delight the people with a public welcome. I shrug off the etiquette of a formal greeting and take her in my arms, inhale her familiar scent.

"I have missed you, wife," I whisper in her ear, and I feel the laughter shake her body.

"And I you, Your Majesty," she says, sinking into a belated formal curtsey for the sake of the audience. Taking her elbow, I guide her toward the palace, speaking into her ear as we go.

"The children are well? The border is secure? I did right in choosing to place you in charge, did I, wife? Or have you married Edward to a beggar girl, wed my daughters to pirates, and sold off all my palaces and replaced me with a Turk?"

Her laughter rings out. It is good to hear it again. It reminds me of another Catherine from a long time ago, a girl I knew when I was little more than a boy. It is as if the intervening years have never happened.

Happiness gurgles between us. I would give all the years I might have left to be alone with her right now but … duty calls, as it always does. There are dignitaries to greet, suppers to attend, papers to sign, but all the time I know she is there … waiting for me, as a good wife should.

November 1544

But the glory of victory doesn't last. Within weeks, people are forgetting to applaud our accomplishments in France and are instead fretting about the cost – both in monetary and in terms of human life. Gardiner does not even try to hide his dissatisfaction.

It is true we are far more vulnerable now than we were before the war. With Spain and France in agreement, England is now totally isolated, unsupported. The Scots and their French allies harangue our northern border, and the continuing struggle on French soil is detrimental to us financially, not least because of the effect on incoming foreign trade.

Our coffers are almost empty, and there is widespread resentment against increasing taxes. The people are tired of paying for what they see as a quest for personal glory. Are they blind not to see that it is for their sake I have fortified the southern coast, building impregnable forts to protect our shores from invasion? The navy that I seek to improve upon is not for my own benefit but for that of the country. My father left a fleet that was both ageing and outdated, and I have done what I can to improve it, but these things come at a cost! The recent refit and modernisation of my favourite ships was funded by monies accumulated from the coffers of crooked monasteries.

I am not a greedy king, I do not crave personal wealth, I covet national security, and I refuse to sit idly on a pile of gold while my country is in peril.

February 1545

Although we do our best, the jollity of Christmas is marred, overshadowed by matters of state. My council doesn't know how to put their troubles aside to feast and make merry as their predecessors did. Even Cromwell knew how to provide a good Christmas table. Their constant harping makes me snap, my temper is stretched, and the tension at court increases.

Katheryn does her best to cheer me but, prey to Gardiner's increasing distrust of anyone with Lutheran leanings, she has troubles of her own.

"I can feel him watching me all the time," she confides with a shudder. "I cannot bear him. He won't be satisfied until he brings me down."

"He cannot bring you down, you are the queen."

Her eyes flicker, and she turns her face away. I had forgotten Gardiner's part in the fall of my other queens.

"The man is a fool. I don't know why I tolerate him."

As long as she keeps her intrigue with the new learning within bounds, she can continue with her interest. I am not a vindictive, controlling man. She warms my bed and my heart and is a comfort in my old age.

That is enough for me. It should be enough for Gardiner too.

With the family around me, we keep a quiet Christmas. While we are gathered at the hearth, I cast my eye over my children. Mary is looking peaked again. Katheryn has asked her to translate Erasmus' paraphrases of the Gospel of St John, and it is causing Mary to entertain ideas she has never considered before. It crosses my mind that Katheryn is trying to convert her, but I hope that isn't so. If the task continues to irk her, I shall demand Mary find something to work on that is more to her taste. Women shouldn't trouble themselves with theology. They were designed for lighter matters. She should really be married, her mind on childbirth and running a household. I must find her a husband; the matter has been postponed for too long. If only there was a way to use her to heal our breach with Scotland and unite the countries under one rule. I run through a mental list of likely Scottish suitors, but none of them appeals.

Yet it is not only our security that I must worry over and our war overseas, but also that which is fought on our own shores, even in our own court! The constant tensions between traditional religion and those who campaign for reform makes court life fractious. The gaiety has all but disappeared from the royal palaces. As fast as Gardiner cuts down a Lutheran, either by fire or imprisonment, so the reformers murmur against him. There must be a way of them reaching some kind of accord.

The furore over the burning of heretics at Windsor necessitated me to finally agree to Cranmer's request to produce a Bible written in English. I could fend off his demands no longer and, initially, I embraced the idea. It seems the ideal way to appease everyone, to heal the breach, but as soon as word spread, the tensions began again.

Gardiner, as I should have expected, detests the idea, calling it a sin against Heaven, and my daughter, Mary, resents it too although, thankfully, she does not speak openly against my decision, as her mother would have.

"Imagine," Cranmer says in my ear, "a country so advanced that its inhabitants can read the word of God for themselves and receive His instruction directly. It would be like a miracle, wrought by yourself."

I nod, seeing his point exactly, but then Gardiner's voice intrudes.

"It is a sin against God!" he cries. "Ordinary men are not equipped to decipher the philosophy of Heaven. Imagine the impossibility of finding a ploughman with the necessary wit, or a woman … for Heaven's sake, Your Majesty. This heresy must be forbidden."

"There is no *must* about it!"

I struggle from my chair and limp angrily from their company, leaving them to curse at one another in private; they can kill each other if they will.

And then I discover that the queen too has been keeping secrets. She has penned a book. All those times I found her closeted away with a pile of manuscripts and a notebook, she was not merely reading or translating, but making a record of her own private heresy.

This will not do at all.

When I confront her, she reluctantly shows me the results of her misguided thinking, and to my surprise, I am reluctantly impressed.

Cranmer is overwhelmed.

It is a small leather volume, gilded and tooled, and inside, the frontispiece reads: 'Prayer and Meditations'. I am surprised at the depth of intellect; although I knew her wit outstripped that of most women, I hadn't realised she was almost as erudite as myself. But all the same, my suspicion is roused, and I wonder if her intelligence is likely to outshine mine.

"I have not put my name to it; it was published anonymously." I glance at her anxious face and, as I continue to slowly turn the pages, my suspicion mellows into admiration. She has included a prayer commemorating my achievements in France, the one that was read in public prior to our embarkation. Before our victory.

"It is well done," I remark at last, and she smiles, releasing her pent-up breath. "I am proud of you," I say, and her fingers slide into my palm, and she lays her head on my shoulder.

We are happy again.

This year, spring is unseasonably wet. Edward develops a cough, and Mary continues to suffer with her usual megrims. Of all my children, Elizabeth is the one that exudes the rudest health, as I did as a boy. While I am distracted with the continuing war and the complaints from my council regarding the emptiness of the royal coffers, Katheryn is kept busy with the children. On one or two occasions, I come upon her scribbling in her privy chamber. When she hastily pushes the papers aside, I do not question what she was doing; it is probably better not to know.

When I am not besieged by trouble, or forced to entertain some visiting dignitary, I take refuge in my private quarters and admit nobody but the queen, or those I regard as close friends. Anthony Denny sets up an administrative department in my privy chambers to be on hand should I need him. He also serves to keep those at bay whom I have no wish to see.

I will admit it to no one, but I am weary. Bone tired. I am ready to return to bed before I have even left it in the morning. My limbs ache, my head aches, my vision is blurred, my breath tainted, and by God, how I thirst.

"You could try to exercise more, Your Majesty." Dr Butts frowns through his spectacles, his eyes magnified, his forehead creased with concern.

"How the hell can I exercise when the pain in my joints is so great?" I heave myself up on my pillows and lie back, panting like a wounded bear. When I glare at him, his neck contracts, his head shrinking into his shoulders, and he rolls his eyes toward the ceiling.

"Perhaps if you begin slowly, a few more steps each day, each time going a little further. You used to enjoy taking the dogs into the gardens … it is not so long since you ran with them in the meadow yonder."

It pains me to be reminded for, in actual fact, it is years since I have done that. I wave a hand toward the hearth, where my hounds are sleeping.

"My dogs are as old as I am, and just as unfit. They no longer hear me whistle, they refuse to chase a ball, they don't even bark at the fool anymore."

Somers sits up at the mention of his name. Butts' face grows longer. Then he brightens, struck by a new idea.

"Then a puppy, Your Majesty! A puppy will cheer you and he will give you such little rest, you are bound to grow fitter."

I scowl. A puppy would be exhausting.

"Is there not some remedy, something that can be mixed with a little camomile to invigorate my blood?"

He frowns, scratches his ear before admitting defeat.

"I will check, Your Majesty, and have a tonic made up for you. In the meantime, perhaps try to get out of bed. Fresh air can only benefit you; perhaps you'd enjoy a stroll with the queen or a ride with your hawks. You always loved to hunt."

He thinks I am still twenty, but my fifty-fourth year is approaching, and I feel every month of it. Every day of it.

As I retreat into myself, I leave more and more of the daily administration to Denny. They even begin to discuss the prospect of a special stamp with my signature carved into it to spare me the trouble of signing so many papers. As my eyesight dims and my inclination to attend to state matters dwindles, the stamp cannot come into being too soon.

"Kate!" I call, and the queen looks up from her seat at the window where the light is better. She puts down her book and comes toward me, tucks the blanket tighter around my knees.

"What is it, Henry?"

"My spectacles. I have lost them; they must have slipped from my knee."

"Again? You have so many pairs, you cannot have lost them all."

She delves down the side of the chair, her body close to mine. I inhale her scent, a fresh outdoors fragrance putting me in mind of lavender and spring. I give her a quick peck on the cheek, and she pulls up, laughing, a pair of bent, broken spectacles held triumphantly before her.

"I fear you sat on them, Henry."

"They creep off my knee. One moment they are pinching my nose, so I take them off, rest them on my knee and then, poof, they are gone, slipped into some unknown realm."

"This is the third pair you've broken this month, and umpteen others have been lost. It is fortunate you had the foresight to order plenty. I will send someone to fetch another pair."

"Ha, very clever."

She turns with a puzzled look.

"Clever?"

"Your pun on 'foresight' when I clearly have none."

"Oh," her laughter tinkles, "I was unintentionally brilliant in this instance, Your Majesty."

As she makes to move away, I catch her hand, draw her back so that I may kiss her fingers.

"I am very grateful, Kate." My voice is husky with emotion, tears pricking my eyes, as they do so often of late.

"For what?"

Once I would have drawn her onto my knee, but I can no longer bear her weight, although she is not heavy at all.

"For your patience with an old man."

"There are no old men in my acquaintance, Sire, and if you should be referring to yourself, I see only a goodly prince, a kind king, a marvellous monarch, a fine fellow…"

"Stop, stop! Before my head grows too big to fit its crown!" We laugh, and when I refuse to release her hand, she sits on my footstool and rests her cheek against my knee.

I pull off her hood that I might stroke her hair, but find it is tightly bound. I sigh, wishing I could run my hands through it, feel the lush thickness of it, testament to her vibrancy, her youth, her fertility.

"Ah Kate, think of the sons you could have given me. Had I only known you in my youth, the times we could have had together."

I exist on memories now. I can no longer manage in bed as a man should, and no longer even pretend that I can. I like to look upon her, I often watch as she is made ready for bed, and some nights I summon her to my chamber, but neither of us expects me to perform. I just hope she has the sense not to stray, not to test the virility of other men. I put my trust in the fact that she is sensible enough to realise the absolute necessity of queenly virtue.

Unlike those who came before her.

Kate raises her head. "What is that noise?"

A hubbub of voices breaks through from the outer chamber. Denny arguing that the king is too busy, indisposed, and can see no one.

"I don't know, but it sounds like trouble…"

"Will you see them?"

"Denny will send a messenger to me if he thinks the matter urgent."

She is just placing her cheek back against my knee when the door opens and Denny himself enters. He halts a few steps into the chamber.

"Your Majesty, we've had word from the border."

"From Eure?" I stop stroking Kate's hair. She sits up and fumbles for her hood, trying to fix it without the assistance of a maid.

"Yes, Sire."

"Show him in."

Kate is on her feet now; she retreats to the window and picks up her book, pretends to read. A few moments pass while I imagine a dozen different scenarios. We have had victory over Scotland; captured the infant queen; and taken possession of Edinburgh. A likelier story is that we've won some skirmish on the border and captured a few dozen more Scots.

Denny returns, accompanied by a messenger who has evidently attended us straight from the road. His face shows signs of a hasty washing, and his hair is damp at the fringes. He bows, perfunctorily and without grace.

"I have ill news."

"A battle?" I ask, with sickness surging in my gut.

"A battle and a loss, Sire."

"A loss."

The physicians are always telling me to keep calm, but I can feel the familiar increase in my heartbeat before the news is given. I know it is not good.

"At a place called Ancrum Moor, our forces under Sir Ralph Eure and Sir Bryan Layton met with those of Arran and Angus…"

Arran and Angus were recent enemies who have now united, allied against us.

"… as our army was setting up camp, the Scots attacked us. Just a skirmish at first, but we gave them chase across the border, most of our force following into what…"

"Into what?"

Feebly, I make the attempt to stand up, my knees shaking, and Kate is somehow at my elbow, supporting me, her calming hand slipping into mine, but I flick it away and wrench my arm from her grasp.

"Into what?" I repeat, my rage simmering.

"Into a trap, Your Majesty. We chased them across Palace Hill, and then down the other side, not knowing that the whole force of the Scottish army lay in wait. The sun was setting, our men were blinded, the smoke of gunpowder blown into our face from the west. We tried our best to regroup, to rally and attack again, but they were swift, Sire. Their pikes twice as long as ours…"

I emit an enraged roar and the messenger cringes, falling to his knees as if the blame were his.

"Henry…" Kate takes hold of my arm again. "It is not his fault. You must not upset yourself…"

"That is not all my news, Your Majesty." The messenger speaks from beneath his arms that are clasped about his head as if to deflect a blow.

"What more?" I bellow. "What more can there be?"

He pants, his red face peeking out, his tongue emerging to moisten his cracked, dry lips. My heart is sick. I know his words before he speaks.

"The mercenaries … the border men from the Scots side who had joined with us … they tore off their English badges and turned against us."

"They switched allegiance … mid-battle?"

He nods, a tear rolling down his cheek. My defeated heart thuds. I wave him up from his knees, but he remains, determined to tell all, determined to send his king even deeper into the mire of despair.

"Our troops, the ones that did not die by the pike, scattered and are lost in enemy territory."

"How many?"

"S-s … they estimate some eight hundred slain and a further thousand missing, possibly taken prisoner. And … and…"

I bite my lip, poke my head forward. "AND?"

"Eure is dead, Your Majesty, and Layton too."

I slump into my chair. *Defeated again?* Is God even watching what is going on here? Has He forsaken me altogether?

With a roar of anger, I sink my head in my hands. Kate waves the messenger away, presses me back in the chair, eases my feet onto my stool and loosens my neck cloth. Sweat drenches my body; my throat is parched, my breath emerging in gulping sobs. I roll my head from side to side on the back of my chair.

"God has forsaken me, Kate. He is punishing me. I have tried so hard to be a good king, an honest man … I don't know what else I can do to win His favour."

"Nonsense, you are just upset. This will pass and when the sorrow has eased, you will see things are not as bad as they seem. Nothing ever is as bad as we think."

She sounds like my grandmother. But even she would despair at so many men lost, and the additional ignominy of defeat at the hands of the Scots.

How Arran will laugh, how he and Angus will congratulate one another on their victory over us. Eure is a great loss. He was an unlikeable fellow, but he did us great service on the border. Some say he committed many atrocities during the course of his duty, but people always speak such things of great men. Sometimes one has to take cruel actions to win victory. It will be difficult to find a leader as competent to replace him.

<u>May - July 1545</u>

Kate is right; after a time, the ignominy of the lost battle ceases to be so painful. The French, galvanised by the Scots' victory, send further troops to their aid. Now, rather than an attacking force, our presence in the north becomes defensive in nature. And it isn't just in the north; my spies in Europe inform us the French fleet is preparing to invade from the south too – I am not sure England can withstand assault from all sides.

But there are some small reasons to smile. In May, Kate's book is published. I have never seen her so delighted with anything. Eagerly, she distributes copies to all her favourites, while I quail inwardly in my fear of reprisal from her enemies.

It is difficult to imagine why anyone should dislike or distrust the queen. She is gracious to everyone, compassionate and loving, and as loyal as a spaniel. In truth, she has barely uttered a wrong word since becoming queen, and if she is ever bored by state banquets then she hides it well. Her inner thoughts never intrude upon her public duty, and she is tolerant of those about court whom she must surely deplore.

Her enemies set up rumours to act as a wedge between us. They hope to undermine our marriage, to test the queen's trust in me, and mine in her. The traditional set even go so far as to push Norfolk's daughter at me in an attempt to lure me into infidelity, but I've known Mary all her life, she was once married to my own son. If I was going to commit adultery, it would not be with her.

Kate and I laugh in private about it, and she even goes so far as to intimate her knowledge of enemy spies to the Spanish ambassador.

"Ah Kate," I say to reassure her. "Even if I had the energy to replace you, I am as far from tiring of you as I am of tiring of breathing."

She smiles. "I know that, Henry. Of course I know that."

Poor Kate, it is not easy for her. Each day she puts on a show, hiding her fear and giving no outward sign of troubles.

But I know her enemies and I watch them.

Gardiner, Wriothesley, Paget, Rich, Norfolk; all adherents to the old faith and lethal enemies to the new. I set my spies to follow them. I must guard Kate's safety, yet I am growing old; when I die and she is Regent, she will be unprotected, and they will be at liberty to turn against her, bring her down.

In early summer, Gardiner finally has his prey in his sights. First, he orders the arrest of Lord Thomas

Howard, Norfolk's own son. He is accused of indiscreetly disputing the scriptures with other members of the court. Dr Edward Crome is also arrested for denying the existence of Purgatory, as is one of the pages for a similar crime. But when Gardiner lays hands on one I call a friend, George Blagge, and sentences him to burning, I can take no more and order his immediate presence in my chambers.

"You will desist!" I roar at the cringing bishop. "You come too close! Even snooping into our privy chamber, even daring to investigate our queen! I will have none of it. Be careful, my lord bishop, lest one day you find yourself on the wrong side of the flames."

A few weeks later, I spy Blagge at court and, delighted to see him once more at liberty, I pause a moment to wish him well.

"Ah, my pig! Are you safe again?"

Blagge, well used to the affectionate nickname, bows low.

"Yes Sire, and had Your Majesty not been better to me than your bishops, your pig would be roasted 'ere this time!"

We laugh aloud, we embrace long, yet I am aware that there is no real humour in the situation. Gardiner is a threat to peace in our realm and must be stopped, yet how to stop him? Isn't it his duty as bishop to protect what he sees as the only true religion? According to Kate, it is everyone's responsibility to fight for it; the problem is that every man's idea of 'true' is vastly different.

My own truth is different to Gardiner's, and different to Kate's too, yet we surely cannot have all men worshipping to their own design. That would lead to chaos. There must be order. In all things.

In mid-July, word reaches us that takes my mind from the queen's peril. The French fleet has been seen heading our way. Immediately, we are on the alert, and the defences along the southern coast spring into action. Dragging myself from my sick bed, I make ready to travel south. It is high time I inspected our fortifications and allowed my troops to see the face of their king. It is good for morale, and my arrival will remind them what they are fighting for.

Taking the queen and a small household with me, we journey to Portsmouth, where we lodge at nearby Southsea Castle. We are greeted by The Lord High Admiral, Lord Lisle, and the vice Admiral, Sir George Carew. I greet them heartily, introducing Kate to those who are not yet formally acquainted with her. Lady Carew curtseys deeply, and when she rises I experience a squirm of guilt, as I always do when we meet.

Her resemblance to her father is marked; he is there in the look in her eye, the shape of her nose. Disconcerted, I stammer and stumble over my words until Kate takes pity and draws Lady Carew's attention to the wonderful tapestries that line the walls. By the time the women have ceased to discuss décor, I have recovered myself and the day continues without hitch.

Leaving the women in the castle, Lisle and Carew show me aboard the newly appointed ships, the Great Harry and the Mary Rose. I visit each deck, greeting the men, asking questions, exclaiming over the weight of the cannon, half-wishing I was young enough to sail with them.

If I were not king, I would have liked to be a sailor. How splendid it would be to sail to new lands, make war against the enemy from aboard ship. On deck, I hold on to the rail, look across the water and imagine it. Do all men dream of an alternative way of life? I warrant some men dream of being a king, yet here I am, a king envying the simple sailor. I laugh inwardly at myself and turn to Carew, who is waiting nearby.

"She's in fine shape," I say. "She has always been one of my favourites. I remember way back when she was first commissioned; it must have been 1511, close to the time my first son was born. I recall I had plans for him to sail in her one day."

Sorrow floods over me. I lower my head, my chin drooping to my chest.

"Ah." Wistful sympathy is rich in Carew's voice. "Every man regrets he did not survive to fulfil that dream." Suspiciously, I glance at him, but find pity in his eyes and nod agreement. It was a melancholy time indeed when we lost our firstborn son. I thought our tears would never cease. I thought Catherine would never cease wailing long enough for me to get her with child again.

Carew breaks my reverie.

"But supper awaits us aboard the Great Harry, Sire. I'm informed the women have already arrived. This sea air will have given you an appetite, I warrant."

When my wife greets me on our flagship, I tuck away the grief I carry for all my lost children, and prepare to do justice to a fine meal.

It is a small gathering, with the Lisles and Carews, and the ambassador of Charles V, who joins us, although I do not recall issuing him an invitation. I have little liking for Francis van der Delft, who entirely lacks the charm of Chapuys, the former ambassador. It is true that the latter and I had our differences. There were days when we hurled abuse at one another. In fact, I also hurled a few cups of wine at him too, but he always had my respect. Even when he conspired against me with Catherine and Mary, and openly urged the Spanish to make war on us on their behalf, I still rather liked him. He was good at his job.

But this new fellow, I cannot abide.

Despite the presence of women, our talk soon shifts to war. Of course, due to the presence of the ambassador, we curb any mention of strategy, but he persistently infers that England is fighting a losing battle. He advises us to just roll over and wave a white flag!

With his elbows rudely on the table, he gnaws at a chicken bone, rinses his fingers in the bowl provided, and speaks with his mouth full.

"If Your Majesty was wise, he would surrender Boulogne. This would not only appease the French but would free up men to fight elsewhere. You might as well submit now as later, cut your losses."

He is a worm. I stare at him with my lip curled, considering whether it would give me more pleasure to string him up to dry in the sun or squash his slimy body beneath my heel.

"We will do no such thing."

I speak coldly, my words clipped, but he doesn't know me well enough to leave the matter there.

"So be it, if you are happy to lose further men, to waste more money on supplies, and alienate even more of your population with extortionate taxation."

My temper, which has been slowly fraying, suddenly gives way and I thump the table so hard that pain shoots up my arm.

I cradle my elbow.

"Enough!" I cry through the pain. "Does no one have a gag to shut this fellow u? Come, I have had my fill of this."

With the next course still untouched, I stalk away from the table, my companions following, murmurs of outrage from the men, small squeaks of concern from the women.

"I thought you were going to string him up there and then, Henry." Kate laughs, making light of the situation and, realising her attempt to diffuse the atmosphere, I laugh with her. Lady Carew covers her mouth with her hand and slowly the others join in, and more wine is sent for. Presumably, the dismissed ambassador is rueing his rash words in his quarters. I hope he can hear our continuing jollity.

"Henry," Kate says, as we make ready for the night. "What was the matter when you introduced me to Lord and Lady Carew? Is there history between you and the lady?"

"Not in the way you infer, no. She was … she is the daughter of Henry Norris … who was executed in '36, along with Anne."

"Oh!" Her face blanches, she puts a hand to her throat. "I'm sorry, I had not expected that reply. No wonder she was a little stilted in her welcome."

"Indeed. He was a good man until … oh, I don't know anymore. Either he was a good man who committed one great sin, or he was a bad man who hid it well in the early days, or he was a good man who died unjustly, at the contrivance of his enemy."

She picks up a comb but does not use it.

"What do you mean, Henry?"

She leaves her seat and comes to kneel before me, fumbling for my hands. With a deep sigh, I stare into her eyes, but find I cannot maintain contact. I close them and force myself to speak.

"It has come to my notice since … that it may all have been conspiracy. Cromwell had reason to want to be rid of every one of the men who died alongside Anne. In fact, he had reason to be rid of Anne too. There was ever discord between them over how the monies from the fallen monasteries should be utilised; Anne wanted reform, Cromwell wanted them abolished and all the wealth channelled into the royal coffer. The truth may well be that Anne and her alleged lovers were victims of Cromwell's ambition. Come to think of it, perhaps I was also his victim."

"Who told you this?"

She speaks anxiously, her grip on my hands tightening.

"Norfolk," I confess.

She sits back on her heels.

"Norfolk," she repeats. "Oh Henry, do you think it is true?"

"I suspect there must be some truth but how can I know?"

"If it was a lie, Henry, it was a cruel one. When did he tell you this, and why? What prompted him to do so?"

I drag a hand across my face.

"I think it was just before Cromwell was brought down. I am surrounded by self-servers, you see. I'm never sure whom to believe. There is no one I can completely trust."

"You can trust me, Henry. But do you see how ruthless men are when their sights are set on a perceived enemy? Norfolk's action was every bit as bad as Cromwell's; they are like dogs feasting on one another's blood! Norfolk ranks among my worst detractors. He and Gardiner will come for me soon, and I pray to God you are ready for them."

"Do you think Anne was guilty? Did you know her?"

"No; I was married or just widowed to Edward Burgh then, and after that I was in Westmorland, far from court ... although we heard stories, of course."

"She was a remarkable woman ... full of vitality. She dazzled every man she met."

"So I've heard. You loved her very much."

"Yes, for a long time I was enchanted…"

"Enchanted?"

"Oh, not literally. I was just dazzled, full of lust, but although she was beautiful and challenging, she was also exhausting. There was no tranquillity, never any peace."

"Not like me, then?"

"You, my love, are perfect."

I kiss the end of her nose and we stare into one another's eyes, each thinking our own thoughts. Just as I am beginning to drift off, she speaks again.

"I always wondered why she would have sinned with all those different men. From all I've heard, she was very clever. I'd have thought, even if she was the most sexually depraved woman in the world, she'd have been too intelligent to ignore the risk of discovery."

"Eh?" I rouse myself, ponder on her words.

"I mean," Kate continues, warming to her theme, "she must have had to tolerate spies, just as I do, just as presumably ... forgive me, Henry ... just as Katherine Howard did. Katherine, I am told, was little more than a silly chit, flirting with danger, thinking herself invincible, but Anne ... she was one of the cleverest women in England. Far too clever than to fuel her enemies' fire against her and commit adultery and treason. Wouldn't she have known her enemies were just waiting for her to put a foot wrong?"

She falls back on her pillow, breathing quickly, as if she has been running. Neither of us speaks again. We lie awake for a long time, staring at the shadowy ceiling. My mind whirls with all she has said. I am astounded at both the simplicity of her argument, and the possible truth of it.

She shifts on to her side, hooks her knee across my legs, her arm across my torso. I can feel her heart beating against the top of my arm. It is a long time before sleep takes me.

In the morning, we wake to a bright blue day and, while we break our fast, word comes that the French fleet has been sighted nearby.

"They are anchored off the Isle of Wight, near St Helen's Point, Sire."

I put down my napkin, abandoning my breakfast.

"Then we must put to sea and meet them in battle. It is clearly meant as a challenge."

"You won't go, Henry! You can't. It is too dangerous!" Kate stands up, wiping crumbs from her mouth as she dashes toward me.

"No, of course not. I would only hinder them. We will watch from the roof; come, you can join us."

Up on the castle parapet the air is bracing, an erratic breeze tugging at our clothes, the briny scent of the sea filling our lungs. I look for Kate, draw her close to me and begin pointing out the different ships. We look on as the sails are unfurled, and my heart swells at the magnificence. They look like a painting and fill my thwarted seaman's heart with pride.

The pennants snap, gulls encircle the masts, and here beneath the wide blue sky, I feel as close to God as I have ever been.

Below us, the wharf springs to life with activity. People are running, sailors hurrying to board ship, their women gathered to wave them off, ragged boys ducking and darting among the crowd in search of mischief.

"Oh no, look!" Kate points as a large barrel tumbles from the back of a cart. It rolls steadily away and crashes into a wall, the contents spilling out; fish slipping and sliding like silver bullion as they spread in a shoal across the pavement. The needy, seeing an opportunity, rush in to take their pick.

"It looks as if they are still swimming," Kate remarks as a boy appears, fills his arms with herring, and runs off, calling to his friends, alerting them to the haul.

"He is going to stink like a fishmonger for the next month," I laugh.

"I daresay he will smell no worse than usual."

I turn toward the voice behind me, my face opening in glad surprise.

"Brandon! You made it after all. They told me you were unwell."

"Ah, it was nothing. Just too much cheese." He thumps his chest before making a perfunctory bow. I grasp his hand, draw him into the company, and we look across the harbour together.

The Great Harry is turning into the wind, heading for the harbour mouth, readying for battle as she goes. The French will rue the day they threatened my realm.

The Mary Rose follows.

"My, what a beauty," I murmur as I watch her sail unfurl. We all pause, transfixed by her magnificence. "Such lines, such grace."

She glides effortlessly through the clustering smaller craft, her deck alive with men, the flags of England flying proud. What I wouldn't give to be one of their number, sailing into battle against a much larger French force, sure of victory. I envy each man, even the lowliest cabin boy.

I stand to attention and watch them go.

Kate touches my elbow, and I bend down while she whispers something in my ear until Brandon exclaims, his voice high and startled, and I turn back again. Something is wrong. I grab his arm and we watch in horror as the Mary Rose begins to list.

Nobody speaks. Nobody breathes. Nobody dares.

The ship heels over, hovers on the cusp of disaster. She will righten, I mutter, she *must* righten. But the gunports, which were open ready to fire, quickly fill with water.

It happens so swiftly, so devastatingly fast, that I cannot move. None of us can. We stand appalled. Helpless! I cry out when the first sailor falls from the rigging. He splashes into the sea, flounders for a while, and then another falls beside him.

Men are sliding across the sloping deck, their screams like the distant cry of stricken gulls. My hand moves to my mouth, my eyes sting and I call out in fruitless warning as a massive cannon breaks free. A cannon I stood beside yesterday.

Nobody hears me.

It bursts through the sides of the ship, surging into the waves, the water it displaces swamping the poor souls floundering nearby. The cries grow louder. All around us, people are screaming, shouting orders; in the street the crowd surges closer to the dock. Women are shrieking, crying, wailing.

I cannot take my eyes from my beloved ship, the men attempting to flee the tilting deck; the men I envied just a short time ago are dying now. Those who do not fall are jumping. In a desperate attempt to avoid or hasten death, they kick off their shoes, and leap into the heaving sea.

There is nothing to be done. It is all too quick. We can only watch and pray as they die.

My heart breaks.

We do not move for a long time after the hull has disappeared. Only the tip of the mast is visible now, but I am numb, unable to speak, unable to clearly think. My companions are likewise struck dumb, and for many minutes we gaze upon the devastation in Southsea harbour. My best ship is lost, sunk beneath the waves, and not a shot was fired.

"God hates me."

"What? Henry, no. It wasn't God. It was… it was…" Brandon's voice dwindles away, he too is at a loss. We all search for reasons. Someone begins to weep, a woman. At first I think it is Kate and I turn to comfort her, but find instead it is the queen comforting Lady Carew. Lady Carew, who has just watched her husband founder with his ship.

I take a step toward them, gently place a hand on her shoulder.

"Lady Carew, my dear lady. I – I don't know what to say…"

She looks up from Kate's shoulder, tries to staunch her tears and attempts to curtsey, tries to pay due respect to her king, but she owes me nothing.

She probably hates me as much as God does.

"No, no," I say, patting her ineffectually. "You carry on, my dear. You do not weep alone; all of England mourns with you."

Just thirty-five survivors out of a complement of five hundred men. I can scarcely bear it. Even the satisfaction of our subsequent victory over the French fleet cannot ease me. My heart is heavy. I cannot rouse myself from gloom. I shut myself away again, pull the curtains of my bed tightly closed. I will see only Kate or Somers, and Denny.

I will never find the strength to face the world again or to continue the charade that is my life; but I must convince them all is well. I am still God's elect, but it is hard when I cannot even speak without weeping.

"You mustn't fret, Henry, you will make yourself ill."

Kate leans over me, concern written deep on her face. At least she loves me. At least there is someone who cares. I puff through my cheeks and attempt a smile.

"I know, but I am weary of affairs of state. Perhaps we should go on a progress after all."

She pulls back uncertainly.

"Are you well enough? I don't think the doctor will advise you to hunt."

I shrug, looking from the window. I don't know what I want. Everywhere I turn, I am confronted with failure. I can find no ease from it.

"Maybe not, but we shall see. Perhaps the country air will give me a new lease of heart. It can only be of benefit to escape the seasonal contagion of the city. I'd like to visit Brandon. I think he is at Guildford; it is some while since we saw him."

I know exactly how long it has been; we last saw him on the day I lost my favourite ship.

As we pass through the countryside, I manage to rouse myself enough to wave and smile at the people who come out to greet me. The sight of the unchanging cycle of the rustic way of life restores some of my flagging faith. There are still some good things to be savoured. There are fresh mown meadows, thick hedgerows burgeoning with birds, there are deer in the woods and fish in the rivers. I can breathe again, and when I hear the excited greeting of a group of peasant girls, I feel younger. My blood seems to flow better here, I go to the table hungry, and I go to my bed tired from fresh air and exercise.

"I feel better for escaping the palace," I remark to Kate as we ride side by side along a country road. "There are no politicians here to plague me."

Her gay laugh evokes a chuckle.

"And it is good to be free from Gardiner's reach," she replies. My spirits sink again. I have no wish to be reminded of it. I scowl and, realising she has doused my good humour, she points to a rabbit sprinting across a meadow.

"Is it a rabbit or a hare? We must have startled him," she says. "Look at his tail flash. It is a good job the dogs are penned up or they'd be after him."

"It is a wonder to me how you can care for the fate of a rabbit. They are put on earth to be hunted. I mean, they are here to feed us, aren't they?"

She shrugs.

"I have some sympathy for them. They mean no harm, yet their life is full of peril. There are dangerous, hungry dogs everywhere. I know the feeling."

My heart sinks further. We are back to Gardiner and his cronies again.

"Well, Madam, perhaps you should be glad we have left your own personal huntsman at home."

She retreats into herself, knowing full well by my use of the term 'madam' that she has displeased me. Others in her situation would have pleaded for forgiveness, claimed they had no intention of irritating me, but Kate, being Kate, says nothing. She allows silence to do the healing.

Brandon greets us. Open-armed on the hall steps, he welcomes us to his home. Inside, they are ready for us, the table already set with a sumptuous banquet, the best bedchamber readied and waiting for us. His wife comes forward, excitedly embracing her friend, the queen.

"I am so pleased you have come, Your Majesty," she says, taking Kate familiarly by the arm. "I can show you those new chairs we have in the parlour. The ones I was telling you about."

We refresh ourselves after the journey, change our clothes before joining our hosts in the hall. Once the meal is over, Brandon invites us into his privy chamber and we gladly accept, pleased to be free of the larger company.

Kate and Catherine Willoughby — or Brandon, as I should rightly call her now — retire to the hearth, while Brandon and I move closer to the window. We sink gladly into our respective chairs, and sigh in unified relief.

"We sound like old men," I laugh, "glad to have safely passed another day without a visit from the grim reaper."

Brandon stares ruefully into his cup.

"I fear he will be with us soon, Henry."

"Perhaps, or maybe we have another decade to enjoy first. One can never know."

"We have been fortunate, you and I."

I raise an eyebrow. He has been more fortunate than I. He is the richest man I know, and the most loyal. I can remember just one occasion when he crossed me. I chuckle aloud at the thought of it. He looks up, puzzled at my sudden burst of humour.

"What amuses you?"

"I was thinking of when you married my sister, how angry I was that you'd stolen such a prize from under my nose. I was already looking out for another king to take her."

He lays his head back against his chair.

"It wasn't done lightly, I can assure you. I was certain you'd never forgive us, but Mary said..."

I think back on my fiery young sister, the queen of France who lost her heart to my lowly best friend. Her image is so clear it is as if she stands before me now.

"I soon came to realise that in exiling you both from court I was only punishing myself. You both had each other while I had no one. I missed you; I had no option but to forgive."

"And I did make her happy."

I look at him, old now and as tired as I, yet it seems only yesterday since we were boys, and I was doing my best to match him in the tilting yard.

"You did. I have long been grateful. There are few men who'd happily take on a Tudor, or even have a hope of managing one."

He laughs softly. His servant comes forward and refills our cups. When we are alone again, Brandon says:

"I miss her still, despite remarrying."

"As do I, Brandon ... as do I."

We stare into the fire, watch the leap and dance of the flames while our minds fill with days gone by.

"Do you remember…"

We both speak at once, break into laughter.

"You speak first, Henry…"

"I was recalling when, soon after I married for the first time, you were dallying with one of the queen's women ... what was her name? She was the friend of Bessie Blount."

"Oh," he frowns, shakes his head. "I've forgotten her name, but I remember her, a big buxom girl…"

"With a laugh like a donkey."

"That's right! Norris had a hankering for her too and when we were drunk one night, he picked a quarrel with me and declared we had to let her choose."

"And while you two were fighting, she went off with … who was it … Compton!"

"Oh yes! Norris was furious, poor fellow…" We sober suddenly, remembering Norris' sad end, but neither of us speaks of it.

"What times we had, Brandon. I am grateful. You above all men have never failed me."

"And never will, Henry. Even were you not my king I would be happy to follow in your wake."

"Really?" I quirk my brow. "That is good to know. It is hard for a king to know if a man's friendship is offered out of love or for what he can gain."

He leans forward.

"The dark is making us maudlin but know this, my king. My friendship with you may have made me rich beyond measure, but I would give up every penny, every inch of the lands I own if you were to ask it of me."

My throat tightens. I cough, flap my hand at him, dismissing his sentiment, but I am touched and he knows it.

"Come," he says. "It is late. We should get to our beds if we are to rise early in the morning for the hunt."

I take his hand, glad of his strength as he hauls me to my feet. I groan aloud as I take the first steps toward the door.

"If my bones allow it, I will see you there, Brandon. I wish you good night."

I am tired beyond measure, but when I climb into bed, sleep evades me as pictures evoked by the recent conversation charge through my mind. It has been a good life; overall, I am lucky. I've had difficulties, but how much worse would those troubles have been without men like Brandon at my side. I thank God for him as my eyes grow heavy, and I drift off into dreams of youth and laughter.

I sleep late. When I finally awaken, my gentlemen are lined up outside, waiting to make me ready for the day. I realise I have probably missed the hunt and Brandon will think me weak, or past it. I submit to the sponge and my beard is trimmed. I have just donned my fresh linen when I hear Kate demanding entrance and I turn from the mirror.

"Let the queen enter," I say, "and leave us alone for a while."

They bow out, the last to leave carrying a slopping bowl of grey water. I am surprised that when Kate pushes into the room, she is clad in her night rail, her hair still in braids. Her face is parchment white, the bones beneath showing strongly. I can see how she will look when she grows old. Instantly, I am on high alert. I cross the room, grab her hands.

"What is the matter? Is it Edward?"

She shakes her head, but heartbreak is written clearly on her face.

"No, no, not Edward. The prince is fine. Sit down, Henry, you mustn't get upset, but I do have some ill news … some terrible news."

I fumble behind me for a chair, slump into it and wait in trepidation for her to speak. She moistens her lips, frowns and grips my hands hard.

"It is Brandon."

"Brandon? What is wrong with him? Is he sick? Too much wine last evening?"

"He - he is dead, Henry."

I snort in derision. Shake my head.

"No, he isn't. We are due to hunt today. I was with him last night. He was fit and well. Brandon isn't *dead…*"

But her face tells me otherwise.

Everything stops, a high-pitched ringing begins in my ears. I grope for words but cannot find my tongue. It is thick and unmalleable.

Someone brings me a drink – the cup is cool in my palm, but I do not taste it. I let the cup fall to the floor. I keep my eye firmly on Kate, absorbing every nuance of expression, every flicker of her eye while she wrestles helplessly with her emotion.

Part of me knows it must be true, but he cannot … he *cannot* be gone. We were talking, laughing together just a few short hours ago.

We are going hunting today.

The door opens, the sound of a woman weeping – loud ugly sobs – wafts into the chamber. How I wish I could enjoy such release, but my own grief is lodged firmly in my throat, suffocating me.

Grief builds slowly; rising up from my belly, constricting my chest, burning my throat, stinging my eyes, and then it erupts in a great angry tide. It pours from my mouth, my nose, my eyes; it consumes my body, extinguishing my will to live.

He is my friend, my oldest friend, my only friend. He must not leave me!

The loss of Brandon is like losing part of myself; it is like losing my mother, my sister Mary, my dearest love, all at once. Apart from Kate, I am now completely alone. Nobody to trust, nobody to confide in, nobody to reminisce of better days. Even Kate is too young to know the man I was, the king I used to be. Apart from Norfolk, I am the oldest man at court, and now I have no friends.

I have killed them all.

Despite his request for a simple burial at Grimsthorpe, I order a state funeral from my own purse, and he is laid to rest at St George's chapel in Windsor. It is fitting for a great man like Brandon to be so honoured. After his internment, having done the best for him I could, I push everyone away, crawl back into bed and hide from the world. Safe in my feathered cocoon, I weep and worry and wish to die.

But kings cannot choose when to die and, eventually, after allowing me time to heal, Kate lures me back to my duties, but they are duties I have no wish to fulfil. Denny puts his stamp to good use, fends off would-be petitioners.

"The king is indisposed," he tells them. "The king is busy. The king is occupied."

In truth, the king is fed up and filled with self-loathing, failing in his duty.

"You must stop this, Henry. You cannot give in to grief like this. You have to fight. I should know."

I look at her, wondering what grief she battles with, but I know it cannot be half as debilitating as my own.

"Why don't we visit Edward, and the girls? It is a while since you saw them. Your son always cheers you."

I sit up, slumped in bed like a pile of pillows, and nod wearily.

"I suppose you are right."

"It is a habit of mine," she replies cheerily, reminding me of the brisk authority of my grandmother. "I will summon your gentlemen to make you ready."

By slow degrees, Kate lures me back to health. I pick up my duties again, although with a heavy heart, but I no longer find joy in court life. I continue to hide away as much as I can, reading and tolerating the antics of my fool. And despite my efforts, misery heaps upon misery.

One by one, my spaniels die, each loss impounding the grief of the last. Each morning and evening, Denny, with no mention of my personal sorrows, runs through the list of essential matters, keeping me informed of the day-to-day jurisdiction of the country.

<u>Spring 1546</u>

With the return of spring, my spirits lift again, and I emerge from isolation and begin once more to seek the company of others. One afternoon, I order my servants to carry me in my chair in search of Kate, and, on entering her chamber, I find her kneeling with Catherine Willoughby at the hearth. They are burning papers. They stop when they notice me, their faces draining of colour.

"What is this?"

I lean forward, pick up a paper from the scattered pile on a chair, and peruse it. It seems to be religious sedition. My heart sinks.

"Kate? Is this treason?" I hiss the words lest anyone overhear.

"No, no, Henry."

She scrambles to her feet, wipes the back of her hand across her cheek, leaving a smudge of soot. "You know Gardiner is after my blood. He will twist and manipulate anything he finds. I am merely taking precautions."

"But does this go against the word of God?"

"No, they are just notes I made while I was writing my books. Idle thoughts and the opinions of others, but the words could easily be misconstrued, as you have just proven. That is why we are burning them."

"Has he threatened to search your chambers? He cannot do so unless he has convincing evidence against you."

"Nevertheless, I have taken the precaution of locking everything private away. He is hunting me, Henry. He is always prying into my business, questioning my servants, my household. He has arrested Anne Askew again and is convinced of a friendship, of collusion between us. He does not believe we have never even met."

I dare not ask if there is any truth in his suspicion.

"Try not to do anything that will upset him. Keep a low profile, stay away from these, these … Lutheran meetings, and I will do what I can to keep him at bay."

Later, after some discreet enquiry, I learn that Anne Askew has not only been arrested but tortured on the rack. It is the Lord Lieutenant of the Tower who brings me word of it.

"They told Knyvet to turn the rack on her, but he refused, Sire, not because of any sympathy with the prisoner but because your laws state it is illegal to torture a woman. I went to see her, Your Majesty. I don't think she will bear any more of it. She is skin and bone, and probably close to death. They need to be ordered to stop. Even if she is guilty, this treatment is … is … she is a woman, Sire!"

"It does not suit Gardiner that she be innocent, so he makes sure of it by way of torture," Kate sobs, butting unceremoniously into the conversation. Her face is lately showing signs of strain, and there are lines around her mouth, shadows beneath her eyes.

Of course it does not suit Gardiner. It doesn't suit him that we should be happy either, or even content. As soon as he has finished with Askew, he will turn his evil intentions upon the queen.

"Denny! Send word to the Tower and order them to cease, and then send Gardiner to me. He goes too far."

It is not the first time the bishop has overstepped the mark and I doubt it will be the last. I send my weeping queen back to her chambers and drum my fingers on the arm of the chair while I wait.

He enters, shamefaced, his cap clasped in his hands. I look at him as if he is a snake.

"You have gone too far, Gardiner. This will not win favour to your cause. Leave the Askew woman alone; a spell in the Tower will be enough to loosen her tongue."

"But, Your Majesty, we are so close to a confession."

I scowl at him, a growl in my throat, and he steps back, drops his hat and raises his hands, fingers splayed, palms up.

"Very well, I will halt the persuasion, but will continue to gently question her ... with respite, so she may eat and pray."

"And sleep, Gardiner. She must be allowed to sleep."

I have often wondered how much truth a man, or woman in this case, speaks under duress. I might well confess to anything if my nails were being torn off, or a candle held to the sole of my foot. How much more might I admit to if my limbs were torn asunder? It is the way of the world, of course, and it serves to free the realm of spies and traitors; if we lose a few innocents on the way I suppose it is the price we must pay for peace.

I wave him from my presence and retreat once more into the gloom of my own company. I lead myself down a dark tunnel of disappointment, along the way I encounter people from the past, people who sinned against me. It is a crowded, unpleasant passage through the dimly lit cave of my imagination.

They are all there, the ragged and the rich, the guilty and the innocent. Peasants, monks, bishops, lords and ladies … queens. Some faces turn to me in sorrow, in regret, others are indignant at the injustice they suffered at my hands. I am not the king of this place, I am just a man, naked and negligent, and vengeance is theirs. They come for me, arms outstretched, nails extended.

I start awake, and when I shout into the darkness, something scuttles from the shadows. It stops at my side. Reaches out a hand; long, thin fingers crawl across my knee.

"Lord King?"

"Somers." I puff out my cheeks, almost crying with relief. "I thought you a demon, crawled from Hell."

"I've not been there, my king, not yet."

He clasps his hands together, hunches his shoulders and chuckles, but I am not yet ready to be amused. I rub a hand across my face, and my palm comes away moist. I wipe it on my doublet and grope for a cup.

"Where is everyone?"

"You sent them all away, Sire. On pain of death, if you recall."

"So I did, I had forgotten. Go and fetch someone to stoke the flames."

He scampers off and I am alone again, alone in the dark with my thoughts. I click my fingers, but my one remaining dog is deaf. I call his name, but he sleeps on. Desperate now for the lick of a warm tongue, I take my stick and thump the floor. Ball raises his head, and clambers to his feet, as doddery as I, and ambles toward me. Hoisting him onto my knee, I ruffle his coat, and he licks my face. My heart warms and the dark spirits melt away into the four walls again.

I am laid low with my leg. Once more it has swollen to almost twice its normal size. I have nothing but dismal thoughts to dwell upon. I will be no better tomorrow; there is very little to look forward to.

Oh, the physicians scurry around, trying this remedy and that, but since the passing of Dr Butts a few months since, my health has steadily deteriorated. Should I ever bump into him in Heaven, I will see him charged with treason for deserting me at this late hour.

Even the antics of Somers cannot rouse my spirits. Kate visits every afternoon and reads to me from various pamphlets she has discovered. This evening she stays later than usual, so we might take supper together in my chamber. Afterwards, as the wine flows, our talk turns liturgical and we spar, in a friendly manner at first, but it soon becomes heated.

She is such a stubborn woman and will not be corrected. The taut set of her chin irritates me as much as her flawed rhetoric, and since I have no wish to fight, I send her to her bed … alone.

I am frowning into the embers of the fire, wondering why my father neglected my education so. No mention was ever made of how to end a war initiated by one's own hand. My tutor never touched on how to rid the realm of hordes of dispossessed monks without creating anarchy. Now the monasteries are gone, there has been an unprecedented rise in vagrancy and crime. It is beyond me; other than hanging them, I can find no remedy. I am still frowning over the state of the realm when Denny slips through the door.

"Your Majesty, the Bishop of Winchester is outside seeking audience."

"Gardiner?" I twitch my blanket higher around my knees. I have nothing else to do so I nod my permission. He comes in, the skirts of his robes swirling about his legs as, full of purpose, he approaches me at the hearth. I do not smile, but scowl as I mutter a greeting.

"Your Majesty, I hope I find you well."

He sweeps a bow.

"It must be clear you do not," I retort, indicating my bound leg raised on its stool, the array of remedies on the table at my side.

"Well, I hope it is nothing more than the usual."

He takes a seat without being asked and I wonder when I have ever encountered such an odious man. What does he mean, 'nothing more than the usual'? Just because an ailment is recurring, does he think that makes it more easily borne? It becomes harder, each attack biting deeper, each recovery shorter until at last it consumes you. Pain, constant, unceasing agony eats at your mind, your comfort, your humour, until there is nothing left but pain.

"What do you want?"

"Ah, yes. What do I want?" he repeats irritatingly, and clears his throat before continuing. "It has long been my concern, as you know, that the court is rife with … with heretics, Your Majesty."

"Indeed. And what harm do they do? There are some who believe me to be a heretic. I can't imagine Cranmer is going to murder anyone in their bed. He is a good man, despite his beliefs."

His eyebrows shoot up to meet his thinning hair.

"Your Majesty must understand that a heretic is sly, his rhetoric is insidious and can infiltrate even the most innocent courtier. You will have witnessed the way some of them work, I am sure. It is easy to inadvertently nourish a serpent to our bosom when…"

"You mean the queen, don't you?"

He starts, appears astonished at such an idea, and pretends to consider the question. I glare at him, daring him to continue.

"Well, it wasn't the queen I had in mind in this instance, but now you mention it, Your Majesty, many of her friends have Lutheran connections. If she did indeed intend to surreptitiously convert Your Majesty to her heretic way of thinking, would you, if you'll pardon me, notice it until it was too late?"

The image rises in my mind of Kate's panic when I came upon her burning papers. Was it guilt or fear that made her react so? And she does harp on about the wrongs of the traditional faith; she makes little secret of her heresy, even from me … her king. If she has indeed been seeking to convert me, then she has no right.

I've seen the books in her secret library with my own eyes. I know sedition when I read it. What if the kindness and love she shows me is a mask, concealing her true self, her real intentions? What if she doesn't love me at all?

The rhythm of my heart changes, the beat becoming hard and sickening as I realise how vulnerable I am, how far I have allowed her to reach into my soul. My next words issue from my lips as if someone else is speaking.

"Look into it then, Gardiner. Question her servants, re-examine the Askew woman. Discover the truth."

And all the time he is taking his leave of me, I want to bite back the words, retract the order, and have him thrown into the deepest, darkest pit.

But something stops me.

June 1546

I sometimes wonder if there is a devil sitting on my shoulder, casting ruin on all my plans. Since I became king, nothing has turned out as I had hoped. I craved military glory, to be remembered as a warrior, like Edward IV or Henry V, yet my military endeavours have all ended in ignominy.

I admit only to myself that my victorious return from Boulogne was feigned. I won no real glory, certainly no foreign ground, not when measured against the financial cost. What I really need is a way out of this war without the shame of surrender, but I cannot lose face, we cannot simply retreat. I will not order my men to come running home with their tails between their legs.

They all let me down.

My greatest generals. Norfolk complaining of hunger and fatigue leading to great losses at Montreuil. The letters he sent demanding we send relief are even now at my elbow. Later, when I ordered his son, Surrey, to replace him so that he might join Brandon in defence of Boulogne, the tone of his messages did not improve.

The letters do not read like those of a seasoned campaigner. When they finally abandoned Boulogne, which was so hard won, and bolstered the defence at Calais, they claimed they had not abandoned it at all but left Lord Poynings in charge.

Poynings! Who was such a hardy fellow that he dropped dead a few months later!

My anger would have been greater at the time were I not besieged on all sides with sedition at home, my health, my marriage, the abysmal state of the economy. All these months later, I am still wrestling with the same myriad problems and know not where to turn, what decision to make, and there are very few I trust enough to ask their advice. Even those I rely on are working to their own ends.

I have no doubt about that.

Surrey, unsupervised in France, does well at first. I honour him, creating him Lieutenant of the King on Sea and Land, and I am proud of his successful attack on the Ardes. *This is more like it*, I think; more action, less sitting around waiting for our enemy to starve.

But even as we win in France, the Privy Council besieges me daily with complaints of the financial cost of war. And they are not wrong. Together with the conflict in Scotland, it has cost us more than two million pounds, and all this while my people at home suffer hunger and pestilence.

But we are winning the war, we cannot stop now! It is unfortunate, however, that the power of his position goes to Surrey's head. Before long, I begin receiving word of behaviour unseemly in an English leader. He disobeys the direct order of the Council; he ignores the fervent plea from his father to listen to the directives of the king. Ultimately, after a major and humiliating defeat at Chatillon, I demote Surrey and send Hertford to replace him. Surrey is ordered to return home in disgrace, but when he arrives, I am so furiously disappointed that I defer dealing with him while I consider my options. Norfolk comes creeping into my presence.

"I beg leniency, Your Majesty; he is young and foolhardy. We can remember what it was to be young, can we not?"

I look at Norfolk's grizzled face, the years of war written large upon it. I recall the immense strength he enjoyed in his younger years, the insidious self-promotion of his middle years, his unwavering loyalty, despite his religious faith, during the closure of the monasteries. I compare all those years of devoted service with the disappointments of our most recent campaign and it is reduced to nothing.

"I do not recall any of us riding in the face of direct orders. Even when I believed I knew better, I listened to wiser men. I did as my father bid, and I always heeded God, even when I misliked the content of their directives."

Norfolk stares back at me, his lugubrious eyes bloodshot, yellow where there should be white. His face is lined, ingrained with the dirt of many battles. I remember how he threw his nieces at me in a bid for self-aggrandisement. It is not so very long since he dangled his own daughter before me, to distract me from the queen, whom he dislikes for her Lutheran leanings. Now, maybe for the first time, he seeks a favour from me that is not simply for his own benefit.

He begs for the life of his feckless son.

He looks away, shuffles his feet.

"He is my son, Your Majesty. My heir…"

And those words touch me because I, more than any other man, understand the importance of sons.

"I will think on it," I say, waving him from my presence, "in the meantime, keep him out of trouble."

I take supper alone. Only Somers is here, accepting the odd offering from the royal plate, muttering the occasional jest, tormenting the poor dog. He picks up one of Ball's bones, places it between his teeth and tumbles across the floor, coming to a halt beside me. He sits up, his hands flopped before him. If he had a tail, he would wag it.

I regard him humourlessly. "Stop it, Somers. I am not in the mood."

Without taking his eyes from mine, he falls slowly and silently sideways and when he hits the floor he stays there, stiff as a corpse. I continue my meal, tasting nothing, feeling nothing.

"What is that damned noise?" I wake from slumber, my neck stiff from the awkward position into which I have fallen. "Is something the matter?"

It sounds like the world is ending, for someone is wailing as if their heart is broken. And it seems to be issuing from the queen's apartments. I grope for my stick and, rising with a groan, I shuffle off to discover the cause of it.

The doors to her adjoining apartment are thrown open at my approach and I enter to discover Kate, collapsed across a table, her head buried in her arms, sobbing as if her sorrow has no end. Her women are flapping and fussing around her, trying to get her to stop.

"What is it?" I ask the woman closest to me. "Why is she weeping?"

With a scowl, the woman hands me a slip of paper and, after a perfunctory curtsey, she stalks away to continue her ministrations to the queen. I limp closer to the candle and squint at the scrawled words.

Be wary, permission has been granted for a warrant to be signed against you.

The message is unsigned. A cowardly thing that has been written in a hurry. I look up. The woman faces me, her chin set, dislike clear in her demeanour.

"Who wrote this?"

"I told the queen it is likely just mischief because Your Majesty loves her too well to ever allow such a thing to happen."

This woman has courage, or she is stupid. I misremember her name but make a mental note to thank her later for her honesty. I take a few tottery steps toward the queen. The women part to allow me through.

"Kate." I touch her shoulder and she springs up instantly at the sound my voice.

"Oh Henry, how could you?"

"How could I what?"

"You ordered it, you must have. Gardiner can't just make out a warrant for a queen's arrest without your say."

I look at her, my heart breaking at the memories of the long evenings we've spent together, the loving, the spats, her constant and unremitting care for me.

A lump gathers in my throat. I have no desire to lose another wife.

"I haven't signed it," I say, my voice husky with emotion.

She holds on to my arm, struggles to her feet and stands tall, looks me directly in the eye.

"And do you intend to?"

"No, no, of course not."

"What is my alleged crime? Is it against you, or against God?"

"Well," I clear my throat, "that is a difficult question since it is one and the same thing."

Her lips part, she shakes her head.

"I will never understand you, Henry. Tell me, of what crime am I accused?"

"Oh, the usual thing. Heresy, a plot to use your rhetoric on me, of holding illicit conversations, of making subversive arguments…"

"Oh, for Heaven's sake."

"Perhaps we should add blasphemy to the charges too?"

She looks up sharply but notices the latent humour in my eye.

"I admit, Henry, to discussing liturgical matters with you, but I was in no way attempting to persuade you. I was trying to distract you from your insufferable pain, from your many, many woes. It was always just empty debate, to pass the time. I love you, I would never…"

With a surge of gratitude, I take her hand and tuck it beneath my elbow.

"I know, my dear, there is no need to take on so. Gardiner caught me when I was tired, and at a very low ebb. Come to think on it, I think you and I had just had a small disagreement. I was an easy target then, but as soon as I woke in the morning, I knew I'd never act on it. I love and admire you, Kate, more than any woman before."

She opens her mouth, probably to deny the truth of my declaration, and she'd no doubt be right. I am old and lonely, and she is necessary to me.

Far more necessary than Gardiner.

"Come," I say, "accompany me back to my apartment. I have a plan to teach Gardiner a lesson. I think you may rather enjoy it."

The war has cost me dearly and gained me nothing. To offset the mounting debt, I have no option but to devalue the English currency again. The Council warns that such an action will only push prices and interest rates higher, but they can offer up no alternative.

In June, I realise I am left with no option but to agree to sign a treaty with France, ending the war, and part of the agreement is to promise the eventual return of Boulogne to France. It is an ignominious deal and it irks me to do it, but that is a worry for later.

The matter between Gardiner and Kate however gives me an idea of how to deal with Surrey without making reference to his actions during the war. Taking

Gardiner to one side, he listens, his hands clasped, his upper body slightly bent toward me.

"It is about Surrey," I keep my voice low, my sentences as oblique as I can. "It has come to my attention that he has been showing a little too much interest in reform, speaking out in public defence of the Lutheran cause. I thought that might be of interest to you."

His face lights up and I sigh with relief as he scurries off after fresh quarry. Kate will breathe a little easier now. But to my surprise, once the bishop begins asking questions about Surrey, accusers from all walks of life appear from the woodwork, also keen to bring Norfolk's son down.

*

"I have forgotten my spectacles." I grope in the seat beside me, coming up with a squashed book and a mislaid pastry, but not my quarry. I squint at the paper I have been trying to read, but it is no good. I flap it angrily at the queen, who puts down her own book. She summons a woman to her side.

"Margery, run to the privy chamber and find a pair of the king's spectacles, would you. There are plenty lying around."

She rolls her eyes in fond rebuke at my habit of mislaying them as often as I do. We are in the garden where the afternoon sun is a little too hot, so I have asked them to push my wheeled chair into the shade.

Although I cannot join in, it is pleasant to watch the youngsters dancing on the lawn, to listen to the strains of the lute. The women are pretty, and the young men are gallant, and I sit in my chair like some old gargoyle tumbled from the palace roof and watch resentfully.

I would never remark on this allegory to anyone. I never fail to present myself as in my prime. I fool myself, and hopefully those around me, that I am hale, that this recent incapacity is just a fleeting thing.

"I will be recovered come the end of summer," I say, and everyone agrees with me; yet, in my heart I know it will only end in my death.

I am not ready yet to die.

Kate has brought a small pile of books into the garden, but they are not liturgical in subject. One is a book of poetry, written I believe by Wyatt, another lost companion of my youth. Snagged by the latent memory, I begin to reminisce again, as I do so often nowadays.

How I envied him his friendship with Anne. I sent him away, far overseas, so I could have her to myself, just as I have parted Kate from Tom Seymour.

I turn my attention to the queen, and wonder if she is aware of the reason he left so suddenly for foreign parts. I speak suddenly without considering the effect my news might have. Or perhaps deep down, I am testing her.

"Before he fell from favour, Norfolk was suggesting a match between his daughter, Mary, and the younger of the Seymour brothers, Thomas."

"Oh!"

Her book falls from her grasp and she leaps up, scattering her papers in the grass, the pages turning lazily in the breeze. While she fumbles to retrieve them, I notice how pale she has become.

"Whatever is it?" I ask, although I know full well. I take her trembling hand, my heart twisting. She is still enamoured of Seymour. I had hoped she had forgotten. I had hoped it was I who now had her heart.

"There was a wasp," she lies. "I thought it was going to sting me, but it's gone now."

She smiles blithely, but I notice a pulse beating at the base of her throat, the flush that has replaced her former pallor.

"I have relieved Seymour of his mission, and he will be returning soon. We shall have to wait and see what his feelings are on the marriage. It won't please everybody."

"No … yes."

She looks away across the gardens, her lashes fluttering as if there is something in her eye. She pretends interest in her women who are nearby, gathering for another dance, their voices carrying toward us on the breeze. I turn my head, watch their gowns undulate, the clothes a bright splash of colour against the green as they take their places.

"Oh!" one of them remarks, pointing toward the archway cut in the hedge. "I wonder what is happening?"

As one, Kate and I follow the line of her finger.

Gardiner, flanked by a trio of guards, strides purposefully toward us. I reach for my wife, and she assists me to stand. We wait, our expressions grim, although laughter is already bubbling in the depths of my belly.

I know very well his purpose, and so does Kate.

"Your Majesty." The bishop bows low, his guards stand stiffly to attention behind him, pikes raised. "I have a warrant."

Kate's fingers tighten on my arm.

"A warrant?" I ask, as if I have no idea. "For whose arrest?"

"For the queen's, Sire."

Puzzlement creases his forehead, his eyes slide from me to the queen and back again. Kate gives a feigned start of shock, while I look at him in surprise.

"For our beloved wife? I would never sign such a thing and well you know it."

"B – but, Your Majesty, your signature is writ plain upon it. Here…"

He waves the document beneath my nose. I take it from him, pretend to peruse it, and then, tossing it to the floor, I grind it into the dirt with the end of my stick.

"This is a forgery, Sir. I did not sign this."

His face turns a fascinating shade of purple, his eyes flash with furious humiliation.

"B – but I – Your Majesty…" He fumbles for a polite way to call his king a liar. It is the funniest thing I've seen since Will Somers staged a wedding between himself and a pig. And that was many years ago.

I take a step closer, lean heavily on my stick while I thump the side of his head with my right hand. He ducks away, too terrified to move, too terrified to linger.

I thump him again.

"Go away, Gardiner, and leave us alone," I roar, giving full vent to my rage. "Find yourself a worthier quarry than my wife, before I become the hunter and turn my sights on you."

November 1546

As the summer wanes and the leaves turn colour, I am still not allowed any peace. I am tired of governance. My desire is to spend time with my wife and my fool, who sometimes seems to be the most rational man at court.

The tension between the two factions is now at breaking point. Norfolk, having failed to breach the divide by securing a marriage between his daughter and the Seymours, retires in high dudgeon to Kenninghall. They think I do not know how they range themselves against us, each party preparing to take control of my son the moment I breathe my last.

My will stipulates that after my passing, the queen shall be regent; as Edward's mother, there is no other I'd trust to take charge of him until he reaches his majority. This pleases none of them, for no man wishes to be governed by a woman, albeit the wisest in the land. But there is nothing they can legally do about it. I have it written and sealed.

Surrey, having wriggled free of his recent misdemeanours, lacks the sense to lie low. Instead, he declaims loudly that his father, as the leading peer of the realm, should rightfully be given the regency. He argues with George Blagge and, deftly avoiding an outward fight at court, which is against our law, he visits Blagge's house uninvited, where he hammers at the front door, demanding satisfaction. He writes a letter, belligerent in tone, threatening Blagge with dire consequences should he, a mere knight, ever cross the earl again.

Hertford shows me the letter, urging me to take action against Surrey now the indisputable evidence is in my hands. But still I prevaricate, unwilling to order action that will bring the Howards down. The Howards may be out of favour now, but I cannot overlook the lifetime of loyalty that Norfolk has shown us. He has been the strong arm behind the throne since carving a way back into royal favour after fighting for the other side at Bosworth.

But a few days later, when Hertford shows me letters written by Norfolk himself that seem to uphold his son's crimes, I am left with little choice. I had never thought the defection of the Howards would wound me so deeply.

When I raise the matter with Denny, he advises me not to ignore the issue.

"It may not be wise to leave the matter unresolved, Sire, given the … the…"

"Given the fact I am soon to die?"

He steps back, hands raised in denial.

"Oh no, Your Majesty, I was not going to say that but, if the worse should happen … you would not wish your son's tenure to begin with so many wolves circling the throne. It could end in civil war."

"Wolves … a very good analogy, Denny. Most appropriate."

He clears his throat, turns slightly pink.

"I did hear from one in the Howard's employ that Surrey has lately added the royal arms of Edward the Confessor to his own."

"What? He has no right!"

"Exactly, Sire."

"It is almost as if he wishes to spend the rest of his days in the Tower."

"Or worse, Sire."

I narrow my eyes and peer at the seemingly mild-natured man who holds my realm in the palm of his hand.

"Precisely."

I ponder the matter long into the evening. When Kate comes to bid me good night, I am still sitting beside the hearth in my night robe.

"Henry, you must go to bed. Sitting up all night will solve nothing."

I reach for her arm, hold her hand close to my cheek. Her skin is cool and soft.

"I know. I hate to be left without options. I have no choice now but to commit them both to the Tower."

"Norfolk too?"

"Yes, Norfolk too, although the damp may kill him before he reaches the scaffold."

"It seems such a shame. He has been a good servant."

Has he? My mind wanders back down the years: recalling the battles, the advice, the betrayals, the camaraderie, his constancy, his loyalty to the crown. She is right. It is sad that his career should end in ignominy.

Norfolk, getting wind of his arrest, surrenders his lands to the crown, and I accept them gladly but do not revoke the order for his arrest. Kate, sitting with me in the solitude of my chamber, tries once more to take his part.

"Are you certain of his guilt, Henry? There is no doubt?"

There is always doubt. I stare at her for a long time, and although the night only offers me shadows, I know her face so well it is as if I can see it.

"No, I am not certain. In fact, I am well aware that he is the victim of his enemies. But it has to stop, Kate. I cannot let this feud continue beyond my death. I must think of Edward."

December 1546 – January 1547

A drear Christmas season follows, which I am too sick to attend. My legs are so weak they can no longer support me, not even with the use of a stick. If I leave my chambers or even wish to cross to the other side of the room, it is by way of my wheeled chair, my attendants puffing and sweating as they carry me up and down the stairs. If they were to drop me, I doubt I'd be able to summon the energy to order them to the scaffold.

I doubt I'd survive the fall.

Kate orders our meals to be taken in the privacy of our apartments, but I have no appetite. The array of rich food disgusts me. I push away the plate and watch her pick at an apple tart. It takes all my effort to breathe, and concentration is almost beyond me. Several times I drift into sleep while she is still speaking.

Outwardly, it is as if I am already dead. There is not a vestige of pleasure left in life, or at least none that I can partake in. I spent the last dregs of my energy making one last speech at parliament, where I exhorted religious and brotherly unity, urged them to love one another. All we need is love. It is a long discourse, which takes all my effort, but it is my last chance to force them to unite in their care of the prince.

If they ever had any love for me, this is how they must show it.

Even if no one dares speak of it, I know I do not have long left. I am but a shadow of the king I once was, and every man present must know beyond doubt that my death is close.

It is a fearsome thought.

I must make amends before it is too late. There are things I must do. Peace I must make, not just with God, but with my subjects. If only I knew how to begin. If only I could think clearly, if only I could see, if only the pounding in my head, the stabbing in my thigh, would ease. How can I organise my mind when I am so beset with troubles? When I am alone in my bed, I weep at the path my life has taken. Nothing has turned out as I intended it to. I will put things right, I will make confession, I will forgive my enemies, I will not die unshriven. But, in the morning, everything is worse.

The fever is strong, my body slick with sweat, and they are burning fragrant herbs in my chamber to mask the stench. If I had the energy, I'd have someone whipped for such an offence. They have attempted every remedy known to man but to no effect. All night and into the morning I have been slipping in and out of reality, and as death draws closer, I can smell its approach. With each passing hour, my fear intensifies.

It is only a matter of time.

My chamber is shadowy, I cannot see into the corners. The hangings about my bed conceal demons, monsters with the faces of those I once knew, and those I have forgotten. My sins are multitude and those I sinned against are waiting.

Retribution.

And it only grows darker. A candle floats above me, someone places a damp cloth on my forehead. I mutter something.

The face looms close.

"Did you try to speak, Your Majesty? It is I, Denny."

He pauses, waiting for my reply, but I turn my face away, slide whimpering back into delirium. Back to the devils.

There are women laughing; they dance around me, their arms full of babies. There are monks, feasting on the flesh of infants, while in the other corner my boys, my precious sons, are lowered, still breathing, into yawning graves. I call out to stop them, but there are long-dead kings watching; they put their heads together, and their mocking laughter shrieks in my ears.

I am Henry! I try to roar, but the words lodge in my throat, choking me, foaming into a river of sludge at my lips.

"Your Majesty, I think perhaps it is time to make your peace."

Denny's words seem to come from afar. It takes a moment for me to realise he is not another of the devils come to taunt me. I'd never thought him a brave man.

In a moment of clarity, I grab his sleeve. It is thick and warm, and real. Earthly.

I hang on to it.

"Send for Cranmer," I manage to beg, but I cannot be certain I have spoken the words aloud. Sleep takes hold, dragging me down again, and this time when I rouse I am calmer, my head is clearer. It is still dark. I can hear the fire crackling, smell the smoke, the sulphur.

"Oh, you're awake." I turn toward the voice, peer into the gloom where the figure is waiting. At first, I think it is a monk, but when the head turns toward me, a shaft of light illuminates half her face.

I blink at her, aghast.

I had thought if anyone would come, it would be Anne.

"Grandmother?"

Fear bites, my guts turn, my sphincter tightens as she turns her eyes full upon me. She is displeased. But it cannot be her; she has lain in her tomb for more years than I can number. I start back in horror, pull the blankets to my nose.

"You are not here."

I try to look away, but something holds me fast. Our eyes lock. Hers are hooded, cold.

"Am I not? Perhaps it is you who are not here. Have you thought of that?"

She makes no sense. She has no more substance than the air that surrounds us, or the smoke that belches from the hearth. While I fight to evade her eyes, she clasps her hands, fingers threaded together, and her displeased gaze drills into me.

"What sort of king do you think you've been, Henry? Did you listen to even one of our directives? Did you seek to please your father and I at all? It was all for your own good, you know."

"I have done my best."

"Have you? Have you really? As I see it, you have failed on every level. One son. Two bastard daughters. And far too many wives; most of them beneath you."

She sniffs derisively.

"I - I..."

My arm hangs limply from the side of the bed as she carefully deconstructs the excuses I have made to myself for so long.

"And as for the church … and my dear friend, Fisher. Your actions were those of a monster, a heresy, an offence to God. Did you never stop to consider the lessons you learned at my knee?"

"I - I…"

"You were supposed to protect your subjects, Henry, yet you burned them, tortured them, starved them, threw them from their homes."

"No, it wasn't me. It was…"

"Oh, stop blustering. If you cannot face me, what hope will you have of making reparation to your father, not to mention God? What do you think the Lord in Heaven will have to say about your actions?"

"It was all your fault! I tried! God knows I tried, but I was thwarted at every turn. You gave me an impossible chart to follow. Had I been granted a living son, I would have stayed with Catherine. I did not mean to destroy the monks, it was the Pope; had he only allowed the divorce, it would have been different! And as for More and Fischer; they disobeyed me, they refused to accept what I was forced to do. I am their king! And I did not want to kill my friends, Cromwell tricked me with his lies, his overweening ambition. I have lived my life surrounded by liars and sycophants, traitors and whores…"

"Traitors and whores whom you invited into your life, Henry…"

"But I have secured the line, I have a son. I have my heir. I have Edward!"

Edward. I grasp the name and cling to it. My only hope.

"Do you, Henry? For how long you think one small boy will survive the degenerates in whose charge you are leaving him?"

"NOoooo!"

The shadow fades. Replaced by another, and this time the figure is solid, real. With the horror still clinging to me, I hold tightly to his arm.

"Denny, Denny, where is Kate? Send for the queen, I must … she will help me…"

Spittle lodges in my throat. I choke and splutter as strong arms lift me from the pillow, and a bowl is placed beneath my chin. Vile vomit burns my throat. I gape, like a dying fish, my breath stolen, my element falling away. I drop back, exhausted, and reality vanishes again, plunging me back into torment.

I don't want to die. I am not ready. There are things I must do, wrongs I must right, promises I must keep, sins I must recant, sins for which I must be forgiven.

I need Cranmer. Someone is praying. Words that should calm me but somehow don't. I try to call out, to beg them to help me, to fight off the reaper, but they neither see nor hear me. They stand in silence, stricken dumb sentinels about my deathbed, while one lonely voice drones in continuous prayer.

Then, the rasping sound I've become accustomed to stops abruptly. Pain ceases. My head clears. I can breathe easily again.

Peacefully, I drift effortlessly upward, and join the carved devils ranged around the canopy of the royal bed. I follow their gaze downward.

Far below, I see myself for the first time as I really am ... was. I absorb with horror the beast I have allowed myself to become.

There is no goodly prince.

The body is bloated, like a whale washed up by the tide. It is scarred, diseased, and the chamber imbued with the stench of its decay. The cream of the English nobility, those I have spared, pray with bowed heads for the beloved king they all despised.

Is this how I will be remembered? Is there nobody left to recall the golden boy I used to be, or the king I intended to be?

Sir Loyal Heart.

I killed my companions of those halcyon days; their sons live on in disgrace, robbed of their inheritance, their lands. Even Norfolk is imprisoned in the Tower, awaiting death, his son beheaded a day or two ago. Not even Norfolk will survive to speak well of me.

Nobody will remember brave King Hal, the lion of England; the years of my reign will be set down by enemies, twisted and moulded, forged into an awful, unshakeable truth.

And I am powerless to stop it. I stare into the yawning abyss of my own personal Hell and Failure steps out to greet me.

The king is dead. Long live King Edward.

<u>Author's Note</u>

When I began writing *The Henrician Trilogy,* I had no idea how Henry would emerge. As an author, I had to close my mind to the deeds he would commit later in his life and focus solely in the moment. I've written the events from Henry's point of view because I thought it time he was given the chance to tell his own story. It may seem that I've whitewashed him, made him squeaky clean, but I think if Henry were to sit down and tell his own life story, it would be very difficult for him to be entirely honest. He was rarely honest with himself.

Like anyone else, Henry had good intentions and plenty of excuses when things began to go awry. He had been raised to expect his life to run smoothly and when it didn't, he struck out. Once he gained knowledge as to the extent of his own power, he became dangerous, and he was self-deluded enough to apportion blame elsewhere.

I've spent more than four years in Henry's company, and it wasn't always easy. Toward the end, in need of respite, I had to take lengthy breaks to clear him out of my head but, now the book is finished, I already find myself missing him. I guess I have some small touch of pity for the way his life went so horribly wrong. Failed potential is always sad.

The young Henry was eager to please, sociable, brave, fun, romantic. He was endearing, and his relationships all positive. I didn't detect any negative aspects to his character until the death of his brother, Arthur, in *Book One, A Matter of Conscience.* This tragedy, impounded by the subsequent death of his mother, marked the end of Henry's innocence, and his initiation into the responsibilities of an heir to the throne.

Initially, he embraced the new path that was opening up to him and his intention was always to be a good king. He wanted his rule to be very different to that of his father. He looked back to the old days of chivalry and grandeur, but these ideals clashed with the new innovative concepts the world was embracing, and his attempts to mediate between the two just made everything worse.

Henry never doubted he would be a king in the same vein as his heroes; Henry V and Edward IV. He was determined to be the best at everything; the best dancer, poet, jouster, soldier, king, lover, scholar and, more often than not, he was.

As a young king, he was unparalleled.

His marriage to his brother's widow, Catherine of Aragon, was successful. They were married for twenty-four years, most of them happily, but she was his senior by six years, and multiple births take their toll on any woman's health. While Catherine grew old before her time, Henry remained a golden-haired king. With the attention his status and charisma drew from other women, the marriage was doomed to fail.

The thing Henry feared the most was failure, and when, after many years of trying, he was still denied a son, he began to look around for the reason why. He knew it wasn't his fault, for he had sired a son with Bessie Blount, and possibly with other women too. He decided the fault must lie with Catherine.

He needed a way out.

I won't go into a lengthy discussion here about the messy divorce that followed, or the emerging changes in his character around 1536, but as far as Henry was concerned, his next wife, Anne Boleyn, also failed him. After years of fighting to free himself from Catherine in order to wed Anne, he was shattered when the boy she promised him was just another useless girl.

His relationship with Anne was always volatile; they fought and made up, and fought again, just as scores of married couples do. There was no real sign of serious dissent between them until shortly before May Day 1536, when warrants were issued for the arrest of Brereton, Norris, Weston, Smeaton, and others who were later released.

These men, apart from the musician Smeaton, were Henry's friends. In the past, he had sparred with them, dined with them, sported with them. They were not, however, friends of Thomas Cromwell, and just prior to their arrests all three had fallen into dispute with him. As had Anne.

I have long suspected that Cromwell may have persuaded Henry of Anne's guilt in order to be rid of her. The theory continues to intrigue me, and I have taken the liberty of exploring the idea in *Book Two: A Matter of Faith*.

In the second book, Henry's character becomes darker and, during the writing process, I began to experience spiritual exhaustion from working with him so closely. The darkness that existed in England at this time seemed to creep into my life in modern day Wales.

They were certainly dark days. I don't think we can fully understand the impact the dissolution of the monasteries had on the ordinary people of England. In the 21st century, we are not particularly religious, certainly not to the extent of those who lived in the 16th century. Again, I think Cromwell should be given a share of the blame; if nothing else he encouraged the king, and I am pretty certain that Henry would concur with this.

Wolsey closed the first monasteries; he targeted the smaller, less profitable ones. Working with him was Thomas Cromwell, and when the time came for him to inherit Wolsey's position with the king, he lost no time in tightening the pressure on the larger establishments.

The closure of the religious houses threw the realm into unforeseen chaos; not just the uprising that followed, or the cold-blooded punishments that were handed out, but the thousands left homeless, jobless and without recourse to medical care when they fell sick. You can read more about what happened to those directly involved in the dissolution in my novel: *Sisters of Arden*.

People love to hate Henry for the harsh treatment of the northern people, but it was his representatives who passed information to the king. He may have signed the warrants, but Norfolk and Brandon were responsible for the nature and the ferocity of the punishments. Or at least, that is what Henry would tell you.

I think that events during these years, the break with Rome, the death of Anne, the failure to beget a legitimate son, compounded at this time, leaving the king vulnerable. Jane Seymour, gentle, pure and pliable, soothed his feelings of inadequacy. For a short time.

After her death, he did not marry again until 1540, and this has been attributed to the grief of widowerhood. The Council was already discussing his next wife almost before Jane was cold in the ground, but the king resisted. Perhaps the birth of a son negated the need for remarriage. The king may not have seen a wife as crucial now he had proved himself and had the security of Edward occupying the royal nursery. We can only surmise.

Shortly after I began writing *Book Three: A Matter of Time,* I was infected with Covid 19, which not only knocked me out for a week but also left me with exhaustion and a very foggy head. Writing suddenly seemed very hard.

Unable to leave the house, Henry VIII became my constant companion. Even when I wasn't writing about him, I was thinking about him. He even began to appear in my dreams. Writing in the first person, present tense, makes the creation of a story very immediate. Sometimes it was as if I was living it.

As the narrative unfolded, I grew sadder for him. His sense of failure, his depression and despair over the betrayal of Katherine Howard and Culpepper were heartbreaking. It was as if he was in the next room and I could almost hear him weeping, asking over and over how and when he had displeased God.

He really had no idea.

Failure is a difficult thing to live with. Some people choose not to live with it at all; Henry, however, was made of sterner stuff and lived on, refusing to give up.

Exhausted both physically and emotionally by his young and faithless queen, he nevertheless took a new wife after Katherine Howard's execution. Henry was nothing if not optimistic and never stopped hoping for another son, or for something to go the way he wanted.

This time, he selected a mature, proven woman, the twice widowed but still youthful Katheryn Parr. And with a reliable queen at England's helm, instead of sinking gracefully into old age, he plunged the country deeper into impoverishment by embarking on a second war against France.

One thing I have omitted to mention during this rambling author's note is Henry's health. From 1536 onwards, he was plagued with painful ulcerated legs. The verdict is out on a definitive diagnosis, but we do know that occasionally the wounds would close up, pus would build up beneath, his face would turn black, and the physicians would have to lance it. Imagine that! I don't imagine he was the easiest of patients, especially with no pain relief. After the death of Culpepper, who had previously had the responsibility of caring for him, Henry was obliged to train another member of the privy chamber to undertake the role.

Toward the end, there was nobody left to remember Henry as a young man. He was in the hands of men who had little regard for the human being that existed behind the façade of royalty. Henry became a tool, a figurehead the Council preserved, not through love or kindness but because, through him, they obtained power.

And at the very end, as Henry lay dying, surrounded by virtual strangers, the failures of his life must have loomed large. He could no longer deny, even to himself, that his war with France had ended in ignominy. He had just one son and two bastard daughters. The royal coffers were almost empty. He had failed in almost every one of the magnificent feats he had striven to achieve. Even the country was divided, with Catholics ranged against Protestants. And as death drew closer, he would have known he was leaving just one adolescent boy to deal with it all.

I feel I should address the unusual deathbed scene in this novel. When writing in the first person, present tense, it is always difficult to deal with the end of the protagonist life.

In *The Kiss of the Concubine,* I make the reader aware of an 'afterlife' during the opening chapter, and the narrative follows Anne through her life and into the hereafter in the final chapter. In *A Matter of Time,* I needed Henry to voice his regrets during his final hours, but the record shows that he was unconscious for several hours before he passed.

Most of my readers love Anne Boleyn, and I suspect would have liked her to turn up to accompany

Henry to Heaven, but those of you who have read my other books will recognise that the person who does appear at the end, maybe in a dream, maybe in reality, was the best choice of all. And besides, I was left with little option when she demanded a cameo appearance in the final book of *The Henrician Trilogy*.

If you have enjoyed this book, please consider leaving a review, however short, and recommend it to your friends.

Judith Arnopp's books include:

Fiction:
A Matter of Conscience: Henry VIII, the Aragon Years
A Matter of Faith: Henry VIII, the Days of the Phoenix
A Matter of Time: Henry VIII, the Dying of the Light
The Heretic Wind: the story of Mary Tudor, Queen of England
The Beaufort Bride: Book one of The Beaufort Chronicle
The Beaufort Woman: Book two of The Beaufort Chronicle
The King's Mother: Book three of The Beaufort Chronicle
A Song of Sixpence: the story of Elizabeth of York
The Kiss of the Concubine: the story of Anne Boleyn
Intractable Heart: the story of Katherine Parr
Sisters of Arden: on the pilgrimage of Grace
The Winchester Goose: at the court of Henry VIII
The Song of Heledd
The Forest Dwellers
Peaceweaver: the story of Eadgyth
The Book of Thornhold
Daughter of Warwick

Non-Fiction:

How to Dress like a Tudor – Pen&Swordbooks

Made in the USA
Middletown, DE
25 February 2024